ALSO BY IAN MOORE

Death and Croissants
Death and Fromage
Death at the Chateau
Death and Papa Noël
Death in le Jardin
Death and Boules

DEATH AND Déjà Vu

A FOLLET VALLEY MYSTERY

IAN MOORE

Farrago

First published in 2026 by Farrago, an imprint of Duckworth Books Ltd
1 Golden Court, Richmond, TW9 1EU, United Kingdom

www.farragobooks.com

This book is a work of fiction. Names, characters, businesses, organisations,
places and events other than those clearly in the public domain, are either the
product of the author's imagination or are used fictitiously. Any resemblance
to actual persons, living or dead, events or locales is entirely coincidental.

A catalogue record for this book is available from the British Library

Printed and bound in Great Britain by CPI Ltd, Croydon, CR0 4YY

The authorised representative in the EEA is Easy Access System
Europe, Mustamäe tee 50, 10621 Tallinn, Estonia.

Hardback ISBN: 9781788425971
Ebook ISBN: 9781788425988

Cover design and illustration by Patrick Knowles

For Rita and Kev, two of the very best.

Prologue

'Is he dead?' the old woman hissed, a tone of inconvenience laced through her question. It was late in a long day and she slurred her words slightly. Though she had been doing that since just before breakfast.

'I very much hope that he is not!' Valérie d'Orçay fumed impatiently, suggesting that any unexpected demise at this stage would upset her plans enormously. She stepped forward, bent down and checked for a pulse.

'The Electoral Commission isn't going to like this one bit.' Noel Mabit stroked his chin in a way that bureaucrats all over the world stroke their chin. It was with a look of intense concentration and thought, masking the desire to escape the situation and responsibility at the earliest possible opportunity. 'I mean, he's only been mayor for ten minutes.'

'He is not dead.' Valérie's voice was flat. If there was relief, she hid it well.

'What happened?' The old woman, Madame Gondard, was taking another of what she thought was a sneaky slug from a not very discreet hip flask.

'Maybe he just can't handle the responsibilities of high office?' Noel mused. 'It is an honour not to be taken lightly. Maybe we—'

'Yes, yes, yes.' Valérie cut him off brusquely. 'You have lost the election, Monsieur Mabit, it is too late to campaign now.'

A crestfallen Noel Mabit, hitherto the power behind the throne of the small Follet Valley town of Saint-Sauver, didn't need to be reminded of his electoral defeat. For the first time in his long, petty bureaucratic career he had chosen to seek the political spotlight and he had failed. Even his wife had disappeared from the town hall quickly after the count, not wanting to be associated with her husband's ignominious rout. It stung, it stung badly and more so that his victor, by some considerable margin, had apparently buckled at the news, slumped to the floor and banged his head on the sacred desk of office as he went down.

'Should we call an ambulance?' He sighed, as though it were the last thing in the world he wanted to do.

'Here.' Madame Gondard thrust her hip flask forward pretending – badly – that she'd just remembered it was there. 'This'll bring him round.'

Valérie took the flask and sniffed the contents before coughing at the aroma. 'It might finish him off, I think!'

Noel coughed too, not from fumes but highlighting that he had something official to impart. 'There is provision,' he began, 'in the terms of the mayoral contract to help with illness, should the incumbent become, er, incapacitated.'

'What does that mean?' Valérie asked, still hesitating with the flask.

'It means that there are funds set aside in the town budget to pay for a restorative sabbatical. The previous mayor made use of this quite often.'

'You mean, to register him in a health spa?' Valérie decided against the drink, whatever it was, and handed the flask back to Madame Gondard.

'For restorative purposes, yes.'

'Really?' Madame Gondard was on the verge of outrage. 'Is that quite legal?'

'For the benefit of the town as a whole,' Mabit argued. 'For democracy. And for France!'

The old lady took a celebratory and patriotic slug.

Valérie was less concerned about the legality and came to an immediate decision. 'I think it is the right thing to do,' she said seriously. 'He needs complete rest.'

Lying half on the floor and – like a sack of forgotten rubbish – half awkwardly against the wall, Richard Ainsworth, the reluctant new mayor of Saint-Sauver, groaned as if in semi-conscious agreement. In truth he had heard every word, but had decided to keep his eyes closed hoping the whole 'just become mayor' thing actually might go away if he did so. He had been railroaded into political life and he resented it enormously. His campaign had focussed entirely on his weaknesses, but had backfired badly and the result of his landslide had come as a terrible shock. He'd presented himself as someone so hopelessly inexperienced and incompetent that, should he win, Saint-Sauver would likely not exist within the year. The voting public were having none of it and had decided that he was actually the ideal anti-establishment figure, the sort of left-field polemicist that rural France was crying out for.

'But I'm English!' he had argued as a final trump card. Only to be met with the sort of rank indifference and shoulder-shrugging that the French like to employ and which the English will never truly understand. 'So what?' they were saying as an electorate, a nonchalance that always hurt the true Englishman even more as it came inevitability with the jolting realisation that the French actually don't dislike the English; they just don't give them any thought at all.

He groaned again. 'Oh, what happened?' he asked weakly. 'Where am I?' he added, overdoing it a touch.

'Monsieur le Mayor.' Noel Mabit's back stiffened as he spoke. 'Do not concern yourself. You must get well and I will take care of things in your absence.'

'It is important that you recover your health. Very important.' Valérie's voice was definite, though no one, least of all the new mayor, was likely to argue. 'And I know just the place for you,' she added with a touch of mystery.

Chapter One

Richard Ainsworth adjusted himself against the first class carriage headrest and happily dismissed the thought that this was exactly what was wrong with politics today. It was in his nature, upbringing and DNA to feel guilty about the slightest thing, but he decided that in this instance he'd had a rare slice of good fortune and was for once going to try and enjoy it. It wasn't as though he hadn't given the voters of Saint-Sauver fair warning. He had argued passionately that he wasn't the man for the job of mayor and, just a few minutes after the result, having managed to trip over his own feet in dismay, almost knocking himself out, was proof positive of this. He'd nearly become the first rural French mayor to assassinate himself.

He had explained at the few hustings he'd contrived not to miss that he was a man of no conviction whatsoever and that he couldn't give a hoot for farmers, workers or the elderly. He'd admitted that his own finances were parlous in the extreme and that he was therefore likely to embezzle council funds and plunge the town into debt. With a mixture of gusto and contrition he had invented a series of fictional adulterous affairs, which turned out to be a gross campaign error as male French politicians are expected to have half a dozen sexual scandals on their CV as a bare minimum. And then, in a final attempt to end the charade, he confessed to having lied on his application for an Irish passport and that he therefore wasn't European at all and so was ineligible for office. Some wag in the national press had got hold of this and, sensing a long-running story, had arranged, possibly illegally, for Richard Ainsworth to be granted honorary French citizenship. All of which just proved once and for all that there really was no room for honesty in the modern political world.

The electorate knew what they were getting then, so now – and possibly for the first time in his life – he was going to take advantage of the situation and enjoy this first class compartment on the gravy train. He was powerlessly in power, but as President Charles de Gaulle had pointed out about the French, it was virtually impossible to govern a people that had two hundred and forty-six different types of cheese.

He leant back in his plush seat, watching the glorious, late-summer gold of the French countryside slide by. Sipping from his gin and tonic, he nervously dared to raise a glass to himself. So far his luck, carried as always like a fragile vase, was lasting. He was on his way to a French health spa, all expenses paid. He hadn't been to the place he was headed to, Le Havre de Paix, the Haven of Peace, but his experience of French health spas was more than enough for the anticipation to build. The health part was generally optional for a start; there'd be various heated pools and saunas, masseuses on demand and so on, optional extras like mud baths and those ear-candle things, but most importantly there would inevitably be the kind of refined French cuisine which was absolutely on point for a chap who'd just had his shorts blasted by a fiercely invasive jacuzzi. Also, there'd be a well-equipped gym, a sinister sight obviously, but the nagging machines would largely remain as unused as redundant oil derricks, casting morbid shadows like dinosaur skeletons in museums.

It was one of the reasons he loved France so much, why he and his estranged wife Clare had moved there. Partly, in his case, to run away from a doleful unemployment, as a film historian with a PhD no less, an anachronism in a digital age; and partly because the French, certainly outside of the big cities, liked to thumb their nose at everything everybody else enthused about, and do so with equal gusto. They'd even build stuff specifically for the Gallic nose-thumbing purpose, hence an empty gym with adjacent five-star restaurant.

He looked across at his companion, asleep on the opposite seat, with some warmth. Softly breathing as the sun darted through passing trees, it was a sign of Richard's current contentment that he felt lucky they were both here at all. Richard hadn't had a hard life, not by any means, but there were those, the estranged Clare included, who insisted that he had at times seemed determined to make things hard. Maybe, on reflection, he had. He had a tendency to avoid full-on enjoyment, for sure. He was from southern England after all. But for once, just for once, he seemed to be ahead of the game. It had taken some time – fifty-four years to be precise – but he was here, or there. Whichever.

He took another refreshing sip and a memory came back to him, one that for the first time he was able to look at with some gratitude.

It was the first time he had laid eyes on Madame Valérie d'Orçay. She had shimmered down the stairs of his upmarket bed and breakfast, or *chambres d'hôte* to give it its French name, Passepartout the pampered almost regal Chihuahua under one arm, and she had briefly stood on a lower step taking in the room, the room taking in her at the same time. Richard had spent his entire working and personal life watching glamorous movie queens make grand black-and-white entrances, the cameras glued to their soft-focus beauty while the audience were given a moment to get their breath back. Bette Davis, Joan Crawford, Ingrid Bergman, Ava Gardner, a couple of Hepburns, all names etched into Richard's psyche like lovers' initials on a tree trunk and all of which flew over Valérie d'Orçay's head, unless she thought Richard was talking about his beloved hens, whom he had named after the great leading ladies of the silver screen.

That moment had changed his life. He hadn't wanted it to. In truth he had been perfectly content with his plodding existence, living on the fringes of French life, hiding away while his marriage fell apart. It suited him. Clare may have realised it only too late but Richard had long known of himself that he was a watcher, not a doer. But when one of his bed and breakfast guests disappeared, Valérie had insisted on – or rather bullied Richard into – taking action. And he had done so, reluctantly, belligerently, feet-draggingly. He was in awe of Valérie and, truth be told, a little scared too. She was a top-quality international bounty hunter after all, maybe even an assassin – she was reluctant to confirm this point, but hadn't ever denied it either. He had seen her in full flow, despatching attackers with graceful ease like a cross between Rita Hayworth and Bruce Lee. Subsequently they had become business partners in a private investigations agency which had, on a couple of high-profile occasions, succeeded where the authorities had dithered. Valérie's dynamism was perfectly complemented by Richard's… well, whatever Richard brought to the partnership. He couldn't say what that might be specifically, but it was certainly something. Perspective maybe? A dour kind of 'Oh really, must we?' sort of vacillation that attempted to rein in some of his partner's more enthusiastic extravagances.

He was aware that he was living a dream, not *the* dream, but a dream. There was far too much rigour, danger and necessary on-the-spot decision-making to be done for it to be *the* dream. No, it was a surreal reality that he found himself in and while he bucked against it with the hangdog disinclination of a man being dragged around IKEA, it was also the most fun he had ever had. He would never admit to it publicly, nor even to himself probably, but he was loving every minute of it.

All that being said of his newish life, he was happy to be taking a break from the B&B and Saint-Sauver, even if only for a week. He and Clare, though more him, had chosen the place specifically for its peace and tranquilli-ty, its comforting anonymity. That's why Clare had left, recognising that the place was Richard in municipal form.

It seemed, however, that after just five minutes of Valérie d'Orçay's whirlwind presence, Saint-Sauver had become a hotbed of division, rancour, old scores, thievery, rampant bed-hopping and even murder. Valérie loved the place immediately therefore and had stayed as a permanent guest at Richard's high-end *chambres d'hôte*, though she would often disappear to 'do the day job', as she enigmatically put it.

It was well within his rights then, with all this in mind, that he was determined to use this rare good fortune and actually have a proper rest. The bed and breakfast was temporarily closed, his beloved hens had been left in the care of his redoubtable housekeeper, Madame Tablier, who had been left with strict instructions that she was at no point to succumb to her breeding and history and eat one of them, and Monsieur Mabit was in charge of the town council. Richard was going to use his time wisely: rest, yes; eat, yes; maybe even sample some of the Loire-Atlantique wines, yes. But also, work. He felt re-invigorated enough to continue with a book he had started writing almost six years ago. One that he knew would probably never be read or even published and which, therefore, carried no pressure whatsoever. This was a new Richard and he was doing it purely for himself. It was *The Book of Movie Family Trees* and just the thought of it gave him a slight thrill. A childish one even, seeing as he'd actually started the research when he had first fallen in love with black-and-white Hollywood, some time around his twelfth birthday.

A gentle snore came from the other side of the small table and Richard smiled. He was warming to this idea of his work and decided to test his 'movie family tree' faculties with a mental parlour game that he often played. He had to pick two very disparate films and connect them in as few steps as possible. As he was on a train, that was the obvious starting point and the first train-based film that flashed into his mind was *Terror by Night*, one of the last of the Basil Rathbone and Nigel Bruce Sherlock Holmes collaborations. Connect it to what though? A nun, one of a group further down the carriage and wearing large, expensive headphones, was nodding along vigorously to what must have been one of the livelier hymns, so *The Sound of Music* it was. Connect *Terror by Night*, 1946 to *The Sound of Music*, 1965.

'Pah!' he said out loud, garnering some curious glances. 'Too easy.' And in his mind, he went through the simple steps. *Terror by Night*, Sherlock Holmes, *The Sound of Music* with Julie Andrews and Christopher Plummer. Plummer played Sherlock Holmes in *Murder by Decree*, 1979. Too easy. He decided to try another pairing, but was interrupted.

'Tickets, please!' As usual the French train controllers were mob heavy. Four of them in starched blue uniforms, demanding respect and paperwork. It was an old-world approach to intercity travel and though Richard was all for it in principle, it inevitably made him feel nervous, like when driving in front of a police car – he was awash with irrational guilt. He groped in his bag under the table and produced two tickets. His sleeping travel companion looked up briefly, trusting him to carry on.

The guard, heavily and ornately moustachioed, looked grimly at the tickets. *The Lady Vanishes*, 1938, Alfred Hitchcock, Richard thought, another classic train film.

'You have bought a first class ticket for a dog?' The guard's voice dripped with condescension.

'That's not my dog,' Richard replied. 'It's my business partner's dog.'

'And where is she, this business partner?'

'I don't know,' Richard replied, before uttering under his breath. 'She's vanished.'

Chapter Two

And she had too. Valérie d'Orçay had simply just disappeared.

She had made all the travel arrangements for the two of them, including the booking at the spa resort. Separate rooms Richard had noticed with a slight disappointment but no surprise because they weren't that kind of couple. Then she had driven them both to the station in Saint-Sauver, made a big show of forgetting her phone and hurried back home to retrieve it. Richard had waited on the platform for her to return, leaning on a small suitcase and with her Chihuahua under his arm. Both he and Passepartout had a look of resignation on their faces, but again, no surprise. They knew she wouldn't be joining them.

Not for the first time he was left wondering how she managed to be so successful as a bounty hunter cum possible assassin. Presumably the work demanded a fair amount of subterfuge on her part, role playing and so on, yet she was easily the worst liar and actress he had ever met. She had no filters as far as he could tell, no veils, no ability to hide her emotions at all, emotions that generally raged and changed constantly like a stormy coastal sky.

Richard's assumption was that she had been called away for 'work', some last-minute culling of a dictator somewhere or a felon on the run from the authorities. He had no evidence to assume that, but she was prone to these disappearances and it was always, she said, work related. Presumably there was an international twenty-four-hour hotline for these kinds of professionals, like with a plumber or something. Or, more likely, some kind of phone app, like Tinder with menaces: swipe right for political liquidation, good sense of humour essential.

The thing that worried Richard just a little bit was that he wasn't worried. Partly because Valérie always came back, partly because her trust in him was such that she knew Passepartout would be well looked after – she'd made it clear previously that she would never have dared leave her beloved dog with any of her ex-husbands, of which there were possibly eight or nine. Richard had never been able to confirm the number precisely, concluding that that would require a national census. And partly, though this had been a dawning realisation as the soothing, gently somnolent train journey had progressed, because maybe her not coming might actually be a good thing. He adored being around Valérie; she was beautiful, wild and unpredictable, exciting and intoxicating but also, it had to be said, a bit full-on, very demanding and really quite exhausting. She made him question who he really was, who he wanted to be, and in the few short years they had been sort-of together, Richard had, as the modern saying goes, lived his best life. As a previously happily dull individual, he would never in his wildest dreams have imagined this sort of existence. There had been murder, intrigue, a run-in with the Sicilian mafia, stolen art and a particularly nasty incident over vegan goat's cheese. He had been shot at, bloodied in a sword fight, accused of heinous crimes by lazy police officers and brained on at least half a dozen occasions, once with a Napoleonic bedpan.

Which was all well and good, he mused, but not the forced retirement – unemployment – he had envisaged. There was just no getting around the fact that exciting as Valérie was, he needed a breather. He needed to recharge his batteries and that was only really possible if she was getting her own intrigue jollies in somewhere else, while Richard settled down with a good book and his own writing ideas, or daydreaming as Clare would call it. In short then, he was due a break and so far, he was loving every minute.

The muffled train tannoy crackled into action. '*Messieurs et mesdames*, we will shortly be arriving in Nantes, the final destination on this journey. Please make sure you take all your belongings with you and have a good day.' Richard stood and took down his case from the overhead shelf before gathering up Passepartout in his bag cum bed. Richard had already removed the dog's topknot ribbon; he was perfectly willing to take care of the thing – he'd even, if pushed, admit to being quite fond of the little fella – but he wasn't going to carry him around as though the Chihuahua were dressed for the swimsuit round at Crufts. They stood in line with the other disembarking passengers and Richard took a quick glance to make sure he hadn't forgotten anything. He knew he hadn't, but he was certainly and with quiet relief leaving some of his own emotional baggage behind.

The large concourse at Nantes train station was teeming with people as he and Passepartout came through the barriers. The modern glass-fronted station was like an enormous unruly classroom with hundreds of children, who had been on *colonies,* or summer camps in other words, being shepherded back on to the trains that would take them home. If they were disappointed that the *grandes vacances* were coming to an end, it didn't show. The whole place had a celebratory feel to it, a happy atmosphere, and while Richard would normally run a mile from such bonhomie, he soaked it all up with a kind of benevolent warmth. Having said that he was relieved to get out into the fresh air and look for the bus stop and the shuttle service that would take him to his destination.

It was a warm, late August day and the outside of Nantes station felt no less busy than the inside, but there was a cooling breeze that ruffled Richard's hair around the temples, temples that had been greying when Valérie had first arrived and which were now heading to the alabaster end of the colour spectrum. He smiled at the thought. Again, he wouldn't swap it all for the world, but a week's peace was quite literally what the doctor ordered. He read the flyer that he had for Le Havre de Paix and located which bus stop he had to find. He was a little early anyway, so he just let life slide by, a permanent and genuine smile on his face, no longer wary that this slice of good fortune was a trap, but for once allowing himself to enjoy the moment.

He was the first in the queue at the bus stop and could have even gone for a coffee before the shuttle arrived, but the Englishness in him meant that he stood directly under the bus stop sign to wait patiently.

'Monsieur?' A small man wearing a white short-sleeved collared shirt and a black tie approached from the direction of the station entrance. 'Monsieur?' he repeated.

'Yes.' Richard smiled back, his usual caution resting on its laurels.

The man then held up a sign that said simply: 'Doctor Ainsworth, Richard'. It was one of those chauffeur signs you see at airports, one that everyone coming through the exit gates stares at hoping their name is there, even though there's absolutely no reason why it should be.

'Yes, that's me,' Richard said, taken aback slightly by the sign and the title.

'Ah yes, sir.' The small man was quite obsequious in his gestures, which made Richard feel uncomfortable, as did the assumption that he didn't understand the man's native French. 'You see, the *navette*, the shuttle, is not running today so I have been asked to pick you up.'

Richard relaxed. A chauffeur-driven car to a week's rest was even better! 'That's very good of you,' he said, and held out his hand to shake. 'Please call me Richard.'

The man took his hand and grinned, showing a gold tooth right at the front of what was otherwise a pretty dilapidated set of dentures. Then he paused as if he had briefly forgotten his name and said, 'Manu, my name is Manu.'

'Well, I'm very grateful to you, Manu,' Richard said matching the man's smile. 'I'll admit I didn't fancy a bus on a day like this. Is your car far from here?'

'Please,' Manu replied, 'not far. Please to follow me.'

Richard did so, still carrying Passepartout while Manu carried his case. Just around the corner from the station and dominating a narrow side street was an enormous black stretched limousine whose lights flashed as Manu pressed a button on his key fob.

'Were you expecting someone else?' Richard joked, as the boot opened slowly on pressured springs and Manu placed his suitcase carefully in the well.

The question momentarily seemed to unnerve the small man who held up his sign again. 'Doctor Ainsworth, yes?' he asked, a slight hint of desperation in his voice.

'Yes, that's me. I was just joking.'

'Ha! Yes! Joke!' Manu then faked a belly laugh of such proportions, Richard thought the little man was miming appendicitis.

Once he'd recovered from Richard's devastating wit, he opened the rear door and beckoned Richard to get in. It was quite an awkward thing to do while still holding Passepartout, so Richard laid the small dog gently on the pavement as he slid in through the door. Manu reached down to Passepartout, ready to help deliver the dog on to Richard's lap.

'Be careful!' Richard warned. 'He's not that keen on strangers, here let me…'

He was too late. Manu had picked up Passepartout's carry bed before he could intervene but rather than snapping at the strange hands lifting him, Passepartout licked Manu's left wrist.

'Nice doggy!' Manu grinned again and closed the door leaving Richard and Passepartout in the enormous surroundings of the back of the limousine.

'Well, you're a one, aren't you?' Richard questioned the little dog with a touch of grievance. 'It looks like we're both in relax mode then.'

The car glided smoothly into traffic before Manu skilfully drove the limousine around the Nantes one-way system.

'Is it difficult driving a car like this?' Richard asked, the window between himself and the driving compartment open wide.

'No, no. Not difficult.' Manu's reply was more cursory than his welcome had been and Richard guessed that actually manoeuvring a behemoth like this took a fair amount of concentration.

'Ah,' Richard said as they approached the outskirts of the city, still trying to make conversation. 'Le Havre de Paix!' And he pointed at the sign indicating a right turn as they sat at a T-junction. 'Not far now.' This time he addressed Passepartout, excitement in his voice.

Manu edged the car forward and then made a quick turn left.

'Manu, the sign said turn right for Le Havre de Paix.'

'Short cut,' the man replied, studiously avoiding Richard's gaze in the rear-view mirror.

'But…'

'Short cut,' he repeated and at the same time pressed a button on the dashboard. The window partition between the two men closed menacingly and then the door locks snapped shut with a loud and intimidating crack.

Richard closed his eyes and tried to keep calm. Were they being kidnapped? If so, Passepartout was showing a remarkable level of insouciance that Richard simply couldn't match and nor, frankly, was he prepared to. If this was a kidnapping, the main question would be why? Richard's life thus far had been the very model of middle-of-the-road, don't-rock-the-boat anonymity, so he dismissed serious criminal abduction from his mind, for now at least. He felt his pulse racing, however, and he was beginning to get a stress headache. He really had absolutely no idea what was going on, but he had a pretty good idea who was behind whatever it was and he cursed the woman loudly from deep in his leather seat. Manu heard nothing, however, and Passepartout had heard it all before.

Chapter Three

The car came slowly to a halt at a quay just outside of the small fishing village of Picorne on the Atlantic coast. Richard had caught the name as they'd driven through it, while Manu had very deftly negotiated the oversized vehicle through narrow, winding streets of small white-painted dwellings adorned with old lobster baskets. If this was some form of kidnap, their arrival in a black stretched limo in a picture-postcard village was hardly discreet. They stood out as much as an oil tanker on a boating lake.

Like a child who had run out of protest options on his parents' back seat, Richard sighed deeply. He had let his guard down, that was the problem. He had assumed, wrongly, that just because Valérie wasn't present he could relax, switch off for a while, get some of that elusive tranquillity that was apparently going around. He tried one last time, and with no little petulance, holding the flyer for Le Havre de Paix up to the driver's partition. 'I'm supposed to be going here!' he remonstrated. To his surprise the partition then slid open, but just a fraction, and another flyer fell through the gap. Richard picked it up off the car floor, Le Fort Esprit de l'Air, it read over an aerial photograph of one of those old French fortified sea defences. Fort Boyard was the famous one, famous because they had turned it into a venue for one of those awful Gladiator-style game shows, the type where very muscular people pretend to be ancient warriors but fight with what look like enormous cotton buds. His heart sank deep into his grumbling intestines. *Oh no*, he thought, *she thinks what I need is some kind of activity holiday!* The very idea of an activity holiday, in his mind, being the ultimate oxymoron.

He read on:

The internationally renowned Le Fort Esprit de l'Air looks forward to welcoming you. This private island has become a byword for ground-breaking, soul-cleansing management coaching and blue sky thinking.

Richard tutted loudly at the phrase 'soul-cleansing management' – it sounded like a laxative process.

We all get tired, we can all stagnate – what the Le Fort Esprit de l'Air promises is more than a complete break, it's a chance to use your burnout issues and turn them into a valuable, innovative management technique.

Set in a stunning, wild and remote environment with fully equipped gym, pool, sauna, the latest in hot stone Swedish massage and exosphere business think plus a five-star restaurant – we guarantee to disrupt your stasis and turn your current negatives into future positives.

He read the thing through a couple of times more and tried to ignore the 'management coaching' and 'exosphere business think' elements, partly because he wasn't sure what they meant. He fully understood burnout and, while possibly on the cusp of it himself, he worried that he hadn't done enough to really justify such a thing. He concentrated instead more on the pool, sauna, massage and restaurant stuff, deciding that, all in all, when it came down to it, there were probably worse ways to be derailed.

From his rear window he saw a group of people starting to gather near the jetty. It was clear that they were strangers to one another as nobody spoke nor even acknowledged each other, even awkwardly avoiding eye contact it seemed. In fact the only thing they appeared to have in common was their very natural curiosity at the vast and frankly sinister presence of a stretched limousine.

There were six of them waiting and they made a tableau of studied disinterest. Sitting on the low stone wall, their backs to one another, were an old man and woman. If they were a couple they looked like bookends of marital indifference. In fact, from this distance, the only thing they had in common was that they were both smoking pipes: old-fashioned clay churchwarden pipes with long stems. His was stuck through a mound of unkempt facial hair and a tobacco-stained beard, and hers was much the same. Pacing up and down, with a mobile phone held at arm's length, was a much younger, attractive, tanned brunette whose hair – which she toyed with constantly – was the colour of the Caramac bars he'd eaten as a child. She administered some sort of shiny balm to her protruding lips before talking into the phone which in itself was surprising as Richard had already established that there was no signal at this secluded spot. A man with a very large head, very dark hair and broad shoulders had his back to Richard and was staring out towards the sea. He was seated in an electric wheelchair and barely moved except every now and then moving his head slowly from side to side in what looked like disappointment. Another smaller, more wiry man was impatiently either sitting on the wall or pacing up and down, his dapper cream linen suit catching the sea breeze. He was muttering to himself ferociously and looking up as he did so, maybe anxious about the boat trip, Richard concluded. The last member of this eclectic group was a blonde woman who occasionally looked nervously at her companions, while also sticking her chin out at the same time. Richard knew that look. She felt like she didn't belong, but was determined to show that she did. She wore a flowery jumpsuit and straw-heeled sandals, and puffed on a vape occasionally letting out a waft of smoke that made it look like her head was on fire. Richard didn't like the scene at all and thanks to his extensive knowledge of brooding opening film scenes all of his alarm bells were now ringing.

Manu's partition slid partly open again and Richard caught his eye in the rear-view mirror once more.

'You get out here,' Manu said with remarkable cheerfulness considering his role in a possible abduction.

'I don't want to get out here,' Richard replied with heavy indignation.

'You get out here!' Manu wasn't taking no for an answer, which Richard could well understand if his boss was who he thought she was.

'No, you don't understand,' Richard pleaded. 'I don't mind getting out here, just not *here*.'

Manu squinted his eyes, suspecting a trap.

'Look.' Richard tried again, and this time in French. 'I assume I'm supposed to be going to this place, right?'

He pointed at the Le Fort Esprit de l'Air flyer and Manu nodded. 'With them, right?' He pointed at the gathering on the jetty and again Manu nodded. 'Well, I can't just step out of a stretched bloody limo, can I? Presumably I'm supposed to mingle with discretion or something, not look like the sodding president.'

Manu finally understood the point being made, put the huge car into gear again and pulled away. Once they were around a corner and out of sight, he stopped and Richard's side door opened automatically, as did the boot, though Manu remained warily inside.

'Honestly,' Richard grumbled to himself, 'what are you scared of? Me? What am I going to do? Attack you with a bored Chihuahua?' Having grudgingly retrieved his sparse luggage and said bored Chihuahua, both the door and the boot closed. The engine then restarted and without any further communication Manu drove off into the distance. Richard stood for a moment watching him go, before it dawned on him that Manu had made an error. Richard could now just do what he liked; he didn't have to go and join the others at the jetty at all, he could just get a taxi to his original destination instead and enjoy the week that he'd had in mind in the first place. It was a tempting thought for sure. Why should he allow himself to be treated like this anyway? Pushed about against his will or at least without his say-so – the two not being necessarily the same thing. Valérie d'Orçay had absolutely no right to have him abducted and then plonk him straight into what was, probably, knowing her, a right old mess.

He gave it a moment's serious thought, then took a big determined breath, picked up Passepartout and made long strides towards the jetty and whatever fate lay in store. After all, he could hardly hide from a professional bounty hunter, especially while in charge of her beloved dog. He shuddered to think how Valérie d'Orçay might react to that.

When he was within speaking distance of the disparate group, he decided to go all in and adopt the character of the slightly put-upon Englishman, one that felt natural for him.

'Hello,' he said. 'Sorry, are you waiting for me? My train was delayed.'

'I'll say it was,' the crabby old man with the beard said. 'Station's been shut twenty-five year.'

'And your car's longer than a train anyway,' the old woman added, though still keeping her back to the old man.

'Right then!' The old man stood up stiffly. 'Now the doctor's here, let's get going before the tide turns.'

'Doctor?' Richard asked, he could never get used to being addressed that way.

'You are Doctor Richard Ainsworth, aren't you?' the old woman asked suspiciously. She made it sound like an admonishing parent using a recalcitrant child's full name.

'Well, yes but…'

'Get in the boat then!' she barked. 'Before *the captain* here gets into one of his moods.' She pointed her pipe in the direction of the old man, who just rolled his eyes.

'I married a mermaid,' he said joylessly, 'and I've been bashing against the rocks ever since. Come on then!'

With surprising sprightliness he walked across a wide gangplank and into a large one-masted wooden sail boat, which had bench seating around its inside perimeter. He then held up his hand, which his wife went to grab for a lift down. 'Not you!' he yelled. 'Pass me some cases woman!'

'Pascal Durand, I swear you have a meaner temper than an electric eel!'

'And Lilibet Durand…' Monsieur Durand didn't get to finish his sentence as Richard's suitcase landed on his head.

'Bullseye!' His wife punched the air, clearly proud of her aim. 'Next!'

The young woman pushed her way to the front still talking into her phone, which Richard could now see was filming her. 'How I'm going to keep my skin soft,' she was saying, 'I have no idea, with all this salt in the air. And I'm surrounded *literally* by all the oldest people in the world. Literally dinosaurs.' Her accent was difficult to place, almost sort of generic continental, though her English was clearly very good too. On closer inspection she wasn't as attractive – in Richard's eyes anyway – as she had first appeared. Her lips, for instance, were bulbous and heavily collagened, and looked like they belonged to someone else; her eyebrows were painted on giving her the brow look of Groucho Marx while her bosom not only defied gravity, it was possibly the largest piece of luggage on the boat. If there was any trouble, she might be useful as a life raft. Richard realised instantly that these observations marked him down as an old man tutting at the modern world and that he probably shouldn't be looking anyway, but he was in a bad mood frankly and the modern world had had a part to play in that.

'Go away!' The blonde woman behind him was flapping at a wasp that was flying around her head.

'It's just one of God's creatures,' the man in the white suit said in what seemed like an American accent.

'Not one of his best,' the woman retorted.

'Do you mind?' the younger woman asked irritably. 'I'm trying to record. It's only a wasp, just ignore it. A sting won't kill you.'

The blonde woman went fiery red with anger. 'No, but if it stings my face I might end up with lips like yours!' she riposted and at the same time, with a backhand that would have graced Wimbledon, she connected with the beast and sent it hurtling in the direction of the man in the wheelchair, who, Richard now saw, was big all over to the point of obesity. It landed on his thick neck and stayed there for a moment, presumably gearing up for an assault on its new environment. If it irritated the man though, it didn't show; nothing it seemed would disturb the concentration he was giving to the horizon at which he continued to stare. Eventually he turned his wheelchair towards the gangplank, which creaked alarmingly as he drove across it, before, much to everyone's relief, he made it safely to the boat and resumed his silent staring contest with the skyline.

Next came the small, jumpy man in the white suit, who stopped at the jetty edge, closed his eyes and made a cross on his chest. 'Lord, deliver me across this ocean to the destination you have chosen, as you did for the Israelites,' he began quietly, before raising his voice to a screeching, bellowing cry. 'And keep the devils down below, near fiery Hell where they belong!' Everyone was quite stunned. 'Could you give me a hand across?' he then asked softly and politely, before realising that everyone was staring at his gear-change performance. 'Exodus, chapter fourteen,' he said innocently. 'Well, the deliver me stuff is at least.'

The woman in the flowery jumpsuit, recovered from her wasp encounter, stood next to Richard and exhaled another cloud of vape smoke. 'Is it going to be rough?' she asked, and Richard recognised the clipped tones of the Alsace region of eastern France. 'When I first won this prize, there was no mention of a boat trip then either. And it wasn't very pleasant. Is there no other way?'

Captain Durand removed his pipe and scratched his head with the stem. 'The way I see it, lady, your options are limited. I could try and lasso the island, drag it closer. Or you could swim, see?'

The lady let out another vape cloud, like a volcano spewing ash before it erupted. 'Charming,' she said bitterly and clambered aboard followed by Madame Durand, leaving Richard alone on the quay.

'Aren't you coming, Doctor?' the old lady asked.

Richard handed Passepartout to her, with neither of them looking the least bit impressed, while Richard crossed the gangplank with as much suavity as he could muster.

After being watched down the steps by everyone else, he turned to look back at the now empty jetty.

'And then there were none,' Madame Durand said, following his gaze.

'That's just what I was thinking,' Richard replied sullenly, before adding, '1945, 1965, 1974 and 1989.'

Lilibet Durand rolled her eyes.

Chapter Four

In theory, it should have been a pleasant crossing to the old sea fortress. The wind was cooling while the sail flapped as if slightly annoyed by the fact there was also a small engine pushing them forward. There was most definitely, however, a strained atmosphere on board the wooden launch. For what was supposed to be a relaxing retreat, a coveted luxury health spa for haggard world business leaders, absolutely no one seemed pleased to be going and Richard, press-ganged into being there in the first place, was beginning to feel particularly aggrieved.

While Passepartout slept on his lap, he spent the time re-reading the brochure that Manu had given to him, learning something of the place's history. It was one of a series of fortifications along the Atlantic coast built on ocean banks. It had taken over one hundred years to build and at vast expense too, presumably the daily rate of aquatic builders being pretty high. Sadly, by the time it was completed, military artillery had progressed suffi-ciently to leave the fort and others like it along the coast largely obsolete. This particular fort, originally called Fort Saint-Nicolas, had been one of the smallest, designed to hold a small garrison of no more than thirty men. It had then briefly been a prison before falling into dereliction. Forty years ago it had been bought by the owners of a hotel chain who for more than thirty years did nothing with the property, until they themselves underwent a revamp as an organisation and were now in the hands of the sole surviving member of the original billionaire family. The restoration of the island had begun and it had subsequently become what the brochure described as a 'state of the art management hub, harnessing both the edgy originality of executive exhaustion and the power of the ocean to change business stratagems'. Richard, though impressed, felt he'd have preferred it as a prison. Which is exactly what it looked like. It was shaped like a hockey puck rising from the sea, its small defence-minded windows like suspiciously narrowed eyes but with rusty tears staining the grey walls. Remarkably there was a palm tree visible on the roof – which only served to highlight how severe the rest of it looked – like a small colourful umbrella in a particularly nasty cocktail.

The Durands, almost comically detesting one another, spent the entire fifteen-minute trip glaring at each other; the wheelchair-bound man stared sternly ahead like a ship's carved figurehead; the small man read the Bible aloud to himself, which was really quite unnerving; and the two women sat at opposite sides of the boat watching each other intently while at the same time trying to avoid eye contact. It seemed to Richard that there was an awful lot of executive burnout on show and whoever was going to be in charge of 'soul-cleansing' in the next few days would have their work cut out.

All that aside, however, he still felt a surge of excitement as the boat navigated the island to approach the fortification from the west. This gave the place an entirely different aspect. The old fort loomed above them, not necessarily a big structure in itself but its isolation giving it a presence beyond its size, and it gleamed in the afternoon sun. It was almost entirely glass-fronted; an enormous and ornate orangery conservatory gave way on to a large exposed sun terrace which in turn led down to the jetty. The bedrooms, or at least he assumed that's what they were above the orangery, had floor-to-ceiling windows and Richard's first thought was how Madame Tablier would react to the idea of trying to keep them clean. The whole thing, even to Richard's layman's eyes, was an engineering and architectural triumph and the design, which combined what looked like the prow of a luxury cruise ship with the back end of an old van, screamed of pure exclusivity. The view from the mainland was just the rusty old prison fort, but from the front, which only the world's weary blue-sky-thinking business leaders saw as they arrived, it was a thrusting, opulent marvel. Richard saw it also as a massive contradiction; no ordinary person on the coast was allowed to gaze on what the guests had, but what they had to themselves was a giant goldfish bowl. He shook his head. Why was he here? he asked himself. This wasn't his kind of place at all. What was Valérie playing at?

Captain Durand stepped the short distance from the boat to the quay and tied a rope to an anchor set in concrete. Lilibet threw him another rope, the whole thing done in silence. They might not be able to stand the sight of each other but they were an efficient team nonetheless and the group disembarked without any fuss, but also in silence.

'Welcome! Welcome, everyone!' An elegant lady about Richard's age wearing a flowing polka-dot blouse and black pleated trousers stepped out on to the large terrace. She had the brightest red hair Richard had ever seen, completely unnatural, almost defining a new colour in itself, but it suited her rather old-fashioned half-up hairdo and she beamed an enormous welcoming smile. She bent down to kiss a greeting to the man in the wheelchair. 'Herr Schmid,' she cried, 'it's so wonderful to see you again.' It had to be said that Herr Schmid didn't look to be too enamoured of his return visit, but he tried a smile nonetheless.

'Pleasure,' he wheezed coldly.

'Still chatty as ever!' She faked a laugh. 'Now, everyone, just leave your luggage where it is and Bruno here will deal with all of that.'

Richard was no expert in Norse mythology, but if he were ever asked to give a police description of Thor, the Norse God of Thunder, then Bruno would be it. He moved slowly towards the boat, his frame not built for speed. In fact, he was built like the island itself, rising up as pure granite but with long, greying blond hair, a carefully manicured short beard, cold blue eyes and the kind of muscle definition that should really only exist on Greek statues. Richard had a feeling that rather than move each piece of luggage individually, Bruno might just pick up the whole boat and move it about like an airport trolley.

'Bruno,' he said, and it was difficult to know if he was being menacing or just struggling with the word. 'Bruno Leroux.'

The woman in the flowery jumpsuit stepped forward excitedly. 'Bruno "Mangetout" Leroux!' she exclaimed. 'I love your television show! I'm Lea Boudon. We didn't get to meet last time I was here.' Bruno nodded in acknowledgement and his neck muscles rippled like a water bed.

Richard had some vague memory of Bruno 'Mangetout' Leroux. His television show had been a huge hit a few years back when foraging for food had been briefly all the rage. He was a kind of French Bear Grylls, who had spent years in the French Foreign Legion before becoming a celebrity with his own brand of urban scavenging. Initially the French public, who after all were proud of the sheer range of animals that they ate, were intrigued but then appalled when 'Mangetout' fashioned a hearty stew from the rubbish skips on a notorious Paris housing estate.

'Where are my manners! My name is Elise Lafarge.' The red-haired woman flapped apologetically. 'I'll be here making sure you have everything you need for your stay and that when you leave us you'll feel that much happier about things.' Elise looked at the group and Richard saw her optimism wane a little. 'Anyway, let's get you all inside and into your rooms.'

Albrecht Schmid drove his wheelchair through the large double doors of the conservatory followed by Lea Boudon, who already knew where she was going.

'You must be Madame Nevaeh?' There was a slight frost in Elise's voice as the young woman passed.

'Just Nevaeh,' the young woman replied. 'Just Nevaeh.' Her accent had somehow become more exotic than Richard had heard so far, but then he'd only heard her filming herself. She'd said nothing to anyone else.

'Oh, yes!' Elise continued. 'I've seen your Instagram videos, your TikToks – is that what they're called? So refreshing to see a young woman use her body to help others…'

'I am an influencer, madame!' Nevaeh said forcefully and strode into the interior.

'That's what they call it now, is it, dear?' Richard heard Elise mutter.

'And Pastor Gilbert, it's such a pleasure to meet you. So they finally managed to tempt you to come here to visit and in such lovely weather too!'

The small man showed remarkably white teeth as he smiled and shook Elise's hand, then his face darkened in a sudden Jekyll and Hyde transformation. 'I never give in to temptation, madame, for there is evil I have seen under the sun, an error that proceeds from the ruler!' He reached a crescendo, then came back down quickly. 'Ecclesiastes, chapter ten, verse five.'

Momentarily stunned by the pastor's ire, Elise quickly regained her composure. 'No sins of the flesh here, Pastor, just a welcoming afternoon cocktail served in the lounge.'

'Good.' Pastor Gilbert beamed, walking in without another word.

Elise turned to Richard. 'Doctor Ainsworth? My feeling is you might be quite busy, I'm already tempted to brain some of them myself.'

Richard smiled in return. He knew a fellow hospitality worker when he saw one. 'I'm not that type of doctor actually, I'm…'

'Oh, yes! Forgive me, the shrink. Well you've certainly got your work cut out with this lot.'

He followed Elise inside. *A shrink? A psychiatrist?* Inside, his own head was now raging. *Oh, Valérie, what have you done to me?*

Chapter Five

Richard would never have tried to guess at the interior of the place because the exterior was already beyond his expectations, and clearly when the designers and architects had sat down together, budget-setting wasn't part of the discussion. The inside though was simply jaw-dropping. The high ceiling of the orangery connected to what was probably the original outer wall and, inside that, was a large circular room that looked like it may have been modelled on the *Titanic*, but with modern twists. The wood panelling covering so much of the walls was dark oak, but with highly polished brass everywhere too. There were ships' wheels, fake portholes and lifebuoys adorning the exposed red brickwork, and four dark steel, winding staircases leading to the upper floors that used thick naval rope as banisters. In the centre, in a kind of sunken circular area, were four deep-red Chesterfield sofas around a low table with a yellowing globe set into it. At one 'end' of the room was a dining table laid for eight places with crystal glasses reflecting the light from a candle centrepiece, a discreet distance from a grand piano that was turning around slowly on a circular plinth. At the other 'end' was a glass lift which went up to the next two floors.

The first floor was built like a balcony mezzanine and had eight doors set into the front part above the orangery – the bedrooms he assumed – while the other half of the mezzanine circle was a magnificent library. Above that, there was another balcony that went around the interior and underneath the flat roof, half of which was glass again and which gave most of the light to the interiors below. Elise had positioned herself behind a desk on the ground floor in front of a set of double wooden doors that presumably led to a kitchen, servants' quarters and whatever powered the place.

The whole thing was stunning yes, but it was also numbing, like standing in front of a great work of art and feeling awed into a sense of personal inadequacy. His fellow guests, however, were either used to such lavish surroundings, didn't care for the place or had all been there before. Whatever it was, they seemed markedly, almost rudely indifferent to their surroundings. For Richard it felt unreal, like walking on to a glorious film set. The result of that though was that Richard had grown up in Britain in the seventies and eighties and if he'd learnt one thing from, for example, James Bond films, it was that man-made private islands owned by billionaires were rarely, very rarely indeed, a good thing.

He decided not to stand and wait with the others but sit on one of the Chesterfields instead, he – and Passepartout – taking in the setting. He still had no signal on his phone, which was no surprise, and his search for the hotel Wi-Fi had been fruitless so he watched his companions instead. One by one the guests were despatched to their rooms, Herr Schmid taking the lift. Pastor Gilbert took the stairs as lifts were apparently the Devil's work; Lea Boudon did the same, but in the opposite corner, enjoying, in Richard's mind and to her credit, the sheer glamour of them. Nevaeh took the lift too, but waited for it to be empty first, and was once again talking into her phone while doing some kind of writhing as the thing ascended.

Richard and Passepartout were the last at the desk.

'I saw you watching everyone, Doctor Ainsworth,' Elise said admonishingly and wagging her finger at him. 'Sitting there on one of our sofas pretending to just marvel at the architecture.'

'I wasn't, honestly,' he protested. 'I really was marvelling at the architecture.'

She squinted her eyes at him. 'Not something you'd do if you'd been here before,' she said slowly. 'Which you have.'

This obviously took Richard completely by surprise. 'Well, it still gets me every time!' he replied urgently. 'I can just never take it in enough!'

Elise Lafarge looked at him coldly. 'Monsieur, sorry *Doctor* Ainsworth. You're a psychiatrist, you watch and you judge. Well, I do the same; it's my job too in a way. But please, I beg you, do it discreetly; my other guests have far too many skeletons in their closets to be keen on being watched. You might get hit with a flying bone.'

'I shall be as discreet as possible,' Richard said, mustering as much charm as he could, while really wishing to confess that his PhD was in film history and not psycho-analysis. 'I'm here to cleanse my soul,' he added instead, to which all he got was a suspicious shrug.

'You're in the Bezos room,' Elise said, this time forcing a slight smile. 'Fourth one in from the right.' She gave him a credit card key.

'Ah, I think I stayed there before,' he exclaimed trying to win back some trust.

'You stayed in Jobs.'

'Ah, yes, of course I did.'

He was glad to be out of the woman's gaze, though he noticed that she was still watching him from behind her desk as he made his way around the first-floor balcony and past rooms Zuckerberg, Musk and Gates. He hadn't paid attention to who had what room and frankly he didn't know if that's what he was supposed to be doing. It was possible of course that Valérie had simply decided that this retreat suited his needs best and was just letting him recharge his batteries. He didn't linger long on that possibility, however, as it seemed incredibly unlikely. If he was here to find something out therefore, he decided now was as good a time as any to take stock of what he knew so far. First thing was that he was surrounded by some pretty unfriendly people; none of them had bothered to introduce themselves. Neither had he, obviously, but then he was English, it really wasn't his job. One thing he did notice straight away was that there were eight bedrooms and, so far at least, only five guests had checked in. Unless Elise had a room and the Durands and 'Mangetout'. He suspected that the Durands would insist on separate rooms, however, so the maths didn't work out. Assuming there were staff rooms somewhere else then, that left three empty bedrooms and presumably one of those was for their host.

Richard had seen absolutely no evidence to suggest that there even would be a host, but none of the guests, himself included, had looked excited to be here, which in Richard's world meant that they had most definitely been invited. No adult actually likes being invited anywhere, was his considered opinion, hence the heavy atmosphere. Even Elise didn't look like she wanted to be here and she was running the place. He decided it was best to unpack and then explore before coming to any hasty conclusions and he tapped his keycard on the locking panel and stood back as the wide wooden door automatically swung slowly open. His suitcase fell from his right hand and Passepartout nearly fell from the other. He had never seen a room like it; if his jaw kept dropping at this rate he was going to have to wear some kind of padded chin strap.

Firstly, it felt as though, if he stepped much further forward, he would fall directly into the Atlantic itself. He had seen infinity swimming pools, this was an infinity bedroom: the plush, soft deep-pile ocean-coloured carpet curving downwards at the edge and towards a grand window that covered the entire west-facing wall. To the left of the door, the bed – Emperor size if that exists – was a four-poster plumped so much it looked like it was made of clouds, a deep-purple bed-runner adding a touch of class and colour. There was a walnut desk to his right, also facing the sea and hosting an old-fashioned blotting pad, a desk light and a large bowl of potpourri. Further right was a gleaming bathroom with heated toilet seat, porthole cupboards, a roll-top bath and a massage shower. Needless to say there was an electric shutter facing west if you were overcome with the need to give passing ships a glimpse of how the 'haves' went about their ablutionary habits.

He walked slowly towards the window, almost like a high diver approaching the end of the diving board. Passepartout followed just a few steps behind and with understandably more caution.

'I'll say this, little fella,' Richard said to the tiny dog, 'I don't know why I'm here, but so far I've got absolutely no com… ow! Bloody hell!'

Richard walked straight into the window, not having made allowances for just how thick the glass would be, and he put a hand to his bashed forehead while Passepartout gave him a sympathetic look of 'rather you than me'. At least it hadn't smashed and he hadn't ended up on the granite rocks below. A small lump was growing on his forehead, however, and he searched the minibar in the corner, hoping for some ice. It was, he was grateful to see, fully stocked and there was a note on the inside of door which read.

'Welcome back, Doctor Ainsworth, this mini-fridge has been stocked with the choices you have indicated previously. Please feel free to enjoy them at our expense and please contact me if you require anything else.'

It was an unnerving message in that not only had Richard never been here before – he was pretty sure he would have remembered that – but also, whoever the other Doctor Richard Ainsworth was, he had an appalling idea of what constituted a stocked hotel minibar. There were various flavours of something called Kombucha, small *canettes* of 'alcohol free' gin and tonic and diet Pepsi, not even Coke, but Pepsi. Obviously Richard was no psychiatrist himself but he was building a picture of Doctor Ainsworth the shrink that was not at all in the man's favour. He took out a can of Blueberry Essence and Hot Sauce Kombucha and placed it on his forehead, it was cold at least and eased the swelling rapidly.

He sat on the side of the bed and wondered if he should go exploring or just rest up for a bit. The confusion of the day combined with the sea air had certainly made him sleepy but, and though he tried to suppress the feeling, there was also a certain amount of adrenalin running through his body and he wondered if he should make use of this rare form of energy.

He heard a noise at the door and a note appeared underneath it. 'Dinner will be at seven,' it read. 'Please dress accordingly.'

'What on earth does that mean?' he asked himself. He had a nice pair of chino slacks and a collared shirt, but the rest of his case was really just T-shirts and shorts. He opened the door hoping to catch the messenger and ask for more details, but there was no one to be seen. It was then that Passepartout shot out between his legs on to the empty mezzanine and made speedily for the stairs. And he was going up, not down. Richard grabbed his keycard, a poo bag and ran after the little dog.

For a dog with such small legs Passepartout managed to run up the spiral staircase with more ease and grace than Richard, his nimble footwork meaning that he easily increased the distance between the two of them. Richard reached the top eventually and an automatic tinted-glass door slid open to reveal yet another design phenomenon.

The glass floor that he had noticed from the ground-floor lounge area and which provided much of the light below, was actually a swimming pool with a swim-up bar. Next to it was a jacuzzi, another purpose-built area containing a sauna, a steam room, what looked like a yoga room and the inevitable gym. There was also a grassed area with sun loungers and telescopes, and the palm tree that Richard had noticed from the boat trip over, which was actually fake and atop a lantern, presumably acting as a lighthouse. It was all, quite literally, on another level to anything Richard had ever encountered before and he'd never wanted more to be a fatigued international entrepreneur with a desperate need for regular soul-cleansing and blue-sky-thinking updates.

Passepartout certainly felt at home. He was, to Richard's guilt, and after a long day's travel, happily relieving himself in the sandy 'Dog Pen' area. He exited the small fenced beach-like garden via a swing gate and immediately, as he left, a rake automatically cleaned the place leaving it as pristine as a golf bunker.

Richard was shaking his head again at the sheer wonder of the whole place when it suddenly dawned on him that Passepartout had known exactly where to go. So either he'd been here before, suggesting the same about Valérie, or dogs have a kind of defecation homing instinct akin to elephants returning to a specific place to die, which he doubted. His thoughts were then interrupted by some jazzy piano playing from another raised, though covered, circular dais that he now saw was partially hidden behind the swim-up bar.

'*You ain't nothing but a hound dog! Cryin' all the time!*' A small man with an old-fashioned entertainer's perm and wearing an expensive tuxedo was watching Richard as he sang and played. 'This is "Big Mama" Thornton's version by the way, not the later Elvis one. *And they said you was high-classed, well, that was just a lie.*' He finished this remarkable introduction with a few gentle notes. 'I'm Bernie Webb,' he said, 'and I sing what I see!' It was obviously a well-practised line, delivered with an accent of pure Estuary English and a finger gesture suggesting he was a quick-on-the-draw gunman, before adding a further tuneful flourish.

'I'm Doctor Richard Ainsworth,' he said, feeling he should play up to the character.

'*It had to be you…*' Bernie Webb sang in reply.

'…psychiatrist.'

The man slipped seamlessly into The Everly Brothers' 'Love Hurts'.

'Yes,' Richard interrupted, feeling this had gone on long enough. 'Could you stop that, please?'

'*Don't stop me now, I'm having such a good time! I'm having a ball.*'

Richard gave the man a cold stare. 'I mean it, enough. Or I'll have you sectioned.'

Bernie Webb beamed a showbiz smile back at him, but the eyes were empty. 'I'm Bernie Webb and I sing what I see!' he repeated. 'I just thought I'd show you my party piece,' he added, a hint of hurt in his voice.

'Sorry.' Richard felt a little guilty. 'But it's been a long day.' Bernie played a few pleasant notes. 'Are you a guest here too?' Richard asked, hoping it wouldn't lead to another song.

'No, Doc,' Bernie said. 'I'm staff, mate.' And he pretended to doff his cap while still gently, soothingly even, playing his piano. 'I come up here to warm the fingers up before dinner. I've got a posh room though,' he added, apparently distancing himself from the other staff. 'It used to be called Murdoch but I asked the name to be changed to Carnegie, like the hall.'

That's six out of eight rooms accounted for then, Richard noted, ignoring the patter. 'I was going to ask about dinner,' he said. 'I've been told to dress accordingly,' he stressed the word, hoping for an explanation.

'Well no one wants naked flesh at the table!' Bernie joked and added a 'ba dum tish' on the piano. 'It's like an affliction, sorry. Anyway, your tux will be in your wardrobe. Made to measure, Savile Row.' He then, with a wonderful vocal imitation of Fred Astaire, started singing 'Puttin' on the Ritz'.

Richard raised his eyebrows. He hadn't actually looked in the wardrobe yet but was feeling badly out of his comfort zone, not that he had a comfort zone. He walked back to the pool, out of sight of Bernie so he could shake his fist at the sky in another gesture of annoyance at Valérie. He probably overdid it a little but he felt vindicated nonetheless and started wagging his finger in a furious show of defiance. While doing so, out of the corner of his eye, he noticed what he was sure was a face watching him from the yoga room, a very worried, almost grotesque face. He stopped immediately and pretended he'd been stretching instead, the classic cover-up for a loss of dignity. Discreetly he looked again at the yoga room, but the face was no longer there.

He went back to where Bernie was still enthusiastically playing away.

'Did you see that face, in the window there?' Richard asked. Thinking it was probably staff, sneaking in some exercise where they shouldn't.

'No, mate,' Bernie replied. 'I was putting on the Ritz.'

Chapter Six

Richard's initial misgivings about the Bond villain environment were still strong but as he followed behind Passepartout on the stairs down to dinner, he had to admit that he had rarely felt this good. He hadn't had a swim yet, nor a sauna, nor a Swedish massage either but dressing in a top-class, perfectly cut and fitted dinner suit had done more for his confidence than anything else had for some time. He had rarely looked this good and the place, even with the suspicions and ignorance he had as to why he was there, fitted that mood to a tee. He felt somehow important and decided to take the stairs rather than the lift, because it just felt right. Elise had prepared a small bowl of food for Passepartout underneath the piano where Bernie was now tinkling discreetly away with some old standards. The other guests were already there: Albrecht Schmid in his wheelchair; Pastor Gilbert, still in his white suit, pacing at the edge of the orangery; Lea Boudon sitting on one of the sofas, vaping contentedly away; and Nevaeh, in a dress that looked like it might have been sprayed on, chattering into her phone.

Richard stopped two or three steps from the bottom and, carried away by his appearance, decided to speak. 'I always seem to be the last to arrive.' He raised an amused and confident eyebrow. 'Let me introduce myself. The name's Ainsworth. Richard Ainsworth.' He paused, remembering himself. 'Actually, Doctor Ainsworth. Doctor Richard. Doctor Ainsworth. Doctor Richard Ainsworth. I'm a doctor. Richard's the name.' He wisely decided to leave it there, feeling quite disappointed that he'd somehow fluffed his big line after a lifetime of secret in-the-mirror rehearsals.

Elise appeared through the smoke of Lea's vape, spraying deodoriser as she went. 'Well, thank God – sorry, Pastor Gilbert – but thank heavens someone's decided to break the ice,' she said in a hectoring voice. 'Who's next?'

She was met with an uncomfortable silence. 'OK then, I'll go next,' she said irritably. 'My name is Elise Lafarge, I'm the manager-housekeeper of Le Fort Esprit de l'Air. I've worked for the company in other venues for decades, mainly Paris, but this is now the flagship resort and I was brought in for my "kick up the arse" skills. Together with Bruno here, that is "Mangetout" – a name he prefers, though I can't for the life of me think why – and with the help of Pascal and Lilibet Durand we run a tight ship. Every conceivable need is catered for – well, in so far as we can anyway. Obviously there's no late-night Uber Eats or anything like that. We are essentially cut off for the duration of your stay. Also,' she added quickly, 'some housekeeping. There isn't any. We do think it's important that you're not over-pampered, so you make your own bed, keep your own things tidy and so on.' She beamed a very false smile at the room. 'So that's me, who wants to take the next turn?'

Lea Boudon coughed to indicate she was about to say something. 'I'm Lea Boudon and this is not the first time I've been here. I'm very lucky, I won my first visit through my husband's company Christmas draw and my second in a magazine competition. It was one of those slogan things, "In exactly twenty words, say why you want to visit Le Fort Esprit de l'Air?"'

She left it hanging there, obviously waiting for someone to ask what her answer had been.

Surprisingly it was the pastor who wanted to know, obviously a fan of pithy epithets. 'Well?' he thundered.

'My answer was, "I want to visit Le Fort Esprit de l'Air again, because I want to see if it has improved."' She beamed her cleverness at the room, before adding, 'I won this dress in a competition too.'

It was a black full-length off-the-shoulder number with a rather gaudy fake orchid on the one diamantine strap.

'Second prize was two of those dresses,' Elise muttered to Richard conspiratorially.

I am what I am! And what I am…' Bernie sang from his seat at the piano, '…is Bernie Webb. I came, I saw and I couldn't get off the damned island,' he joked. 'Just think of me as part of the furniture.' He finished his brief introduction with a beautiful rendition of the 'Hallelujah Chorus' from Handel's *Messiah*, which prompted the pastor into action.

'I am Pastor Gilbert Rondeau from Montreal in Canada. And…' He paused and bowed his head. 'I used to be in Vegas, a life of sin and iniquity.' This last part was spoken almost as a confession, then the fire and brimstone level arrived. 'Then I saw the light! I read the Bible! And I knew I had to help my fellow man! There is only one law and that is…'

'Yes, but why are you here?' Albrecht Schmid had spoken so little, it took everyone by surprise.

'I understood this place was for sale and I'd like to make this the base for my worldwide church.' The pastor answered very gently, but they all knew what was coming. 'Anyone else looking to buy and stand in the way of the work of Lord God Almighty?' he thundered, pointing at everyone in the room individually. As he was the only one who hadn't 'dressed' for dinner he gave the impression of white-suited purity, but it also made him look rather odd.

In any case, no one answered his question and once again it was left to Elise to mutter that 'not even God could afford this place.' Bernie moved into a rather intrusive rendition of 'The Way We Were'.

'*Scattered pictures…*' he sang loudly.

'That'll do, Bernie.' Elise waved her hand at him. 'Keep it light.'

'My name is Nevaeh, it's Heaven backwards.' She had turned off her phone finally and was addressing the room, standing as though on a film première red carpet. She waited for Bernie to tail off. 'I am Nevaeh, but unlike Madame here…' She nodded towards Lea with a look of mild distaste as if the older woman was an affront to youth and beauty. 'Unlike madame, I didn't have to win a competition, I won at life – I was invited.'

Before any tension could arise from her provocation it was inevitably Bernie that interrupted. '*I found him in the star… In the call… In the blue… But it never was you… It never was anywhere you…'*

He sang and played the Judy Garland standard plaintively and skilfully, and annoying though he could no doubt be, Bernie Webb was far too talented to be a mere dinner accompaniment to pampered, stressed-out entrepreneurs.

'Did you write that for me?' Nevaeh asked without irony. 'It's lovely, but it's pronounced Nevaeh my name, not Never.'

Once again Richard caught Elise's eye. 'I reckon they pumped her boobs up with her brain cells,' she whispered a little too loudly.

'At least I had somewhere to put them in the first place, madame,' Nevaeh riposted, her exotic accent slipping a notch.

Elise smiled widely. 'Well done, you! That's the spirit. A bit of back-and-forth as they used to call it.' She paused. 'So that just leaves you, Herr Schmid.'

Herr Schmid drove his wheelchair out from the dark shadows to slightly less dark shadows; in fact just about the only part of him in the light was his right hand, which gave the impression that it was now somehow separated from the rest of his body. What made it even more sinister was that the nail of his forefinger was black with bruising. 'I am from Germany originally, Hamburg,' he began in a high, rasping voice. 'I was one of a number of financiers for this project.' He rolled back into the shadows.

'When do we get to meet our host anyway?' the pastor asked.

'I'm told that Ian – that is Mr Connor – will arrive soon,' Elise replied. 'Sorry, but that's all I know.'

'Ian Connor?' Richard asked, trying to suppress a laugh.

'That is right, Doctor Ainsworth, Ian Connor. Do you know him?'

Richard smiled. 'I doubt any of us do!'

'Is there Wi-Fi?' Nevaeh interrupted. 'I'd like to look him up and also my followers expect something from me all the time, I really must…'

'Only the Lord has followers!!' the pastor brayed inevitably.

Elise shook her head ignoring the man. 'Sorry, dear,' she said. 'There is no Wi-Fi, no internet. Just intranet, so you can explore the island on your phones or devices, even chat to each other if you like, but the outside world – which you can see of course from the roof terrace – is not contactable.'

'You mean, there's no Wi-Fi at all?' Nevaeh momentarily wrenched her phone away from her face and spoke with the desperation of someone who had crawled across the Sahara Desert and found that the oasis had closed early.

'But we can take a boat back whenever we want?' Lea Boudon asked, a worried look on her face.

'Only if the tide allows.' Pascal Durand came in through the double doors with some bowls and wearing a most unlikely dinner jacket above his baggy denim jeans.

'And if you can be arsed.' His wife followed behind wearing an apron over similar denims.

'Lilibet,' Pascal sighed heavily. 'We've both lived here nearly forty year. For the last time, it's a bloody tide thing!'

'Well, I think that's everyone.' Elise clapped her hands, more to put a stop to the bickering Durands than anything else. 'Guests and staff.'

'There's Monsieur Mangetout.' Lea Boudon's tone clearly suggested that she didn't at all think he should be left out.

'I came here by accident a few years ago and stayed.' The deep voice came from over by the table. 'I now cook and help with restorative exercise classes.'

'By accident?' The pastor didn't seem convinced, his voice accusatory.

Richard saw Mangetout catch Elise's eye and she seemed to nod encouragement.

'I was at the end of my life. I decided to swim into the ocean and never return, my body to be used as sustenance for the sea and all its creatures.'

'I knew it!' the pastor cried. 'Suicide is a sin!'

'Yes, but clearly he survived.' Elise was losing her patience.

'And what happened?' Lea asked.

'He got caught up in one of my nets,' Pascal answered. 'Nearly ruined them he did. Still, we took him in.'

'Good. Now we know.' Elise clapped her hands again.

Richard, thinking about the mystery face he had seen earlier, was on the verge of asking if there were any other staff on the island when suddenly they were all interrupted by a thunderously loud crash that sounded more like a rock fall somewhere, startling all of them except the old Durands.

'What was that?' Nevaeh cried.

Pastor Gilbert, who had hit the floor as though taking cover from an assassination attempt, told them all to get down and that the place was obviously possessed.

'No, not possessed, Pastor Gilbert,' Elise said with irritation. 'Just in the way.'

She stepped over the pastor and opened one of the sliding orangery doors, revealing a large gull lying awkwardly on the concrete floor, its neck clearly broken.

'We told them this would happen.' Lilibet shook her head and looked at her husband. 'Didn't we? We told them this would happen.'

'We did,' he replied sadly. 'And would they bloody listen? No! Put glass everywhere; bloody bird hazard now it is.' Finally, and with some sadness, they had agreed on something.

Another loud bang sent everyone into shock again, the pastor once more throwing himself to the ground.

'Dinner is served,' Mangetout intoned deeply, standing beside a large gong.

Chapter Seven

For once there was an excuse for the moody silence and they ate most of the first course without anyone talking. The shock of the broken-necked gull and the violence of such a needless death rather put a dampener on what was otherwise an excellent *bouillabaisse*. Richard tried to lighten things up by praising the chef, who he thought had been Madame Durand.

'Oh, call me Lilibet,' she beamed at the recognition of her contribution. 'But I didn't make it, Mangetout did, didn't you?'

Mangetout nodded solemnly. 'I call it Atlantic Forage,' he said with a hint of pride.

'Oh great,' Bernie interrupted. 'Plastic bottle tops and prophylactics, just what the doctor ordered.'

Rather than breaking the tension, his joke only deepened it as one by one each diner quietly put down their soup spoon, while at the same time complimenting the originality of the flavours and finding various ways of saying, 'I want to save room for the main course.'

All except Nevaeh, who had barely touched her soup anyway and who had an anxious look on her face. 'We're not eating seagull, are we?' And while some, Richard noticed, rolled their eyes at what they judged to be a naive question, it was, to his mind, a very pertinent enquiry.

'Not tonight, dear,' Elise said soothingly. 'Even Mangetout can't turn fresh food around that quickly.' There was relief from most quarters at the news.

'You know technically, seagulls don't actually exist. They're just gulls,' Lea Boudon said patronisingly. Her competitive instinct – after all, that's why she was here – was open and aggressive and constant.

'I just saw one hit a window,' Nevaeh replied sulkily, clearly still shaken by the event.

'Yes, but that was a gull, not a seagull,' Lea persisted.

'It was a gull that came from the sea! What difference does it make?' Nevaeh's eyes flared angrily and it was obvious to all that the two women, so very different, were going to be at each other's throats for the entire stay. Lea Boudon came across as a bully, while Nevaeh was touchy and had a short fuse. Richard thought that one would have to be less sensitive to survive the world of a social media influencer, but clearly not.

'Does it happen a lot?' the pastor asked, directing the question at Elise but getting an answer from Pascal Durand.

'All the bloody time!' he said with some anger and Richard noticed his wife just touch his arm to calm him down. An oddly warm gesture considering their constant squabbling.

'I'm afraid he's right,' Elise said, helping Mangetout clear some of the dishes. 'Especially in the evening. You haven't touched your soup, Herr Schmid, are you not hungry?'

'I am tired,' he replied simply.

'We told 'em!' Pascal Durand was obviously very upset by the death of the gull. 'It's not natural. I lived on this place more of my life than not and it was better before this, this…' He was struggling to describe the place at all. 'This business hippy twaddle!'

Business hippy twaddle seemed the absolutely perfect description and Richard made a mental note of it.

'But why do they do it?' Nevaeh might not have been the sharpest knife in the drawer, but at least she was curious and as a result of that, she probably helped a lot of other people who preferred to hide their ignorance, Richard concluded.

'It's the reflection, dear,' Lilibet said. 'The windows reflect what's behind the gulls, so they think they're flying safely into the horizon. Only they're not, it's glass.'

'All of that side used to be a nesting ground,' Pascal shook his sadly. 'Gulls, gannets, puffins. You don't see many puffins now, maybe a few.'

'Sometimes the birds fly deliberately into the window, well male ones do anyway.' Elise sounded more inconvenienced than passionate like Pascal.

'Why?' Nevaeh was shocked at the thought.

'They think it's a rival, dear, on their territory, but they just end up attacking their own reflection. Still, that's men for you.' Both Lea and Nevaeh, finally on common ground, nodded in sage agreement.

Silence descended once more, the women having come to a blanket agreement on men in general and the men, knowing how these things generally go, deciding not to argue. The main course was a welcome arrival then, especially as – and much to everyone's obvious relief – it was announced as pork tenderloins and was not in any way bird shaped.

Richard decided to try again, the previous talk of reflections having jogged his memory and, he was quietly proud to admit, his investigative instincts. 'This really is very good,' he said, nonchalantly crumbling some bread. 'It must be quite something for just the four of you to keep this place running. Do you not take on extra staff when you're full?'

There wasn't an immediate reply, though he thought he noticed a nervous look pass between the Durands.

'No, Doctor, there's no need,' Elise replied fussing around the table. 'We have everything covered in the kitchen and the rooms aren't made up every day like normal hotels.'

'Oh.' Lea seemed put out. 'Yes, I'd forgotten that. I don't understand it myself.'

'Well, there's a number of reasons really: one the environment.' The Pastor harrumphed at Elise's explanation. 'And two, it's not part of the ethos of the place. Mr Connor's belief is that the modern businessman or woman is far too pampered and that's what causes their burnout. They reach the top, have all the trappings of success, people running around after you and so on, and they lose their edge, they lose the common touch. He calls it the Roman Empire Disease.'

'Business hippy twaddle' it might be, Richard thought, but there could be something in that. 'It must be exhausting for you though,' he said simply instead.

'We're fine, Doctor.' Her reply was rather tart and the thought occurred to him that she might think he was a spy, a business psychologist sent by head office to come and keep tabs on staff performance. Whatever it was, he didn't want to push the idea of there possibly being someone else on the island fort just yet and certainly not in public. There was always the possibility of course that maybe – just maybe – it had been his own reflection in the window after all.

After dinner was over they mostly moved to the Chesterfield sofas; just Albrecht Schmid stayed apart while Pastor Gilbert endlessly restless, paced up and down. Richard sat next to Passepartout while Lea read a magazine that was on the coffee table. Nevaeh stared blankly at her phone, looking quite lost without the use of its primary function of connectivity. Bernie meanwhile was back at the piano and playing quite beautifully while also filling in for various wind instruments with some skilful mouth trumpeting. Elise even joined in with him at one point as they sang a glorious version of 'Well, Did You Evah!' from *High Society*. Elise capturing perfectly the crooner drawl of Bing Crosby as they both belted out, surely with some irony, '*What a swell party this is…*'

As the evening went on, Bernie continued alone; his trumpet solo with a gentle piano background on a Miles Davis medley was particularly soothing, Richard thought, and he began to feel very tired. *Why was Bernie there?* he wondered. He was neither proper staff nor proper guest, but certainly a talented musician and performer and also – it seemed quite obvious by the amount he was drinking – not entirely happy with his situation. For once Richard, not a great fan of the internet, as it had put him out of a job after all, really wanted to search for some information. It was Elise who clapped enthusiastically as Bernie reached the end of the song and after a brief moment everyone else joined in as well. In the end, of course, why Bernie Webb was there was also a question Richard could ask of nearly all of them. He didn't even know why he was there. It was a question which only Ian Connor – he chuckled at the name again – could really explain.

As the gentle applause died down and Bernie took a theatrical bow, a new sound echoed around the large room. 'Good evening, ladies and gentlemen, this is your host Ian Connor.'

Everyone looked first at each other and then accusingly at Elise, who just shrugged and shook her head to indicate that she had nothing to do with it, whatever it was.

The male voice had a soft Irish accent and a playful quality that under other circumstances might have put the listener at ease. 'Welcome back to Le Fort Esprit de l'Air,' it began. 'I'm so sorry I wasn't there to greet you in person, but I promise to arrive shortly. Believe me, I wouldn't miss this for the world! It'll be fun! In the meantime, I'm sure Elise and the team are looking after you all.'

Everybody eyed each other nervously.

'I don't like this!' Pastor Gilbert shouted. Presumably, Richard suspected, this was not the disembodied voice he was used to hearing and his own voice caused the recording to pause.

Richard, on the one hand, had been waiting all evening for something like this to happen; all the signs plus Valérie's string-pulling interference had suggested as much. So far everything had had the appearance of an elaborate game, a sophisticated theatrical set-up to divert high rollers from their temporary miseries. On the other, he had to admit, Valérie herself was not one for frivolities, so why would she organise for him to take part in a game? He took another sip on his drink, trying to look calm while in reality he was trying to make up his mind. If it wasn't all a charade, he thought, it was potentially dangerous, quite possibly murderous and therefore much more up Valérie's street. He gulped, hoping nobody was watching him. Danger and murder are two things that any sensible individual would run a mile from, especially Richard who liked to run away at the slightest sign of small talk let alone potential death. This was different though and he rather alarmingly felt a surge of adrenalin that was fighting with his more usual retreat signals. All his life he had sat transfixed in front of a screen watching this exact kind of controlling set-up, one that would inevitably lead to an evening of rancour, suspicion and death. He had loved it, but had been outside of it. Now, he felt he was actually *in* a film, an interactive cinema experience that played on all of his senses, and even if the usual Richard would fight against such things, the intoxication was overwhelming. It had all the ingredients of a classic murder mystery, films he loved and rewatched over and over again. This wasn't just *And Then There Were None*, this was *The Cat and the Canary, Clue, What a Carve Up!,*

After the Thin Man. He was almost hyperventilating as the films tumbled around his mind. So yes, the adrenalin was flowing, the nervous excitement bubbling away. Valérie had done it again. She had read his mind and booked him on a murder mystery weekend, an immersive experience that would give the sense of live cinema that he had always dreamt about. He settled back in his seat and waited for the game to begin. He even chuckled quietly to himself, *Ian Connor*! What a wonderful twist that was.

Chapter Eight

Richard leant back into the deep leather sofa as Passepartout snored, resting his head on Richard's lap. Guiltily, after all the fist-shaking, he had to hand it to Valérie, this was perfect. His daughter Alicia had once asked him – he vaguely remembered that it was some kind of school project – which period in history would he travel back to if he had the use of a time machine. He hadn't needed to think for long; Egypt, he'd replied definitely. The little girl's eyes had widened on the assumption that her father, hitherto having shown little interest in the wider geo-political world, had chosen to see the pyramids being built or Cleopatra's parades or even the Suez Crisis or the Six Day War. All of her classmates had their parents scurrying around the swirl of time either killing off at source future murderous dictators or averting conflict and famine with modern enlightened thought but her daddy was a true original.

'Yes?' she had followed up excitedly.

'Yes. 1978. The set of *Death on the Nile*... Ustinov, Davis, Smith, Niven, Lansbury...'

His thoughts were rudely interrupted once more.

'You have been gathered here tonight to listen to the following indictments.' Ian Connor's voice had developed a sombre tone and Bernie's background piano playing perfectly matched the new ambience. 'Herr Albrecht Schmid, you secretly tried to remove me from the board of my own company and threatened to withdraw your funding if that does not happen. Traitor.'

If Schmid was upset or even queried the accusation it didn't show, he was still half in the shadows anyway and made no sound.

'Madame Nevaeh, you stand accused…'

'Actually, it's just Nevaeh.' She waved an accusing finger and rolled her head aggressively. Again, her voice briefly interrupted the playback.

'…of hideous hypocrisy. You were paid to spread positive awareness of Le Fort Esprit de l'Air and you responded to that arrangement by describing the bed linen as lame. Traitor.'

Nevaeh crossed her arms teenager-style and responded to the accusation. 'Honestly, how was I to know there's an accent on lamé?'

'Pastor Gilbert Rondeau. I offered you sanctuary from your taxation troubles and you repay me by claiming this place is possessed and that only your ownership can exorcise it. Traitor.'

The pastor for once remained entirely impassive, not even looking upwards.

'Elise Lafarge. This company has looked after you for most of your working life and yet you steal from us almost on a daily basis. Traitor.'

Elise rolled her eyes. 'Honestly, a few bits of cutlery. It'll hardly break the bank.'

'Madame Lea Boudon. You and your husband won a competition to stay here. And your review on Tripadvisor was two stars, "*I wouldn't pay for it!*" You didn't pay for it, dammit! Traitor.'

'Bernie Webb. On the run and in trouble, I gave you safety, with only one caveat. That you don't play any Liberace! Traitor.'

If this was a game, Richard was noticing that nobody was laughing, especially at this latest accusation. On the face of it and in all respects a minor crime and one that any lounge pianist might make, but Bernie clearly didn't get the joke and his face, despite the excess of wine, drained of colour.

'Doctor Richard Ainsworth. A clinical psychologist of world renown…' This should be interesting, Richard thought. 'I give you a lucrative contract and the best room – what do you do? Complain that the wall sockets aren't close enough to the bed! Traitor.'

Again, a minor grievance, but Richard felt pretty sure that in his life before becoming a B&B host he had more than likely left exactly that complaint.

'Bruno "Mangetout" Leroux. This island saved your life and how do you repay me? By siding with a television company behind my back, just so you can be on TV again. Traitor.'

Bruno stood impassively, saying nothing.

'Pascal and Lilibet Durand. I kept you on this island, fed and homed you. And how do you repay me? By reporting the company to the World Wildlife Fund! Traitors.'

The Durands both exhaled from their pipes simultaneously, but like the others, and with the exception of Nevaeh, they didn't deny the accusation.

'Ladies and gentlemen, how do you plead?'

'Turn it off!' The pastor was the first to respond as silence enveloped the room. Only Richard was smiling, enjoying the show immensely and marvelling at some really authentic performances. In particular he felt that the pastor was really into his part and he predicted big things for the man if he was lucky enough to get a break.

'I don't know how it was turned on!' Elise was flapping around and looking at Mangetout for assistance. He didn't give the impression of someone who knew his state-of-the-art audio playback systems with any great intimacy though, not unless he could boil the parts down for soup at least and it was Richard, with a warm, genuine smile on his face, who offered to help.

'Everybody start clapping,' he dictated, leading the way. They all looked at him as though as a psychiatrist himself he was in sore need of a colleague's support, but as Richard led the way, they slowly joined in. As Richard had already worked out, once they had together reached a certain level of noise, the recording started again.

'Welcome back to Le Fort Esprit de l'Air, I'm so sorry I wasn't there to greet you in person, but I promise to arrive shortly. Believe me, I wouldn't miss this for the world! It'll be fun! In the meantime, I'm sure Elise and the team are looking after you all.'

Richard, now thoroughly enjoying himself, made a big scene of following the speech around the room, before eventually sitting back down next to Passepartout on the sofa and opening the globe set into the coffee table. In it were small, obviously very powerful speakers and a small antenna, and next to them a green button which Richard pressed. The button turned red, and Ian Connor's voice stopped abruptly after the sentence, 'You have been gathered here tonight to listen to the following indictments.'

He sat back on the sofa unable to hide a rather smug grin and looking like he expected a high five from the still bored Chihuahua.

'*You're so vain*,' Bernie sang, a trifle cruelly in Richard's opinion, but it did nothing to dent his confidence.

'I asked you people a question; how do you plead?' Ian Connor's voice, though with a heavy hint of exasperation, once again filled the room and at the same time burst Richard's fragile bubble. Everyone else in the room turned to give him a look of extreme disappointment, tinged with pity. Even Passepartout finally opened his eyes and, with an added touch of betrayal, began to wag his tail with no little enthusiasm. Richard gave him a stern look, which changed nothing.

Slightly shakily Lea Boudon stood up, as usual a vape cloud hogging her head. 'Well, I plead guilty!' she shouted up to the ceiling. 'It wasn't very good last time! The pool was cold and… and… he played Liberace!' She pointed accusingly at Bernie Webb, who downed the glass of wine sitting on the piano and then started playing a quite furious version of 'Chopsticks'.

'Do you know what this is?' He also shouted up towards the ceiling and wherever he thought Ian Connor's voice was coming from.

'That's "Chopsticks",' Nevaeh replied.

'Exactly! Written in 1877 by Euphemia Allan under the pen name Arthur de Lulli. Liberace did a *version*! Do you know how prolific the old creep was? He was in the business for four decades, he released a hundred and eleven albums! Do you know how many songs he wrote? Bloody none, mate!' He banged away at the keyboard once more before pouring himself some more wine.

'I have tax problems, sure.' It was the pastor's turn to defend himself, but he was being rather cagey too. 'Governments of this world are godless. I use my money to help the poor and needy, not for war or climate change programmes or… or welfare for the heathen!'

'So you don't pay taxes then?' Elise concluded. 'You see, I thought the Bible said…'

'Never mind the Bible right now, lady. I said this place was possessed and here we are talking to the underneath of a goddamn swimming pool!'

It was quite the slip-up for a man of fervent religious belief, but he also seemed to have a point. Where was the voice coming from?

Nevaeh walked to the centre of the room and looked about her with an air of serious concentration. 'How do you think he's doing that?' she asked rhetorically. 'Do you think…' She seemed to be on the verge of a major breakthrough and her breathing increased. 'Do you think it might be… Wi-Fi?'

It was inevitable that Bernie would have something to say about such a let-down and he didn't miss his cue.

'Then you go and spoil it all by saying something stupid like I…'

Before he could reach the end of the sentence he made a grab at his throat and began choking. He stood up unsteadily and his face turned puce. Lea Boudon screamed as his other hand knocked the wine glass off the piano; it landed on the rug and earnt a filthy look from Elise. The pastor moved as far away as he could, obviously feeling that whatever possessed the island had now taken residence in the diminutive figure of showbiz journeyman Bernie Webb. For his part, Bernie continued to stagger wildly around the room, still choking and bouncing off furniture and other people like a pinball in a machine. Everyone recoiled from the horror and pain on his face, except for Schmid, who seemed not to care at all, even when Bernie almost fell in his lap. There wasn't one person Bernie Webb didn't approach, as if he were searching for whoever had done this to him. He lurched painfully at Nevaeh, who also screamed, before eventually he fell dramatically down the few steps to the sofas and landed at Richard's feet. Richard too recoiled, though he had had a feeling something like this would happen from the start of the evening. It's always the piano player first, he'd told himself.

Bernie made one last grab at Richard's leg, looking up at him in severe pain and desperately pulling at his own shirt collar. Finally he collapsed face down in the plush rug, his hand slipping off Richard's calf and on to the floor. Suddenly all the lights went out, plunging them into darkness, the only light coming unexpectedly from a lightning storm out at sea, followed by deafening

thunder from the open terrace doors. The lightning briefly lit up a silhouette along the orangery window. It was
the figure of an elegantly dressed woman holding a gun,
which was pointed directly into the room. Passepartout's
tail started to wag wildly and this time it was Richard
who screamed.

Chapter Nine

After a moment the lights came back on and briefly every-one looked at each other in suspicion and annoyance.

'Does that happen often?' The pastor's muffled question came from behind one of the sofas, though he still had enough about him to act as a potential buyer.

Nobody answered.

Lea was now completely obscured by a vape cloud, the pastor was on the floor again, Schmid hadn't moved, Nevaeh was recording herself, and the staff had remained exactly where they were. The silhouette of the gun-toting woman was lost because of the artificial light, though Richard now knew that Valérie was on the island, as did Passepartout, who looked disappointed that his mistress had not stayed around to greet him.

Bernie Webb still lay motionless on the floor at Richard's feet.

'Is he dead?' Elise asked, and although there was a touch of anxiety in her voice, there was also an element of extreme inconvenience. 'Can anyone else play the piano?' she added, pointing at the instrument and directing every-one's attention to it.

'OK, Bernie, you can get up now.'

The voice was Ian Connor's, only this time it wasn't through any hidden speakers, it was live and the man himself was sitting on the piano stool. He wore an immaculate dinner suit and had thick black-framed glasses perched tightly on a handsome face. Richard couldn't pinpoint his age; he could have put him anywhere in his thirties if it wasn't for the fact that his face was so serious, melancholy even, that it aged him by a good twenty years on top of that. His forehead was creased into a frown that suddenly disappeared with a flashing smile briefly showing perfect teeth, before morphing back into a frown again. The smile looked like it had taken a great deal of effort.

'I said you can get up now, Bernie! Always milking it. Jeez, he never knows when to stop.' Still Bernie Webb's body stayed still and Richard had the distinct feeling that things had not gone exactly to plan. He bent down to feel for a pulse and then jumped back in shock as the man suddenly sat up and grinned at him.

'Ha!' he laughed. 'Fooled you, eh?'

Connor shook his head like a tired parent. 'Sorry, Doctor,' he said, his eyes reproaching his piano player. 'And I suppose I should also apologise to everyone for my rather showy entrance. It didn't seem right to just meet you all. I wanted to create a bit of atmosphere.' He stood up from the piano stool allowing Bernie to reclaim his seat. 'A very good performance, Bernie, a little hammy as usual, but you had everyone fooled I think.' Everyone just stared at Connor. Some people are like that, they can dominate a room just by being in it and Ian Connor had charisma by the bucketload clearly. All eyes followed him and he knew it. He walked slowly around the perimeter of the room and behind Herr Schmid in the shadows. He had film star good looks too, but there was a hint of vulnerability about him as well, a touch of what seemed to Richard genuine sadness, and it showed as he leant on the bars of the old German's wheelchair.

'Well, now that everyone's finally here…' Elise started fussing around the room, 'perhaps we can arrange some nightcaps.' She took a tray from a buffet cupboard and passed it on to Bruno. Meanwhile Bernie, back at the piano, played something discreet and anonymous to smooth over the mood.

'So, were you here all the time then?' Nevaeh asked. 'Spying on us?'

Connor tried to smile again, but for whatever reason didn't feel motivated to see it through.

'I was, Nevaeh, yes. Though not spying as such and don't worry there aren't any cameras. I was just making sure that my guests were being looked after and that, of course, you were paying attention. Sorry it wasn't live-streamed on Wi-Fi for you.'

'Only a devil would hide in the shadows!' Pastor Gilbert's face was taut with anger while he pointed a right-eous finger at Connor. So far, by Richard's reckoning, the pastor had hit the floor three times that evening. Granted, he didn't have far to go, but neither did it look like he was quite ready to face his maker yet; the man was obviously very highly strung.

'Not just devils, Pastor, accountants that break the law too.' This time Connor did break a smile, though again it came and went quickly. The pastor found a seat and sat down, not taking his eyes off his host, a scolded look on his face.

If this is a game, Richard thought again, *it feels very authentic.*

Bruno returned with a tray of drinks, presumably, just like the suits hanging in the wardrobes, already knowing what everyone would be wanting. Much to Richard's relief he found that the doctor he was standing in for preferred hard liquor before bedtime and he sipped at a very fine single malt. Frankly, he needed the stimulus. If this really was a game it was pretty close to the bone and why hadn't Valérie come in? Was she here hunting someone down? Was she here to protect someone or to assassinate someone? Or did she just miss Passepartout and feel the need to make sure he was alright?

He had no idea how to answer any of these questions and decided to ride it out for the time being. To wait and see what the host Ian Connor – though he still doubted that was his real name – had up his sleeve after all the frankly low-rent and absurd accusations, none of which had been denied.

He did not have to wait long.

Ian Connor moved to the empty dining table and turned the end chair, which had a long wooden back, to face the room. He then sat in it as though it were a throne and he was the king. He crossed his long legs and swirled his brandy around the glass, his lips curled slightly upwards and even the lighting changed once more, a spotlight solely on him.

'It was interesting,' he began, his eyes only on the brandy which was leaving a film on the glass, 'to watch you, all of you, not even try to deny the accusations.' Now he raised his eyes and looked on each person individually. 'I realise of course, in the grand scheme of things, that an unkind Tripadvisor review, or missing spoons or even the work of Liberace and the World Wildlife Fund are small fry.' He took a sip of the brandy, while Richard reflected on how in the past he had spent days in a terrible mood just because of a bad Tripadvisor. 'But that's just it,' Connor continued. 'It's the small things and they add up, right? Until the whole lot is a big thing.' He stood up, obviously agitated. 'Like when you watch a documentary on fish or something and the camera shows this enormous beast just below the surface, and you think like wow! What is that? It's bigger than a blue whale! But it's not a blue whale, it's not one fish, it's a massive shoal of millions of little fish. You get me?' He thundered the question into the room and most people muttered barely audible replies.

'Actually a blue whale is a mammal,' Lea Boudon offered tentatively. The look on her face suggested she should have kept the fact to herself, but her competitive instinct had overridden it.

Connor sighed deeply and looked to the ceiling. 'We just added another fish to the shoal,' he said defeatedly.

'But what is this all about, really?' The pastor was upright again. 'I mean, OK, you're a little annoyed but is that why you invited us here? Just to say you're upset with us, because, you know, I have a flock that needs tending and if…'

'Oh belt up, man, will you?' Connor didn't sound angry, just tired, and he sat back down again. 'I've had enough. I've had enough of you and I've had enough of this.' He spread his arms wide seeming to indicate the entire fort. 'And this!' He threw a dozen or so banknotes on to the floor in front of him and nobody moved for a moment, before Lea and the pastor proceeded in an unseemly and distasteful scrum for the cash.

'Oh that's tacky,' Elise said loudly, while Nevaeh filmed the spectacle and Bernie struck up with, *'Money makes the world go around…'*

Richard sat back down next to Passepartout. His mind was in total confusion. He still didn't know if he was participating in a game or not. An outsider enmeshed in a creative holiday, the rest of them all playing a role. So far, everything had pointed to a version of Agatha Christie's *And Then There Were None*; Lilibet Durand had even said those words on the quay. But the piano player hadn't died, the host had turned up and now there was this rather grotesque scrabbling around on the floor for money. Not that Richard didn't need money, but he wouldn't wrestle for it. Then there was Valérie, lurking in the shadows somewhere. She had arranged Richard's presence here, but again, why?

'I see you, Doctor Ainsworth, taking it all in, no doubt making judgements on us all.'

'Only God can judge man,' the pastor cried, his reflexes not dissimilar to Bernie's, his words briefly distracting Lea, and he grabbed a handful of notes straight from her hand.

Richard watched them, but was aware that in turn Connor was watching him. He didn't feel at all qualified to respond, but knew that he really must do so. If it was part of a game, he must play on. If it wasn't a game, he might be in danger if he revealed his true identity as a non-psychologist; and it wasn't just Connor watching him, everyone was now. He pretended to pick at some dust on his trousers and took a sip of whiskey for courage.

'So, Doctor, what do you say?' Connor's attitude was mocking. Either he knew Richard wasn't a real psychologist or his attitude to the world of mental health wasn't a positive one.

'Know thyself,' Richard began, scrabbling around for a film quote that might fit the situation. 'Know thyself,' he repeated. 'I would say that there lies the beginning of wisdom.' He started to walk confidently around the room, though his legs felt like jelly and he couldn't remember the exact quote he had in mind. 'You know, to erm… defeat man's oldest enemy.' He turned to face Ian Connor from the other side of the room 'Vanity!' he blustered. 'Will we though? Let us hope.' He walked out of the room and on to the dark sun terrace offering up an apology for his mangled nonsense to the scriptwriters as he did so and hoping that no one else had recently watched Montgomery Clift in the 1962 film *Freud*.

He took a very deep breath of sea air. Whatever storm there had been had passed and the night, all too quickly for Richard's liking, had become still and calm. Behind him he heard questions being asked. Questions like, 'What the hell was that all about?' and 'Should I put know thyself on my Instagram?' That was good enough for him, as someone once said, 'If you can't convince them, confuse them.' His relief was short-lived, however, as he heard the cock of a gun in the darkness.

Chapter Ten

Richard stood frozen still, afraid to move. Some restorative holiday this had turned out to be; he was more strung out now than he had been when he left Saint-Sauver. Plus, he now finally concluded, with an armed Valérie on the scene this was very likely not a game at all, but some kind of elaborate, potentially lethal set-up of which he was most probably an insignificant, if not entirely expendable, pawn. That's of course if it even was Valérie.

'Valérie?' he asked, hoping he had that right.

'Is that you, Richard?' He had been right and she sounded annoyed. 'Quick, you must go back in, I need you in there, not out here!'

'Yes but…'

'Richard!'

'OK, OK, but I mean, it's a bit much. Is this a game or not?'

'Yes! And it's about to start!' She remained in the shadows somewhere to his right.

'About to start! But I'm exhausted already!'

'Go back in, Richard!'

'Hello? Doctor Ainsworth?' Elise had appeared silently behind him, making him jump. 'Were you talking to yourself? Is that a good thing in your profession?' she asked sarcastically.

Richard turned to face her, hoping the darkness was hiding the beads of sweat on his forehead. 'Yes, well,' he started, playing for time, 'as I said, know thyself. So I was just, well… getting to know myself.'

He could feel her eyes staring at him sceptically in the darkness. 'Are you going to re-join us,' she said eventually. 'I think Mr Connor has something he'd like to say to us all.'

Connor had resumed his throne while the other inhabitants of the room were arranged like a scattered audience in a nearly empty theatre.

'Glad you're back with us, Doctor!' He flashed one of his smiles, almost like a lighthouse itself, warning of danger ahead. 'I don't blame you for wanting some fresh air though, it's stifling in here.'

'I adjusted the air conditioning just as you instructed, Mr Connor.' Elise seemed a little hurt that she hadn't achieved perfection.

'It's not the room temperature that stifles me, Elise, it's the smell of greed.' He looked around the room again, his disgust obvious to see. 'You've all taken from me,' he said quietly. 'All of you. Whether that be money or trust, you've all chipped away at me like a sculptor on a block of marble. So, in a sense, you see before you your own creation.' He stood again. 'Well, I've come to a decision. Instead of taking little chunks, why don't you just take the whole stinking lot?' He opened his arms wide, but did not smile. 'Why have a little, when you can have it all?' There were some mutterings among the guests, mild insincere protestations that Connor waved away. 'Imagine… Pastor

Gilbert, imagine. You wouldn't have to buy this place, it would be yours. I'd give it to you.'

The pastor's eyes widened and the greed that Connor had mentioned was clear for all to see. 'You mean I'd get this place for nothing? No strings?'

'No strings.'

The pastor smiled and then the flame came back to his eyes. 'Get thee behind me, Satan!'

'I'm in front of you, you incorrigible fraud, but if you don't want it…'

'I didn't say no!' the pastor fired back immediately.

'Or you, Lea Boudon, no more kowtowing to your husband's boss and his wife. This would be yours, imagine what you could do with it, the social standing you would have?' Lea sucked furiously on her vape as if she were learning the bagpipes.

'Elise…' Connor's voice gained a further edge of cruelty. 'A lifetime of serving others for no credit whatsoever, you could steal all the cutlery you wished.

'Bruno Mangetout, your own island and no doubt TV series. Pascal and Lilibet, ah, if this island were really yours, you could return it to what it once was.'

'We could just put curtains up,' Lilibet said, offering a practical solution.

'You'd still get a reflection woman; it's still glass!' her husband hissed back.

'It wouldn't be the same, Pascal Durand, and you know it!'

They continued bickering and Connor clapped his hands to interrupt them. Unfortunately, as Richard had suspected, this triggered his previous introduction and once again his voice echoed around the room. 'Good evening, ladies and gentlemen, this is your host Ian Connor.' Connor clapped again and the thing stopped.

'Who else?' he spoke quickly, trying to hide his frustration. 'Ah yes, Nevaeh. You're well aware just how short-lived your influencer career really is, you're not actually as dumb as you make out. What are you, twenty-four?' Nevaeh nodded slowly. 'Tick tock, literally, my dear. You could install Wi-Fi of course; actually there is Wi-Fi but only I have the password and you'd all have to know way more about me before you could guess it. And none of you do, I'm just a meal ticket.'

'*Food, glorious food!*' sang Bernie and immediately marked himself as the next target.

'Not just a meal ticket of course, I am sanctuary as well, aren't I? A hiding place where no one ever goes. Isn't that what Simon and Garfunkel sang?'

With a painful grimace on his face, Bernie fought off the temptation to play the tune but it looked as though he had little control over his hands and voice. '"Mrs Robinson's Affair",' he stammered through gritted teeth.

Richard had recognised as such, the theme tune to *The Graduate* but couldn't understand why it would cause Bernie such pain. At least it wasn't Liberace though.

'And you, Doctor?' He turned to Richard. 'You've always expressed a desire to have your own clinic for high-paying, gullible patients. This place would be perfect, would it not? You could even get into the real money.' He rubbed his thumb and forefingers together menacingly.

'Real money?' Richard asked, though he had no idea why and, as his mouth was so dry from the tension, how.

'Yes, the er… Dignitas route. What did you write once? People really ought to be put out of their misery.'

'But that's illegal,' Richard replied. He could feel his temper rising, though it had to be said it was mainly aimed at the armed woman on the terrace. 'Isn't it?' he added cautiously.

'Ah.' Connor regained his seat. 'Not here it isn't.'

'What do you mean?' the pastor asked, obviously hooked by the whole idea, so much so that he forgot to spout the relevant commandment.

'This is *my* island,' Connor said forcefully. 'My family's company bought the rights to the place and in agreeing to take it off the hands of the French government, it was made an island state. I am the law here. I pay no taxes, the rules are mine, only people I allow here visit. This is my country. Though it could be yours.' This time he didn't so much as flash a smile as manoeuvre one into position, leaving him looking like a hungry crocodile. 'Now, just think, what could you all do with your own country? No tax, no fear, no servitude, no laws, no competition.'

'And you'd just give that to us, am I right?' The pastor was very eager indeed.

'You see, Albrecht?' Connor threw the question over his shoulder. 'Look at them, they're right here!' He opened the palm of his hand and drove a finger into the heart of it. 'You said this place had no power, well it has, old man, and it always did have, even when I was young here and you came to see my mother.' He smiled knowingly. 'Of course, it could be yours now, all yours.'

'What's the small print?' Lea Boudon interrupted, a reasonable question under the circumstances.

'Ah.' Connor's eyes lit up. 'Spot the professional game player.' He swilled his glass again. 'All ten of you will find, under the pillows on your bed, a brown envelope. There are nine envelopes as I've counted you two as one.' He pointed at the Durands, who didn't look delighted by the news. 'In each envelope is a contract. The contract has been signed by me, and witnessed by my legal team. All you have to do is sign it and the island is yours.'

There was a brief moment of stunned silence and then the pastor, Lea and Nevaeh made a bolt for the stairs while Bruno ran towards the double doors at the end of the table and behind where Connor was sitting. 'This is God's will!' the pastor cried, pulling Nevaeh back by the shoulder.

'Age before beauty.' Lea joined in, almost trampling the younger woman underfoot.

'There is just one teeny-weeny little catch!' Connor had raised his voice and everybody stopped still in their tracks.

'A catch?' Richard asked.

'Yes, Doctor, a catch. You see I might have made a little, itty bitty little mistake. I may have put the wrong contracts in the wrong rooms.' He smiled again. 'Oopsie.'

Connor let the news sink in.

'Wait a minute.' The Pastor obviously didn't like the sound of this. 'Are you saying that if I were to grab the contract in my room, it might have this lady's name on it?' He pointed at Lea.

'I know, right? I am *so* clumsy!'

'And if I were to then produce that contract, this place would be hers?'

'What can I say? To err is human…'

The pastor sat down and gave this some thought, they all did.

'You did this deliberately!' Nevaeh cried, dusting herself down.

'Tut-tut, such cynicism in one so young. Though, you're right of course. What you must all decide is how you go about getting the right contract, the one with your name on it. Teamwork, subterfuge, theft… what other ways are there? How do you even go about finding who has your contract? Really, it will be such fun.'

'I don't understand.' Bruno stepped forward and addressed Connor directly. 'What do you get out of it?'

Connor looked frozen for a moment. 'I get peace, Mr Mangetout, I get some rest. This place has brought me nothing but misery and I want out.'

'Won't you miss all the money?' Bernie asked, for once not in three-quarter time rhythm.

Connor shrugged and for the first time Richard sensed he really was lost for words.

'We could all just band together and split the profits,' Lea suggested with an uncharacteristic sense of teamwork. 'And then bump you off!' Richard felt almost relieved that she hadn't completely changed.

'You could,' Connor replied, a tired look in his eyes. 'But I'm afraid, for your sakes that is, that I have taken insurance against that. You may come in, Valérie!'

he shouted towards the doors of the terrace. Immediately and silently Valérie appeared from the shadows behind and placed a hand on his shoulder, making Connor jump in fright. 'I keep telling you, don't do that!'

Richard was relieved that he wasn't the only one she shocked in that way. Again there was silence in the room as they took in the appearance of Valérie d'Orçay. She was dressed in black leggings half covered by knee-length boots and topped with a tight-fitting black turtle-neck jumper. Her shoulder-length hair was plaited. Her face was stern and she said nothing, all in all giving the impression that she really was the insurance Connor had mentioned and that she shouldn't be crossed. Of course, the gun helped. The same gun which Richard usually had to ask her not to leave lying around the kitchen back home.

Everybody who had hitherto been standing now sat, except for Elise who wandered about collecting glasses. Connor said no more. He had thrown down his gauntlet, dangled the bait as it were, and was waiting patiently to see how it played out.

'We could simply destroy the competition's contracts!' The pastor, exalted, thought he'd hit on a solution.

'Sorry, Rev.' Connor smirked. 'They're all coded and joined on some cloud or other. If one goes, they all go. Poof!' He threw his hands up.

There was more silence.

'Well, I think I'll turn in.' It was Bernie who spoke first. 'I'm going to sleep on it.' He closed the keyboard and was shaking his head. 'I'm not even sure it's a game I want to win,' he said sadly.

Elise came towards Richard and picked up the glass that was on the chair of his sofa. She leant in closely as she did so. 'Excuse me, Doctor,' she whispered into his ear. 'Could I borrow you for a moment? It's Herr Schmid. I think he's dead.'

Chapter Eleven

For a moment Richard just stared at her, blinking furiously as he did so. He felt like blurting out that not only was he not that type of doctor, a psychiatrist; but he wasn't even that type of doctor either – he had a PhD in film history. Nobody else seemed to notice that Elise and he were talking, so wrapped up were they in their Machiavellian calculations of how they could get their hands on the right contract, the one in their name. Then he noticed Valérie watching him and there was a look in her eye which he had seen before, countless times. And not just from Valérie, but from Clare too. And his daughter Alicia. And his mother. It was a look of 'don't let me down now, Richard, I'm counting on you.'

He raised a quizzical eyebrow, buying himself some time. Then he stood up, stretched his arms wide and yawned loudly. 'Well, I think I'll go to bed too,' he said, to no one in particular and made for the staircase under which Albrecht Schmid was sitting, shadowed, in his wheelchair. Elise was already moving in that direction as well, handing her tray to Bruno as she passed him. She bent down as if to talk to the old man in the wheelchair.

'What's that, Herr Schmid?' she said loudly. 'Your wheelchair needs charging and could I give you a hand? Of course!'

It was pretty appalling acting but no one, other than Richard and, he guessed, Valérie, was paying attention anyway so he offered to help and they wheeled Herr Schmid to the lift and made what felt like an escape but actually wasn't. The very nature of the design of the place, a glass lift, a mezzanine floor for the bedrooms, meant that they were never out of sight of the others, if of course they had been watching something else other than each other. Richard and Elise made their way silently around the mezzanine corridor before Elise used her master key to open the old man's room. Richard closed the door behind them and leant back on it, letting out a deep breath as he did so while Elise turned on the lights.

'Well?' Elise badgered him. 'Can you make sure? Is he dead?'

'You want me to do it? I thought you might have already checked!' He regarded Herr Schmid with a look of both disdain and horror.

'I was worried about how quiet he was, then I checked for a pulse and I couldn't find one. I want you to check now.'

'Why me though?'

'Because you're a doctor, that's why!'

'Oh yes, I forgot about that,' Richard conceded. 'I'm not that kind of doctor, though.'

'Oh for heaven's sake, surely you know where the pulse is? Or do you people only do mother fixations and gaslighting for money?'

Richard felt a bit stung by her caustic approach, but moved over to the wheelchair anyway. Herr Schmid was sitting bolt upright, still wearing those enormous glasses, though maybe his head was slightly to one side. Apart from that, however, he didn't look markedly different to how he'd looked when he was alive. If he was dead, that is. Richard took a deep breath and despite being even more repulsed by the dead man's bruised fingernail picked up the right wrist, feeling for the radial artery. The old man's flesh felt soft and slightly moist and it brought back a horrible memory of going to London Zoo as a child and being made to hold a snake by one of the zookeepers. Schmid's skin felt the same, clammy and cool at the same time, meaning that Richard didn't waste long in his pursuit of a pulse, there was none.

'He's dead alright,' he sighed.

Elise sat down on the bed and shook her head. 'Well that didn't take long, did it?'

'What do you mean?' Richard asked. 'How long do you want me to give a pulse?'

'No, not that. I mean, it didn't take someone long to act, did it?' She was shaking her head as she spoke and looked a little frightened too.

'You mean, you don't think it's natural causes?'

'Most likely not.' She looked at him quizzically. 'You don't seriously believe he died of natural causes, do you?'

'I don't know how he died! But it's a bit quick to be jumping to conclusions, don't you think?'

'No, I damn well don't!' she replied harshly. 'One minute Ian Connor lights a competitive win-at-all-costs fuse underneath everyone and the next minute someone dies… that's quite some coincidence, don't you think?'

Richard sat down next to her and noticed she was weeping. 'Did you know him well?' he asked softly.

'No,' she sniffled. 'I'd met him a couple of times the first time I worked here. He was always very nice.'

Richard was confused. 'Sorry, I don't understand. Why are you crying then? If you didn't really know him that is.'

She took a tissue from her sleeve. 'Because I'll get the blame, that's why. Mr Connor doesn't like surprises, or what he calls "events". He says if you're paying attention, nothing should be a surprise.'

'He doesn't seem an easy person to work for.'

'He's not. He's scary. You saw him downstairs, he's a control freak.'

Richard didn't know what to say. 'You could win the island in his competition, I suppose. Then you'd be the boss,' he joked. Richard often thought that taking a light-hearted approach to very serious situations was a good way of lightening the mood; sometimes it worked and sometimes it didn't. This time it didn't.

'I don't want this godforsaken place!' she hissed loudly. 'I only came back because I ran out of money in my retirement. I need to work.'

They sat in silence for a moment, both perched on the end of the bed while a dead Albrecht Schmid sat opposite them in the wheelchair. Eventually it was Richard who broke the silence.

'Of course, we shouldn't really have moved the body then,' he said with a weary sigh. 'If he has been bumped off – and that really is just speculation at this point – we should have left him where he was and told everyone.'

'And start a panic?' Elise shook her head. 'Anyway, do you think they'd care, any of them? They're far too interested in their own greed. All they would want to know is whose contract does he have.'

They both looked at each other and then simultaneously turned to look at the made bed and the plump pillows, which were presumably hiding a brown envelope, as Ian Connor had described, containing a contract bearing the name of a lucky guest.

'I really think this is a police matter,' Richard said unconvincingly. 'Nothing else should be touched, cause of death should be established and so on and so forth.' He tried his best to sound like a medical professional.

Elise shook her head. 'That won't happen though, will it? You heard what Mr Connor said, he *is* the law here. He *is* the authorities.'

Richard frowned. 'What about his security guard?' he asked, trying to sound innocent. 'Presumably she has some independence and she would certainly like, possibly even need, to be told what's happened.'

'How do you know that?'

'What? How do I know?' Richard felt he had said too much. 'Well, wouldn't you? There you are, a respectable body guard person, and five minutes after you turn up someone's dead. I'd say that's a stain on your record, possibly.'

'I don't know.' Elise thought about it. 'I suppose she's the only one not in the game, so maybe it's a good idea.'

Richard decided to capitalise on the moment. 'I've worked with security over the years,' he lied. 'All very hush hush and when they're detailed as a personal bodyguard they'll keep information like this to themselves, not alarm the client.' Elise didn't seem totally convinced. 'I think it's the best way to move forward.' He tried again. 'In my experience, if you keep this kind of stress to yourself, ourselves, it can create what we call in psychiatry, er, a muddle.'

'A muddle?'

'Yes. A muddle. I mean there is some Latin name, but er, well, muddle just about covers it.'

Elise looked back at the pillows. 'What should we do about the contract?' she asked, apparently in agreement.

'We should definitely leave that untouched. There might be fingerprints on the envelope.'

She nodded and came to a decision. 'OK, I agree with you,' she said. 'We should lock him in here and speak to this Valérie woman. She looked like a sensible, no-nonsense type.'

Richard again tried to look non-committal. If he hadn't been hamstrung by secrecy he would have wholeheartedly agreed with the 'no-nonsense' bit, and rolled about on the floor laughing at the sensible part.

'I should probably give her the master key as well,' Elise continued. 'I certainly don't want it. I'd be suspect number one if anything else happened.'

Richard saw her point and agreed. Elise locked the door quietly behind them and they made their way back downstairs where only Ian Connor and Valérie now remained.

'Have they all bumped each other off?' Richard asked, forcing a laugh. Nobody else bothered to do the same.

'I suspect,' Ian Connor drawled, sounding a little drunk, 'that they're all planning their next move. Who's weak? Who's strong? Shall I play it nicely or aggressively? I would have thought, Doctor, that you would have something of a head start in the mind games department, don't you think?'

'I'll go and lock up,' Elise interrupted before turning to a stern-looking Valérie. 'Do you want me to show you around, madame. It might be quite useful for you and there's only one master key; don't ask me why, apparently it's extra secure that way.'

Valérie nodded and they left in the direction of the orangery. Connor watched them both intently. 'Always employ a woman as a bodyguard, Doctor Ainsworth. As Kipling said, "The female of the species is deadlier than the male…"'

'Ah yes,' Richard replied, just about resisting the temptation to respond with his own thought, '*Deadlier Than the Male* was also a 1967 Bulldog Drummond film.'

Connor turned to face Richard, a serious almost tortured look on his face. 'I asked you a question, Doctor. I think you have an advantage over the others. Go on now, tell me your next move.'

Richard hadn't even given the game, if that's what this was, any thought at all and his natural instinct under any situation was always one of survival. The fact was, though, that someone in the fort had a contract with his name on it, while he had a contract with someone else's name on it.

Everybody, and on paper that included Richard, had both a bargaining chip and a motive. 'I think, Mr Connor,' he said slowly. 'That you have created a very dangerous, poisonous situation and I can see no good coming from it all.'

Connor laughed, but it was a hollow laugh. 'I know!' he cried. 'And I've got the best seat in the house to watch you insignificant little creatures tear each other apart! I can't wait for it to start.'

It already has, Richard thought sadly of Albrecht Schmid, *it already has*.

Chapter Twelve

Richard sat on the end of his bed, looking through the window and into the darkness of the sea. Every few seconds there was a light that passed from the fake palm tree lighthouse on the roof, which had a brief soothing effect as it reflected on the sky. It was now two in the morning and despite it having been a long, exhausting day, he was wide awake and expecting a knock on the door at any moment. In one sense he was extremely relieved that Valérie had shown up, but he was also really, really annoyed that she had shown up too. He had been looking forward to a rest, a pampered week on the coast with good food and nothing to worry about but hiding his tummy by pulling his shorts up too high. Even if it had been a murder game, he'd have been happy with that. Sometimes mental distraction can be a rest in itself, they say. Whoever they are. But the death, as yet by unknown means, of Herr Schmid had changed that. He no longer felt this was a game. He wasn't, as he had briefly thought and hoped, surrounded by consummate actors putting on a show for his benefit, pretending to play greedy, ambitious, downright unpleasant characters. Instead, he was on an isolated island, controlled by a sadistic billionaire and peopled with genuinely greedy, ambitious and unpleasant characters. Hence he was relieved that Valérie was here, only if it wasn't for Valérie, he wouldn't be here and he resented that.

As usual, she elicited in Richard massively conflicting emotions. He loved being in her company, she was intoxicating, but then he also hated being in her company because inevitably it led to some kind of danger and Richard feeling inadequate, out of his depth and a bit like a spare part. He did feel that he had grown into the role of being her partner, but she was definitely in control and at times he felt no more empowered than Passepartout the Chihuahua.

He had wrestled with these conflicting emotions since returning to his room. He had left Elise, Ian Connor – whose charisma and draw had dimmed with the lights – and Valérie downstairs to finish closing up for the night. He had heard two doors shut along the corridor, presuming that was Connor and Valérie, and then waited. Only he hadn't just waited and that upset him a little. The temptation of knowing that a contract for the ownership of the island resort lay under his pillow had, eventually, proved overwhelming. In the end then, he was no better than the other guests, grotesques all of them. They were like all the kids in *Charlie and the Chocolate Factory* and Richard had considered himself above them: he was Charlie. But having ripped open the envelope he realised he was actually no better than Veruca Salt. Then, having read the contract, he realised something even worse. If Albrecht Schmid had indeed been killed by a rival, that would make whoever held Schmid's contract a suspect. Richard re-read the contract.

This contract (dated) is to confirm that Lane Bridge Holdings passes over all deeds, ownership and legal rights of Le Fort Esprit de l'Air to... (insert name here)... Herr Albrecht Schmid.

He groaned and fell back on the bed, nearly squashing a sleeping Passepartout. By rights it was he that should be sleeping soundly, perhaps in a fug of a post three-course meal, red wine haze; having swam, jacuzzied and been massaged into dreamy fatigue by a...

'Get up, Richard, this is no time to be lying around like that!'

He fell off the bed, fortunately on to the thick rug and landed at her still-booted feet. 'It's polite to knock, you know?'

'And wake up the whole corridor? Don't be ridiculous, Richard!' And she picked up a grateful Passepartout who licked her face repeatedly.

Richard managed to get to his feet with as much dignity as a man in his mid-fifties sporting striped pyjamas can manage and regretted not keeping his dinner suit on. He had anticipated her visit after all.

'How did you get in?' he asked, making his way to the minibar. 'Kombucha?'

'No!' The look on her face heavily implied that Valérie was no kombucha fan. 'I used the master key. Elise Lafarge gave it to me.'

Richard opened the *canette* and took a gulp, winced and shook his head. All the great spies, private detectives and genuine patsies given the runaround by a dame, a *femme fatale*, had a whiskey or a whisky or a bourbon.

Richard was in M&S nightwear, sipping from a small can of sweetened, effervescent mushroom tea. Bogart would be spinning in his grave.

'She did not say why she gave me the key though.' She tapped the key in the palm of her hand. 'She suggested I look in on Herr Schmid before I went to bed, but again she gave no reason why.' Valérie was pacing the room now, essentially having a conversation with herself as if Richard wasn't there. Richard himself was struggling to keep down his Cantaloupe and Spicy Jalapeño Ginger Mango fruit-based iced tea and wished he hadn't started the thing.

'Do you have a minibar in your room?' he asked, deciding rightly that she didn't need him in her conversation so he might as well start his own.

'What was that?' she asked distractedly. 'Oh yes, of course.'

'Does it contain anything that isn't designed for children or post-adults?'

'I don't know, I haven't looked. Why?'

'You haven't looked!' Richard was aghast; this was the final straw after such a trying day. It was the kind of behaviour that just went against all credible reports on the positive aspects of human nature. What kind of person registers into a hotel and *doesn't* check the minibar status? It's part of the whole experience. Minibars are vital to a hotel room. You spend your entire stay being wracked with guilt because you've either spent twelve pounds on a teaspoon of gin, stocked an empty fridge with cheaper products bought at an off-licence, or tried to keep drinks cool in the bathroom sink because the hotel ripped out their minibar for no reason other than 'economics'. Richard loved a minibar. How anyone could be so incurious as to not open theirs immediately they'd put their case down was utterly beyond him. He really had no grasp of the woman's mechanics at all. Granted, when travelling she might be using firearms and needed to be a little cautious with alcoholic beverages, but even so. It was always going to take a lot to knock Valérie off the pedestal Richard had put her on, but this was quite a shock.

'Why would she ask me to check in on Herr Albrecht Schmid?' she asked herself, Richard's foot-stomping inward tantrum going quite over her head.

'I can tell you bloody why!' He was by now unable to control his temper.

'Richard!' she hissed at him. 'Please keep your voice down. Nobody knows I am here and I don't want anyone to think we are together!'

'Well, ain't that the truth,' he whispered bitterly, before continuing quickly. 'I can tell you why she asked you to check in on the old man... he's dead, that's why!'

She looked at him in complete surprise. 'Dead? How?'

'I don't know how.'

'And how do you know that he is dead?'

He sighed and sat on the bed again. 'Elise told me downstairs. She said she *thought* he was dead and would I like to confirm it for her?'

'But why did she ask you?'

He wasn't altogether impressed by the tone in her voice. 'Because she wanted a medical opinion that's why.'

'But you're a...'

'Eminent psychiatrist as you well know! You set me up for this Madame d'Orçay. I was supposed to get a week's proper holiday, but oh no, we couldn't have that, could we? You had to spoil it and throw me into a snake pit!'

'I had no choice, Richard! I needed someone on the inside and I saw your name, or someone with your name on an old guest list. I looked you… him… up on LinkedIn. Doctor Richard Ainsworth, prominent psychologist, studied at the University of Sunderland, nineteen eighty-seven to nineteen ninety-two. Struck off twenty nineteen.' She looked absurdly pleased with herself.

'Struck off! What on earth did I do? He do?'

'I did not ask him when I found him. I gave the man five hundred pounds to stay away for the week and he took it. He was behind with his rent, he said.'

'So he's doing well for himself then?' Richard was almost, though not quite, out of sarcasm.

'I think he is very unhappy, but how interesting, no?'

'What is?'

'That there is another Doctor Richard Ainsworth, like you. You're a doctor too. On LinkedIn, there were a lot of Richard Ainsworths…'

'What do you want us to do, set up a support group for each other?'

'Oh, you are impossible sometimes!'

'Only sometimes? I've got some catching up to do then!'

They both sat down on the bed, their backs to each other, exactly as the Durands had done on the boat trip over. After a few minutes, Valérie stood and left the room, closing the door quietly behind her. Ordinarily Richard would have been greatly concerned by this turn of events, but as she had left Passepartout behind, he knew she wouldn't be gone long.

When he heard the door open again, he resumed his sitting position, his back to the entrance. For once, he'd been right and internally he punched the air, as he'd had absolutely no real confidence in the position he had taken at all.

'There,' she said and he gratefully noted a slightly apologetic tone before the dull thunk of glass hit the thick duvet. She had a small brandy from her minibar and the bounty made him remember trick or treating on a Halloween night as a youngster. The early days of Halloween in the UK, before it became Americanised, when people gave more begrudgingly.

He knew also – and this once again produced a raging internal battle – that if he were to start drinking now, it would look the wrong side of desperate.

'Thank you,' he said stoically. 'Maybe later. There's work to do.'

He told her what had happened with Elise and Herr Schmid, and how he had advised Elise to give Valérie the key in a way that left the woman no choice. As it was, she was only too happy to be rid of it, but there was no harm in hyping up his part in the suggestion.

'Brilliant, Richard!' Valérie said. 'Brilliant!'

'Well, it would be if I wasn't now the prime suspect. If any foul play is suspected, that is. I have Schmid's contract.'

Her look became more serious. 'That is a problem, but as you say, only if he was murdered. Did you see whose contract he had?'

Richard shook his head and explained his reasoning behind not looking: fingerprints.

'I think we should check,' Valérie said, climbing off the bed. 'I might also be able to see if he was killed or whether it is natural causes. Maybe…'

'You mean, go back and rifle the corpse? Shouldn't we inform your boss? I'm assuming he would want to know first.'

Valérie shook her head. 'I do not think, really, that he would care. He despises you all.'

'I can't say I really blame him; we're a pretty unlikeable bunch.'

They both stood at the same time and Richard decided to at least put on a dressing gown and some slippers. Then Valérie opened the door, made sure that no one was around and led Richard back to Schmid's room and his dead body.

She unlocked the door silently and ushered Richard through before slipping in behind him and re-closing the door. Richard turned on the light and then immediately turned it off again.

'What are you doing?' a startled Valérie whispered.

'Are we in the right room?' Richard asked nervously.

'Yes, of course, why?'

He turned the lights back on. 'Because our corpse has gone.'

Chapter Thirteen

There are moments in life that can literally stun you into inaction. A level of stupefaction overtakes the body meaning that any further physical effort is rendered utterly impossible. There are also moments in life that can stun a person, almost like a cattle prod, into the exact opposite. For Richard, this moment was the latter. It had been such a long day that he took the disappearance of Albrecht Schmid's dead body as a personal insult, an event aimed squarely and disparagingly at himself. This was no time for measured reflection therefore, no time to sit quietly by and consider the facts. This was a moment to ransack the place like a demented burglar and find evidence of the man, if not the corpse itself.

It was Valérie who decided to take the sitting-down-let's-look-at-this-logically approach and she perched on the end of the bed, chin resting on her knuckles, elbow on the knee.

'Do you mind?' Richard asked irritably. He had looked everywhere and he was now tackling underneath the bed.

'Oh, Richard, you could hardly hide a wheelchair under the bed!' Valérie complained, though she moved her legs anyway.

She was right, of course, and Richard stood once he had made sure of that fact and shook his head mournfully.

'I don't get it,' he said for the umpteenth time. 'I just don't get it.'

'Are you sure he was dead?' she asked, in the way people reply with 'where did you last see them?' to the question 'have you seen my car keys?' That is, with no apparent thought at the potential volcanic consequences.

'Of course he was dead!' Richard exploded. 'I may not be medically trained but I know when there's no bloody pulse. I've got a swimming safety certificate, you know?' he added, as if that were all the affirmation needed.

'And Elise could feel no pulse either?'

'That's right. That's why we brought him up here, just to make sure.'

'Then somebody must have moved the corpse.' Valérie's tone was totally matter of fact, a simple unarguable state-ment, one that sent Richard tipping over the edge.

'You don't say!' He was practically having convulsions. 'You don't think it just moved to the next world via the disabled access ramp then?'

'Oh, do calm yourself down, Richard! You are making enough noise to wake the dead!'

'A bloody good thing too!' He was rapidly losing all grip on his temper, if not sanity. 'Then maybe we can ask the slippery old fox where he's taken himself off to!' He paused, and made a big show of closing his eyes and taking deep breaths. 'There is one place that I haven't looked,' he said, with surprising calm and determination.

'Where?' Valérie asked, her eyes wide at the potential breakthrough.

'The minibar,' he said seriously, as though he'd discovered the secret of alchemy.

Some fifteen minutes later, when neither had spoken and both had been sitting deep in thought, Richard – mollified by half a miniature Irish whiskey and miniature Coca-Cola like a baby after a dose of Calpol – was more sanguine about the situation.

'Let's look at this logically,' he said and began pacing the room. 'Albrecht Schmid was definitely dead, right? Elise and I left him here while we decided what we should do. She was scared to tell her boss, Ian Connor, and wanted no part of it. She decided therefore to give the fort's master key to you. We, in an effort to confirm that he was indeed deceased, come to the room and find the body gone.'

'Yes.' Valérie was much happier now that Richard had calmed down, even if had just stated the very obvious and offered no further insight. 'There are some issues from that though. One, did Elise give me the only master key?'

'She said it was the only one,' Richard answered.

'Ah yes, that is what she said, but is that the truth? Also, and please do not fly away from your handle, it is possible that Herr Schmid was not dead. He was a very fat man…'

'I think they prefer the word larger, these days.'

'He was a very fat man and I know from experience that a pulse can be hard to find with fat people and old people.'

That simple statement raised a whole load of questions in Richard's mind, but he decided it was best to concentrate on the present, which was opaque enough without further distraction.

'So you're saying that two people missed that he was actually really not quite dead and that he's now taking a late-night, early-morning roll around the grounds, is that right?'

'It is a logical possibility, Richard.' Her voice was stern. 'Something else – why was Elise scared to inform her boss?'

'She said she would get the blame, that's why. That Connor didn't believe in surprises. If you're doing your job, nothing should come as a surprise. That's his mantra.'

'Silly man!' Valérie rolled her eyes.

'What about him, anyway?' Richard asked. 'He's your employer too – what's he like? What's all this nonsense about? And firstly, what's his real name?'

Valérie looked on the verge of answering the first two queries, but suddenly stopped in her tracks at Richard's final question.

'What do you mean what is his real name?' she shot back, sensing a criticism of her own truthfulness.

'I mean his real name,' Richard said slowly. 'It can't be Ian Connor, that's too absurd.'

Valérie gave him an odd look. 'Why can it not be his real name?' she said, not bothering to hide that it was she who was on the verge of losing her temper this time. 'Do you think that I am so, so laissez-faire that I do not do a due diligence on my clients?'

'Look, no…'

'Do you think me so unprofessional that I have not made many, many enquiries about this so silly man?'

'No, all I'm…'

'You insult my abilities with your "cannot be his real name"! Pah!' And with that she grasped his whiskey glass and downed the remainder of the drink.

'I hope there's another one of those.' Richard sulked.

Valérie's reaction was of someone who did not drink whiskey often and for a moment she looked like she might keel over backwards before relaunching her attack. 'Explain yourself, Doctor Ainsworth!'

Not even Richard then, but Doctor Ainsworth. Richard took a step back. 'Let me speak, Madame d'Orçay,' he said, holding his hands out in a placatory gesture. 'Ian Connor is a joke name. It has to be.'

'Why does it have to be? It is not funny.'

'No, not funny haha, just a joke name, made up. Look, I know this is a silly question, but have you ever seen the film *And Then There Were None?*' She shook her head. 'None of them? There are at least four cinematic versions: 1945, 1965, 1974 and 1989.' She said nothing, but continued to glare at him. 'You may know it by its other title, *Ten Little Indians?*' She stepped closer. 'Anyway, the point is this,' he added hurriedly. 'Ever since I arrived, I've had this feeling about it all not being real. I thought it was a game at first. I thought you had kidnapped…'

'Redirected.'

'OK, I thought you had,' he used his fingers as speech marks, '*redirected* me here to take part in a murder game. So much reminded me of some of my favourite mystery films. There's a conflict of interests game, set up by the host to divide the guests, that's *The Last of Sheila*, 1973.'

Valérie's eyes narrowed. 'There was the fake thunder and lightning, that's *Murder by Death*, 1976.'

'I do not need the years, Richard.'

'Sorry, I can't help it. You have no choice. There's the remote island set-up, *Evil Under the Sun*, 1982. There's a touch of *Rebecca*, 1940; *The House of Fear*, 1945 and…'

'Richard!'

'Right. Connor. In *And Then There Were None*, and actually it was Lilibet Durand who mentioned it first, it's from a nursery rhyme. In *And Then There Were None…*'

'Which version?' she asked, losing patience.

'Ah, all of them. In *And Then There Were None*, a disparate group of people are invited to an island and each in turn is murdered until there is just one person left, the killer, you see?'

'But why did they go?'

'What? Why did they go?' Richard had had this problem with Valérie before, her mind was so brutally logical that anything fictional requiring on the part of the audience some willing suspension of disbelief was beyond her scope. 'I don't know why they went, but they too had to listen to a list of their supposed crimes read out, by their host.'

She nodded. 'And this host was called Ian Connor?'

Richard responded animatedly as though Valérie was close to guessing the answer in a game of charades. 'Yes!' he cried. 'Well, sort of. The host in the films is called U. N. Owen.'

'Not Ian Connor at all then!'

'No, bear with me. U. N. Owen – it's a made-up name, really it means "Unknown". You see?'

'Ah, yes. U. N. Owen, unknown. Very clever. But it's still not Ian Connor.'

'No, but say Ian Connor very fast – what do you get?'

She looked at him dubiously, while for his part he was almost beside himself. 'Ian Connor,' she said slowly. 'Ian Connor,' this time a little quicker. She narrowed her eyes. 'Ian Connor Ian Connor Ian Conna In Conna, *Inconnu!*' she shouted, then in a whisper: '*Inconnu!* But that is French for unknown.'

'Exactly! It's the same set-up.' They hugged slightly awkwardly.

'And what happens next?' Valérie said, not exactly pulling away, but as good as.

'Well, actually, the piano player chokes to death.'

'Which Bernie Webb tried to do!'

'Yes, and he was played by Charles Aznavour in the 1974 version.'

Valérie frowned. 'Is that relevant?'

'No,' Richard admitted. 'I was just trying to throw in a cultural reference that you might know.'

Valérie sat back down on the bed. 'There is a slight problem though, Richard.' Her voice was slightly apologetic. 'He really is called Ian Connor.'

'Oh, he can't be!'

'I'm afraid he is. He was born in County Cork in nineteen eighty-eight. His father was called Connor, from a long line of Connors. He really is called unknown.'

A deflated Richard sat down next to her again. 'That's a shame,' he said eventually. 'I thought we were getting somewhere.'

'He is a very unhappy man, I think. He built up the company after his parents died, a workaholic. A genius too, so I am told, and he is a billionaire. But, for whatever reason, it is not enough for him.'

'Hence the game, like some kind of sport. Is he married?'

'No. And apparently he has no friends at all either.'

Richard stood up in frustration. 'There must be something. I can't believe that with all the coincidences I'm getting he hasn't set this up for a darker reason.'

'Do you think he moved the corpse of Albrecht Schmid then?' Valérie asked, her business head back on.

'I don't know,' Richard admitted. 'But somebody did.'

'Who would want to…' Valérie stopped mid-question as the truth dawned on them both at the same time. If the contract was gone, it could be anyone apart from Richard, which he regarded as a relief. If the contract was still under the pillow it at least ruled out that person as the phantom corpse mover.

They both made a dive for the pillow, rolling around ignominiously on the bed as they grasped for the envelope until a red-faced Richard stopped himself and, in gentlemanly fashion, allowed Valérie to open it. She tore it open urgently and read the contents breathlessly, a little red-faced herself.

'This contract (dated) is to confirm that Lane Bridge Holdings passes over all deeds, ownership and legal rights of Le Fort Esprit de l'Air to… (insert name here)… Madame Elise Lafarge.'

Chapter Fourteen

Richard had been hoping to face the morning refreshed, but when the alarm went off at the not too ungodly hour of 8.15, he still felt pretty rotten. The day before had been so full and long it now felt like he had binge-watched a particularly gruelling and unbalanced television boxset, but not in series order. There was no narrative, or at least the narrative kept changing and he had no idea what was going on. And then it dawned on him that he hadn't even set an alarm, but that it had been done for him. 'This isn't a retreat,' he grumbled, staggering out of bed, 'it's a bloody boot camp.'

He managed to focus his eyes and saw that Passepartout was waiting patiently at the door to go and do what dogs need to do first thing. Richard didn't feel like dressing in a hurry and as it was clear Passepartout knew the layout of the place like the back of his paw, he opened the door to let the little dog out and called a warning down the corridor after him, telling him 'not to talk to any strange dogs'. He turned back into the room and had his breath taken away, again, by the majesty of the view. It was so beautiful, so calm he felt like dropping to his knees and worshipping it. It was so all-consuming in its serenity, he could have wept.

All his life he had only really wanted to be left alone, to bother no one and have no one bother him. He had loved Clare, but they had both known really that she was out of his league. He loved his daughter Alicia, had grown to tolerate her husband Sly, and would later in the year have his first grandchild, which he realised for the first time, he might actually be looking forward to; but this, this was all he'd ever really need. The Atlantic Ocean, calm now, a few clouds reflected on its surface and giving him a beatific vibe that no drugs, no religion and no one person could give him. It was intoxicating. And, he realised greedily, it could be his.

Somewhere in the old fort was a contract with his name on it; alright he wasn't the Doctor Richard Ainsworth on said contract, but possession was nine-tenths of the law, right?

He could wake up to this view *every day*, he could feel this tranquil *every day*.

Passepartout scratched at the door and Richard begrudgingly tore himself away from his private vista, like a child told to stop looking at a screen.

Fifteen minutes later, after a quick shower, they descended for breakfast at much the same time as everyone else; presumably the alarm was set the same for all. Connor and Valérie were already there, as were the Durands and Bruno setting out the breakfast buffet, while a testy-looking Elise fussed about, coming in and out of the kitchen area. She shot Richard a worried look and almost imperceptibly shook her head to indicate that she hadn't said a word.

Boy, thought Richard, *have I got news for you.*

A subdued Bernie was playing lightly on the piano, a glass of wine already perched on the top.

'Welcome, everyone,' Connor said brightly, though the smile was still like a television during a storm, flickering on and off. 'I trust you slept well?'

'I'd like to talk to you, Connor.' The pastor had a determined look on his face. 'I think we can do business.'

Connor sighed. 'My dear Pastor, you don't get it, do you? I don't want to do business. That's the point.'

The small man, still clad in a white suit, sat down disappointed.

'Poptarts?' Nevaeh said suddenly, pouring herself some juice.

Connor looked at Elise.

'I'm sorry,' Elise said, 'but we don't have them.'

'No, I meant, is that the password for the Wi-Fi? Poptarts.'

'No.' A look of intense despondency came over Connor's face. 'Is that the sum total of your night's thinking and reflection?' he asked.

'No!' Nevaeh retorted. 'Of course not. Scalextric?' she resumed after a brief pause. Connor shook his head sadly. 'I'm just trying to think what my older brothers had as children.'

'Well,' Connor decided to move on quickly. 'Now we've heard from the CEO of Nevaeh Influences, representing her four million worldwide followers, has anyone else come up with a plan for how they might get their hands on their contract and this place?'

Richard thought that Connor's demeanour was a bit lacklustre. He was trying to sell the big idea and, granted, he had a captive audience, but he came across like a gameshow host on a no-longer-popular quiz show. His heart didn't really seem in it at all; in particular, the eyes gave it away. They were distant and not really in the room.

'I'd like to just ask outright who has my contract?' Lea Boudon demanded. 'I'm sure we can come to some like, timeshare arrangement.'

Once again, Connor hung his head in dismay. 'Is that it, Madame Boudon? Where's your competitive instinct? Where's the thrill of the game? Bernie, what have you come up with?'

This seemed to galvanise Bernie somewhat and he played the classic shock horror dun, dun, duuun sting on his keyboard. 'I don't know, boss,' he slurred. 'On the one hand I don't want to be on this island forever and on the other hand I *really* don't want to be on this island forever. If I win, I'm on this island forever.' He ended this vague sentence with a quick, energetic rendition of Frank Sinatra's 'That's Life', which did nothing to improve Connor's mood.

'Oh, lord,' he moaned. 'Mangetout?'

'I am willing to sell my contract to whoever wants it,' he said quietly. 'But only if I can still use the island for my TV show.'

'Now we're getting somewhere!' Connor looked a little cheered at least that somebody had a tactic in mind. 'Pascal? This is your home, I keep you here, where will you go if you lose?'

'The way we see it,' Lilibet interrupted, 'whoever wins will need staff, so we'd like to stay on.'

'And create a bird sanctuary,' Pascal added defiantly.

'You said you wouldn't bring that up now, that's for later on!' his wife admonished him.

'I'll make my case now, woman, and stop telling me what to do!'

'But what will you do if you win?' Connor shouted. 'Hire masters to serve? God, that's dull. Elise!'

'What?' a startled Elise asked, grabbing at a set of pearls nervously.

'What would you do if you had the island?' His voice was menacing. 'More importantly, what would you do to get it?'

Elise looked about her like a cornered cat. 'Oh, I haven't got time for that now!' she cried. 'I've got lunch to prepare!' She disappeared through the double kitchen doors.

'Doctor Ainsworth, you're keeping very quiet.' Richard naturally knew that his turn would come, but he still didn't have anything prepared. Then he remembered the real Doctor Richard Ainsworth and decided that was the way to go. 'I'd sell it,' he said. 'Pay off my debts and stop letting other people's problems bother me.'

He was very pleased with his answer, even if it elicited a look from Valérie suggesting that that's exactly what Richard would do, which he had to admit might not be a bad thing. Either way, it finally broke their host.

A thoroughly deflated Connor sat down. 'Where's Schmid anyway?' he barked angrily. 'He should be here by now. He's not as incapacitated as he makes out. Bruno, go and knock on the old man's door, give him a chivvy-up.'

Bruno bounded up the steps, three at a time, and everyone watched him, in particular Richard and Valérie, who exchanged a quick glance.

'Right then,' Connor resumed, 'this morning's plans.' He sat at the table and pulled a napkin on to his lap while everyone watched his movements just like the night before. Connor started buttering some toast. 'After breakfast,' he began, his first bite still tumbling around his mouth like linen in a washing machine, 'you'll have an hour or so free to yourselves. Explore – there's the pool, the bar, the gym, a library. Do what you like. Measure up for carpets, seriously, knock yourselves out.' He took another bite.

'Goldfish?' Nevaeh asked.

'Never had pets,' Connor replied, without missing a beat. 'From eleven o'clock, it's time for work. Well, it's time for our resident psychiatrist to work anyway.'

Richard started choking on his coffee and a hovering Valérie moved forward in what appeared would be an effort to slap his back. It wasn't and she deftly removed Passepartout from his lap before he was covered in coffee. 'Excuse me,' she said, at least making it sound deferential.

'Work?' Richard managed to spit out eventually.

'Yes, Doctor, work! Time to earn your keep now. Time for the resident trick cyclist to do some quackery.'

'Do you think that's wise?' Richard tried to sound professional. 'You have put everyone under such an enormous anxious strain already. It might prove too much.'

Connor looked at him coldly. 'Oh, I do hope so,' he said flatly.

'In my professional opinion…' Richard tried again.

'Your professional opinion, *Doctor*, will be given when I ask for it. Bruno, where's Schmid? Is he there or not?'

'There's no answer, sir,' Bruno shouted down.

'Trust him to try and be different,' Connor growled.

Richard noisily replaced his cutlery. His calm inner sanctum from earlier in his room had now been shattered. He didn't like bullies, never had. Not unless they were attractive women and in that case, he unfortunately couldn't help himself and rather enjoyed the experience if he were honest. But he wasn't going to allow this charmless megalomaniac, albeit a billionaire charmless megalomaniac, to behave like that.

'I think you'll find, Mr Connor, that Herr Schmid is dead,' he said and rather nonchalantly popped a grape into his mouth. Everyone immediately fell silent, except for Elise, who dropped a bowl coming through the doors and Bernie, who began to play something appropriately inappropriate, but then backed out of it.

Immediately everyone started firing questions at Richard. 'How do you know?' 'Where is he?' 'How did he die?' 'Whose contract did he have?' and so on, but Richard stayed silent.

'Is this one of your oh-so-clever mind games, Doctor?' Connor asked with a look that suggested he was quite impressed with Richard if it was.

'In a way,' Richard replied coolly, though inside his stomach and his mind were taking it in turns to bungee jump off a cliff. Then he decided to put into action the idea that he and Valérie had discussed, though it had been hers, just before going their separate ways the night before. That everyone should know Herr Schmid had died; Richard would announce it at breakfast, but that the two of them should then gauge the reaction when the room was found to be empty. 'I felt for Herr Schmid's pulse when I took him to his room last night, there was none. I said nothing of this to Elise, however, not wanting to alarm her. I wanted to tell you privately, but some narcissistic trait in you demands that everything be made public. So there you are, here we are.'

Connor began nodding his head slowly. 'OK then,' he said quietly. 'Let's go and look. Everyone. Together.'

All of them made their way up the stairs or by the lift in silence. There was nervous tension in the air as some contemplated whether this was part of the game Connor had laid out, a tragedy or worse. Once they were all outside Schmid's door, Connor had them line up against the handrail so that they all got a view. Valérie waited by the door, key at the ready.

'You should take notes, Doctor. You might be able to use some of this in your one-on-ones later.' Richard didn't like the look in Connor's eye; it was pure callous enjoyment. 'OK, Valérie,' Connor said. 'Open the door.'

Valérie carefully unlocked the wide disabled access door and swung it back on its silent hinges. A gasp went up, Lea Boudon screamed and fainted into Bruno Mangetout's arms. Richard could quite easily have done the same, because Herr Albrecht Schmid was there in front of them, motionless in his wheelchair, his head fallen to one side.

Chapter Fifteen

Bruno held Lea Boudon's flopped body tightly, stopping it from falling to the floor. Lea, not fully unconscious, was clearly enjoying herself, however, and was taking longer than seemed reasonable to right herself. Meanwhile, it was Valérie who took charge.

'I must ask,' she demanded, putting herself in the door threshold, 'that no one come any further into this room. This is now a crime scene and it must be treated as such. It must be kept uncontaminated.' Richard, in part in awe of her chutzpah, her speed of thought and her elegant silhouette against the large window, also hoped that she hadn't just flipped sides and was determined to call in the real authorities all of a sudden. His fingerprints were so all over the place it might as well have been an art installation. They were especially abundant in the minibar, a bad sign if Schmid had been poisoned.

He was aware also that Connor was looking at him and he affected a face of deep concentration, which in practice is never that far from a face of deep frustration, which is what Richard actually felt. It seemed to him that Herr Albrecht Schmid was far more active in death than he had been in real life. Richard had certainly deposited his dead body here after dinner. It was not there later that night. It was now back in the room shortly after breakfast. The man was proving a positive menace.

Connor started shaking his head. 'Right, everyone.' He even clapped his hands like a tour guide. 'Take ten minutes, do what you have to do and we'll reconvene in the pool area. Ten minutes, got it?'

Everyone, understandably in a state of shock, muttered their acceptance of the arrangement and shuffled off, giving whoever was next to them a wide berth. All except the limpet-like Lea, who Bruno hadn't yet managed to release back into the wild. And Elise, who looked at Richard searchingly for some guidance. Richard felt the least qualified to give it frankly, but he did give a short nod and a wink to suggest that he was fully in control of the situation. He, Connor and Valérie stayed behind. Connor grabbed Richard's arm, pushed him towards Valérie and they all crossed the threshold together. Connor slammed the door behind them, but not before Passepartout had followed them in.

'What, in the name of the sweet Mary Mother of God, is going on here?' he asked. Richard and Valérie looked at each other innocently, but fortunately the question wasn't directed at them. It was directed at himself. Not strictly rhetorically, however, because he was demanding an answer of himself too. Richard raised his eyebrows, but said nothing. Valérie scooped up Passepartout with one hand and had the other on her shoulder-strapped gun holster at the same time. 'This was not supposed to happen at all. So why did it?' Connor carried on his extraordinary, highly personal tête-à-tête as if neither of them were there in the room with him, pacing up and down as he did so; and to be fair to the man he was conducting a pretty thorough interrogation. 'There's no such thing as a surprise,' he concluded eventually. 'This is not natural causes.' Finally he turned towards Richard and Valérie. 'This is not natural causes,' he repeated firmly. 'But we'll say that it is.'

'It might be natural causes!' Valérie retorted.

'Oh, I like her,' Connor said to Richard. 'She never thinks for herself! She is so on my side.'

Richard tried to avoid Valérie's eye, which he guessed was probably looking at a quick contract termination.

'She might be right,' Richard ventured.

'Oh, come on!' Connor looked from one to the other. 'No way. I pit guest against guest and one of them winds up dead. Really? Like, have you never seen a film in your life, Doctor?'

This time it was Valérie's turn to step in before Richard began spouting the classic *Halliwell's Filmgoer's Companion* from A to Z; not as deadly as her gun but in many ways just as disabling.

'I think we must check if Herr Schmid's contract is still under the pillow as it should be,' she said, walking between the two men, brushing them apart with some force. She retrieved the envelope and made a big show of ripping it open as opposed to the careful, even delicate procedure the night before. She handed it to Connor, who read it slowly and bounced his head from side to side weighing up the information.

'OK. So from our original ten in the game, we have eight left,' he said, giving it the oomph of a sports commentator.

'How so?' Valérie asked.

'Obvious. One is dead, Schmid. And one didn't take her contract when she had a clear opportunity to do so, if she was the killer that is. That leaves eight.' He leant in close to Valérie. 'If I were you,' he said quietly, 'I'd look for whoever has Schmid's contract. That's your killer, right there. OK, see yous upstairs.'

He left the room looking as happy as Richard had seen him since they'd met the night before.

'What if he actually knows who has whose contract?' Richard asked nervously, knowing full well that Schmid's was in his possession.

'I don't think so,' Valérie said seriously. 'I was with him when he did most of the organising and that silly man likes chaos.'

'How can a man who likes chaos hate surprises?' Richard asked, confused.

'Because, Richard, the two are not the same. Especially when the chaos is of his own making.'

Richard nodded sagely, but frankly didn't buy any of that. It sounded like typical management speak to him, all snake-oil salesmen oxymorons dressed up as 'I saw that coming' logic. Pure business hippy twaddle, as Pascal would say.

'If you say so. Will the body be OK in here? He's not going to turn up in the pool later is he?'

'No.' Valérie shook her head sagely. 'I think he will be fine here now. How low does the air conditioning go in this room, Richard?'

He went to the controls and managed to turn it down to a very chilly eight degrees. 'That should keep him cool enough for now,' he said.

'Good.' Her reply was stern, but distant. 'We will come back together later. Now we must go upstairs.'

Richard shrugged. 'He might not be here later, judging by his current record.'

They followed Passepartout up to the next floor via the stairs and were blinded by the late-morning sun that hit them as the tinted automatic doors slid open. By the time Richard's retinas had stopped burning and he was able to focus, what was before him was like a stock photo from a holiday brochure. These people had been shown the corpse of a fellow guest just ten minutes earlier and had seemingly decided to choose Bacchanalia and sun-worshipping as a collective coping mechanism. Even Pastor Gilbert had swapped the white trousers of his suit for white shorts. He'd kept his white jacket on though and added a white flat cap. He looked like a cross between a lawn bowls umpire and a choir boy. He was lying on a sun lounger reading the Bible out loud, but also inaudibly, which again gave off a rather sinister aura.

The Durands occupied two ends of a sun lounger and had made no concessions to the heat of the day other than to sit under its parasol. Inevitably they had their backs to each other and were sucking hard on their pipes while regarding the rest of the party with very obvious suspicion. It was clear too that the way they were sat meant that if one were to stand up suddenly, the other would be catapulted off. Richard rather liked them and thought with an unpractised psychiatrist's eye that the lounger/catapult situation was a perfect metaphor for their marriage.

Bernie was at the piano, almost certainly his happy place, and playing a slowed-down jazzy version of 'Club Tropicana', while Lea and Bruno sat nearby at a table. It was clear that Lea was trying to convince Bruno to dance with her and the poor man – and Richard knew this feeling well – looked terrified at the prospect. It was certainly not something the Foreign Legion had prepared him for. Elise fussed about the place, walking from lounger to table asking if anybody wanted anything and occasionally throwing a nervous look in the direction of her boss, who would sometimes respond with a glance of his own in what looked like a successful attempt to unnerve the poor woman.

Connor himself sat shirtless on an underwater stool at the pool bar, leaning back and letting the sun bronze his pink hairless body. As Richard had tried to make clear, he wasn't *that* kind of doctor, but he knew enough to know that a pale Irishman and intense sunbathing are rarely a good mix. Nevaeh was sitting on the stool next to him, whispering something that neither Richard or Valérie could make out. She had changed into a bikini that was exactly the same colour as her tanned skin, making it look like she was actually topless but that her nipples had been airbrushed for public decency.

Richard felt decidedly overdressed in his elasticated slacks and polo shirt. How Valérie would cope in her black get-up he didn't like to contemplate.

'Ah, Doctor, Valérie. So, is it natural causes do you think?'

Richard began to um and ah, and was therefore grateful when Valérie decided to answer for the both of them. 'It is almost certainly heart failure,' she replied definitely. 'Isn't it, Doctor?'

'What?' Richard was caught by surprise. 'Oh yes, almost certainly.' He had worked with Valérie for long enough to know that this wasn't necessarily a falsehood. In their experiences together, he'd learnt that many things could bring on heart failure and it did not rule out a nefarious alien influence.

'Well, it's very sad obviously. And I'll get around to notifying the authorities later. My island, my rules and all that. For now that is. Who knows? It may be one of you soon who has that unhappy duty to perform.' Connor looked anything but unhappy and nobody else was exhibiting any outward signs of grief either. 'Of course, it increases the chances of a win for those remaining…' And with that statement hanging like a storm cloud in the air, he slid off his stool and swam the entire length of the pool underwater, emerging at the other end with the inevitable hazard warning light of a grin on his face.

'When you say that increases the chances for of one us,' said Lea Boudon, a stickler for rules and detail, offering Bruno some brief respite from her attentions, 'does that mean that you know whose contract was in Albrecht's possession?'

Richard felt a sharp elbow in his side. 'Albrecht?' Valérie whispered. 'Not Herr Schmid?' It was a good point that Richard hadn't picked up on, though he had noticed that no one was questioning the decency of carrying on with the game.

'I don't have the contract,' Connor said over his shoulder as he climbed out of the pool, revealing himself to be wearing the most indecent swimming trunks

Richard had seen since the seventies and the heyday of the Grattan catalogue. No wonder there was no moral panic at continuing his game, the man was utterly shameless. 'Valérie here has the contract. It belongs to somebody here now, which means they are playing, but with no chance of winning.' Now there was a reaction. Suddenly the group, unperturbed by the death of a fellow guest began vocally objecting to Connor's mischief in a robust way, like footballers surrounding a referee.

He held his hands aloft, almost like a Roman emperor demanding, not appealing, for calm. 'Anyone is welcome to drop out of the game at any time,' he said slowly, looking from one to the other. 'Any time,' he repeated.

There were no takers and Bernie began to sing 'Hotel California' to break the silence. It didn't fit to Richard's mind: *could* you check out any time you like? *Could* they never leave?

Chapter Sixteen

An hour or so later, Elise, fussing as always and clearing things away, looked at her watch. 'Is that really the time?' she said loudly. 'Sorry to drag you away from your downtime, Bruno, but if you could put Madame Boudon down for a second, we need to go and get lunch prepared.'

Bruno reluctantly broke away from Lea Boudon, the couple clearly having struck up quite a mutual attraction. So much so that Richard wondered if it really was vape smoke that surrounded them or the smouldering of a new relationship. Lea got up languidly from her lounger and made her way to the indoor gym, humming to herself happily.

Ian Connor watched her go and snorted derisively in her direction like a pantomime villain. 'So, Doctor,' he said, swivelling on his bar stool and turning to Richard, 'what about these one-on-one sessions then? Now seems as good a time as any, don't you think?'

Richard definitely did not think so at all. 'Maybe after the shock, we should perhaps allow people some rest?' he argued, but was immediately countermanded from an unlikely, but typical source.

'Nonsense, Richard! Sorry, Doctor,' Valérie said, appealing to Connor at the same time. 'You must speak to them while they are vulnerable, no?'

'I think ethically, madame,' Richard responded through gritted teeth, 'that is something of a grey area.'

'Maybe,' Connor interrupted. 'But she's right. It's like any business, Doctor, you'll gain nothing if your opponent is comfortable.'

There was a nasty edge to Connor's voice this morning and Richard would have liked to think that perhaps he was more affected by the death of Albrecht Schmid than he cared to outwardly show. It wasn't generally in Richard's nature to give the benefit of the doubt towards people, but there was something in Connor that felt familiar. Was it disappointment? Fear? He couldn't put his finger on it. A desire to escape the reality he'd made for himself, perhaps?

'I've wrestled with life for many years,' Richard said enigmatically, not actually intending to say the words out loud, especially as he was misquoting again, 'but I'm happy to state I finally beat it.' It was supposed to be one of his favourite quotes, uttered by James Stewart in the film *Harvey*, about a man who is thought to be insane but who may actually be wiser than everyone else. *That part was apt at least*, he thought.

Connor, however, looked impressed, as though he felt Richard might have read his own thoughts. 'I'd like to sit in on your sessions, Doctor,' he said. 'I'd like to see how you work.'

'Ah, no, that won't be possible I'm afraid,' Richard insisted. 'Completely unethical.'

Connor looked disappointed and a little angry too, as he wasn't used to not getting his own way. 'I understand,' he said quietly.

Richard put a hand on the man's shoulder. 'Are we ever really afraid of something we understand?' he asked seriously, this time leaning on something that sounded like Fred Astaire in *Carefree* playing a psychiatrist opposite Ginger Rogers. Inside, and completely against his natural instincts, Richard was enjoying himself immensely. It wasn't just that he was more relaxed now that Valérie was there, it was something else. When he had first stepped into the grandeur of Le Fort Esprit de l'Air it had felt like being in a film. He'd even been assigned a role, the psychiatrist, and he was now drawing on his immense back catalogue of film history and dialogue and immersing himself fully in the part. OK, so he had mangled the quotes horribly so far, but if anything that seemed to be working to his advantage. He was beginning to realise that film dialogue about psychiatry, certainly as he remembered it, made sense. Whereas his half-remembered ramblings actually gave him an air of batty but unquestioned expertise. Nobody quite knew what he was talking about and it leant him scientific gravitas.

'I would suggest, however,' Connor was not to be completely put off, 'that Valérie here sits in with you.'

Richard thought that a very good idea too, but for the sake of appearances felt he should put up some sort of objection. 'Again, ethically...' he began.

'Ah, have it your own way then.' Connor sounded bored now.

'Of course,' Richard replied, lowering his voice, 'we don't know for sure that Herr Schmid wasn't killed, so some protection would be welcome.'

Connor gave him a thin smile. 'You're right, Doctor, we don't know that for sure at all. It might even have been you.' He held Richard's gaze for an uncomfortably long time, before giving a curt nod of assent towards Valérie and then slipping off his stool and swimming away again. He rose a few metres down the pool. 'Oh, and just in case you're in any doubt,' he called back, 'you can trust Valérie. I have done a very thorough check-up on her background. Her file says she's clean.' He sank below the surface again and Richard wondered if that was a file he really wanted to see or one to be avoided at all costs.

For her part, Valérie was clearly wanting to skip over the whole file thing very quickly. 'Who shall we start with, Richard?' she asked earnestly.

'I don't know,' he whispered back. 'I really am not that kind of doctor!'

Valérie gave him a disillusioned look, like that of a pushy stage mum whose hot-housed offspring was now refusing to walk out into the limelight.

'Lea Boudon,' Richard said immediately, for fear of letting her down. 'She's on her own at least.'

They found Lea on the walking treadmill, a bottle of water in one hand and vape in the other. She had discarded one of her flowery jumpsuits and revealed a much better figure than the rather large clothing hid. She was concentrating and counting her steps out loud. 'One hundred and six, one hundred and seven...' She noticed them in the mirror. 'Six hundred and two, six hundred and three… I'll be with you in a second,' she said, puffing out her cheeks. 'I just want to get to my six-ten target.'

'No problem.' Richard tried to affect an air of therapist calm. He and Valérie went to pour themselves each a coffee and sat at a table waiting for Lea to finish.

'Ah that's better,' Lea said, sitting down. 'It's been quite a stressful morning what with one thing and another, hasn't it?'

'It has.' Richard nodded sagely, overdoing it slightly. 'Does it worry you?' he asked. 'The death of Albrecht Schmid?'

'I didn't know him!' Her answer was immediate, too immediate for Richard's liking, though if asked he wouldn't have known what he meant by that; nonetheless he could see Valérie thought the same way.

'Of course not,' Richard smiled. 'But any death can bring up memories of those who we have lost…' He now sounded more like a sanctimonious vicar than a man ostensibly of science and he knew it.

'Nope. Not with me,' Lea replied through a fog of mint-scented vape. 'I'm not the sentimental type at all.' She tapped immaculate fingernails on the table.

'I like your nails very much,' Valérie commented and it was easily the most un-Valérie thing he had ever heard her say. 'Did you win that manicure in a competition?'

The usual alarms went off in Richard's head and he felt like leaving the room as soon as possible, and just letting the two of them just get on with it if it was going to get catty, but Lea laughed.

'She's probably a better judge of character than you are, Doctor!' she roared. 'No, I didn't. It's Valérie, isn't it? Can I call you Valérie?'

'You must,' Valérie gushed.

'Well, Valérie, no. I paid for them, as I pay for everything.'

'You didn't win a competition to come here the first time then?' Richard asked.

'Oh, yes, I did. But it wasn't my husband's company, it was mine. I own and run a light engineering company. We are *very* successful,' she added proudly.

'Why haven't you contradicted all the stuff about your husband and his company then?' asked Richard suspiciously.

Lea gave him a patronising smile and then turned her eyes to Valérie. 'Men, eh?' She rolled her eyes and Valérie nodded sagely. 'I learnt very early on, Doctor, that if I were a woman in the engineering industry I would struggle. And if I were seen as successful, the other companies would collaborate and turn on me. All my attempts at getting finance and investment were denied, then I had an idea.'

'You hired a man to front for you?' Valérie interrupted with a world-weary tone.

'Exactly!' Lea smiled again, but her eyes shone with anger. 'I re-presented the same business plans and the same engineering ideas to the same investors, all through an out-of-work actor I hired for the job. My boyfriend at the time was going to do it, but he ran off with my secretary. Some male stereotypes never die. Anyway, the money came rolling in and still does. I'm not Ian Connor money, but I do OK.' She leant back in her chair. 'So, what do you think of that, Mr Psychiatrist?'

He felt like giving her a round of applause frankly, but instead sifted through his brain rolodex of psychiatry-related film quotes and came up with a winner. 'That's business,' he nodded in admiration. 'Half of it's luck and half of it's the right trousers.'

Lea graciously accepted the acknowledgement of her achievements. 'I like that,' she said. 'One of yours?'

'No, a colleague of mine.' Richard covered quickly, not revealing it was another of his film misquotes, this time from a screwball comedy called *That Uncertain Feeling*. 'So you have no family then?' he asked, for something to say.

'I didn't say that,' was the very pleased response. 'I have a daughter. I adopted her at a very young age and she's planning to go on and take a degree in engineering.' She smiled proudly. 'I hope she'll take over the company one day.'

'I admire you both,' said Richard genuinely, no need this time for a quote.

Valérie was also impressed and especially, it seemed to Richard, with him and how he was adapting to his role, which inevitably caused him to relax and make a fatal mistake. He went to put his hands behind his head, further to continuing his word-perfect acting with more lines ripped from cinema history, but unfortunately knocked over what was left of his coffee. It spilled on to the table.

'Oh, Richard!' Valérie admonished him, but moved out of the way before she was stained. Lea vaped, but didn't otherwise react.

Richard – and he would for ever more be proud of this – reacted quickly. 'So, madame.' He stared at Lea. 'What do you make of this shape the spilled coffee has made on the table? What does it say to you?'

Lea laughed loudly and playfully elbowed Valérie, who tried and failed appallingly to hide that she didn't like that kind of familiarity. 'Oh, he's good, isn't he?' Lea barked.

'I apologise.' Richard smirked, enjoying himself again. 'A clumsy way to introduce the famous Rorschach test, though some call it the inkblot test, but I prefer to take people by surprise!'

Valérie raised her eyebrows at this. From her point of view she could count on the fingers of one finger how many times Richard had surprised her. His estranged wife, Clare, even fewer. He could easily have explained that his very limited knowledge came from a rare film from 1958 called *Screaming Mimi*, but as it was about a neurotic stripper working in a nightclub called 'El Madhouse', he decided to stay silent in front of the two ladies in case they judge the psychiatrist harshly.

Lea was still chuckling, but looking at the spilt coffee intently nonetheless. 'Well, it looks like a land mass, doesn't it?' she said thoughtfully. 'An island maybe? Possibly even this island and that bubble, that one right there in the middle is Herr Albrecht Schmid.' The bubble burst. 'Yes,' she looked up at them both. 'Poor Albrecht Schmid, running out of time. Pop!' she added, with a twinkle in the eye. 'And before his time, I'll bet.'

'You do not believe it was natural causes, then, madame?'

'No! Does anyone? With this silly competition that our host has set up, no!'

'Is that why you fainted when you saw the body?' It was clear to Richard from Valérie's tone that she didn't feel fainting was really in Lea's character.

'Oh no, dear! I fainted because I was next to Bruno.' She smiled. 'And I always get what I want.' She stood up to go. 'I'm going to shower before lunch, I think. I'll tell you this though, if you're looking for suspects then that Bernie Webb is worth talking to. I mean, why can't he leave the island?' She picked up her water bottle and left them at the table.

'She definitely knocked off Schmid!' Richard hissed, though they were now alone.

'You are so sure he was knocked off?' Valérie asked not unreasonably.

'Well, I am now, yes, because she did it. He was obviously one of the investors who turned her down, it's simple. She's taken her revenge here, on a lawless island.'

Valérie nodded. 'Perhaps, Richard, perhaps.'

They both stood up to leave as well, but as Richard approached the glass door, he spotted something on the window. There was an oval shape, very obviously lips which had kissed the glass. They were very faint, but Richard was struck by it and realised that this was the window where he thought he'd either seen a face or his own reflection the afternoon before. He pointed it out to Valérie, who shrugged as if it was unimportant, but Richard bent down. He knew what it was, children do that to windows, kiss and blow their cheeks out, at the same time creating condensation and maybe writing something on the pane. He breathed on the area to reproduce the effect. The lips became clearer and then above them, written in capitals, was the name IAN.

Chapter Seventeen

'What do you make of that?' Richard asked as they got into the lift. The pastor had still been chanting away in the pool area and directed his righteous ire in the direction of Connor and Nevaeh, who were sunbathing on adjoining loungers. Everybody else had gone, either to prepare lunch or to get ready for it.

'What do I make of what?' Valérie sounded distracted.

'The name on the window, that's what!' Richard couldn't understand her diffidence on the matter. 'I think it speaks volumes about our host. He's a child basically and all this game, or whatever it is, is just a tantrum.' He shook his head. 'I'd like to get him on my couch for a few minutes, it's obviously mother related!'

'What do you mean it is mother related?' Now he had her attention.

'I don't know,' he admitted. 'I'm just immersing myself in the character.' A thought occurred to him. 'Were you two already here when we arrived?'

'Oh yes,' she replied as the lift descended. 'He was determined to watch you all from the moment that you landed here.'

'And the staff knew, obviously?'

'Oh, yes. We came over yesterday on the Durands' boat.'

The lift came to a smooth stop at the ground-floor lounge, but before they stepped out Richard had one more point to make. 'I don't think he was watching us from very far,' he said urgently. 'I think I saw him hiding in the gym.'

'But why?'

'Because nobody uses the gym, that's why.'

'No, why hide, why not use cameras or surveillance? How do you know that it was him, anyway? It might have been your own reflection, you know?'

'It might not have been him, no. But it certainly wasn't my reflection. Because my reflection doesn't behave like a child and nor would it write "IAN" on the window.'

She looked at him, still unsure of his point, but before she could answer, Bernie played them an introduction as a greeting.

'Strangers in the night, two lonely people…'

Richard had the distinct impression that, drunk though he clearly was, Bernie was being ironic in his choice of song. Valérie and he were meant to be strangers after all, colleagues in a billionaire's fake psychology experiment, but they were certainly not acting as if they'd just met. But then that seemed very much to be the fashion around the place. Lea and Bruno, Nevaeh and Connor… He tutted loudly, it was like some oldies' love island and the thought made his stomach churn.

'Ah, Monsieur Webb.' Valérie beamed a smile at Bernie, who returned it with a forced smile of his own.

'Watcha, Val!' he replied, in a cockney accent. 'Rich. Well, if it isn't the good cop, bad cop of the men in white coats brigade. Come in, take a pew, it's just me and you…' He played beautifully for a minute or two while they listened. He was right, they were the only people in the lounge area.

'Can I start the questions this time?' Valérie whispered to Richard.

Richard wasn't sure. He was beginning to like his role as chief investigator and felt it had gone rather well with Lea Boudon, quite revealing in fact. 'OK,' he replied, also in a whisper while Bernie continued to play. By his tone he wanted to make it clear he was against the idea of Valérie taking the lead. 'But you have to be subtle. Remember these people are highly strung individuals and one of them may even be a killer.'

Valérie gave him a filthy look, suggesting that he really should not be questioning her abilities as either an investigator or as a woman of immense empathy. She decided not to answer him and turned to Bernie Webb instead.

'What are you running away from, Monsieur Webb? Why are you hiding?'

Richard tried not to shake his head in dismay; instead his eyes just blinked repeatedly in shock at Valérie's total and completely unfiltered approach to people. He decided to intervene.

'What my colleague means,' he shot Valérie a look as he spoke, 'is that you are clearly a very talented man, almost like a human jukebox…'

'Ha!' This seemed to delight Bernie enormously. 'That was my stage name for a while!'

'Well, I'm a big fan.' He gave Valérie another look before she could interrupt his flow. 'So, I guess my question is, with all that in mind, why are you here? A court jester for burnt-out business executives?'

Valérie let out a petulant sigh of exasperation. 'What my colleague means is…' Her voice was rich with irritation. 'What are you running away from and why are you hiding?'

'Blimey, you don't muck about do you, Val?' Bernie replied and then broke out into song again. '*She's just a devil woman…*' He stopped, his heart clearly not in it. 'Oh, I dunno,' he said, returning to a more gentle lift music tune. 'It's not such a bad place really, is it? I mean people pay thousands to stay here, don't they? And I've got it for free.'

'But it's obvious that you don't want to be here,' Richard said with some sympathy. 'Almost like you're trapped.'

'Like you are hiding!' Valérie added with some vehemence.

Bernie played some more and despite his inebriation was weighing up how to answer. 'I am hiding, I guess,' he admitted sadly.

'People never really run away from anything,' Richard began sagely, but before he could embark on the quote from *Psycho*, Valérie interrupted.

'From who though?'

'Oh, madame,' Bernie emphasised the word. 'Isn't it obvious? I'm hiding from me! I'm on the run from me! But you know the problem with that?' He looked seriously from Valérie to Richard, who remained silent.

'I keep bloody finding me, don't I?' He cackled at his own observation, but it was a mirthless, empty laugh which broke as he turned back to his keyboard and began singing beautifully.

'"You Know I'm No Good"?' Richard asked softly. 'Amy Winehouse?'

'Bless her, yes,' Bernie replied. 'Now there's someone who knew about self-destruction, not this half-life I lead.' He banged angrily at the keys and took another long drink from his glass.

'Do you never leave at all?' Valérie asked, her voice softening at last.

'I did a few months ago,' Bernie said, his voice low. 'The island was emptied while they did another refurb. I was only gone about a month, spent the whole time in some casino in Nantes and then hurried back here as soon as I could. And you know the worst thing that happened?' The other two both shook their heads. 'I followed me back here! Bloody idiot.' He started playing 'Me and My Shadow'.

'So you are addicted to gambling, monsieur?'

'You bet, Val!' He cackled again. 'And I'd love to play poker with you! Seriously, I'm a weak man and there's no temptation here other than this stuff.' He held up his glass.

Richard, not a card player himself, had often made the same observation: Valérie would never be able to hide her emotions around a card table. His thoughts were lost, however, as his mouth started moving again in response to Bernie's self-assessment of his weakness. In his head there was some perfect dialogue from the David Niven classic *A Matter of Life and Death*, something about a weak mind not being strong enough to hurt itself or something and so saving itself from insanity. He fought to resist saying it out loud, however, and instead thought about changing the subject entirely. Maybe even trying the inkblot test that he had accidentally introduced with Lea Boudon, but he knew those things would just be a trigger with Bernie Webb. All of them. Rorschach, word association, ambiguous stimulation, all of them would result in: 'I'm Bernie Webb, I sing what I see!' showing his human jukebox wares. Much in the same way, Richard was loathe to admit, that he himself was prone to do with films. Clare had once described these cinema fact and quote outbursts as a form of Tourette syndrome, which didn't seem far wide of the mark at all. And now he'd found a fellow sufferer.

'Did you know Herr Schmid?' Valérie asked, choosing her words carefully for once, no doubt hoping it wasn't the name of a hit song.

'No, not at all.' Bernie continued tinkering at the piano. 'He came here once before when I was here, but he didn't talk much.'

'It must have been quite a shock that he died of natural causes like that,' Richard pushed.

Bernie looked doubtful. 'It would indeed be a great shock if he died of natural causes!' he joked. 'But no one believes that. Our wonderful host has put a target on our backs, hasn't he? And I've got so many targets on my back I look like a shooting range! Bang! Bang!' he shouted with a grin. 'Now, do I go Sammy Davis Jnr or Cher?'

Just then there was an awful sound as another large sea bird came crashing into the orangery windows, sliding down slowly before coming to a rest on the ground, its fate the same as the previous evening. Richard and Valérie both stared in horror at the sight, whereas Bernie seemed almost to have missed the incident completely.

'You know, my bet – not that I make bets anymore – my bet is on the Right Reverend,' he said above his playing. 'There's something not real about him and if Ian Connor was right that Schmid had some kind of investment in this place that he would pull, he might have been refusing to sell it privately. *I'm just talking in my sleep*,' he added in song, as he hadn't sung for over a minute.

'Do you really think so?' Richard asked. 'I admit he's a bit intense, but all the same… a man of the cloth?'

'Nah, mate, he's no man of the cloth that one. He's a fraud, trust me.'

'How do you know?' asked Valérie, in a tone that strongly suggested she agreed.

'Because, madame, I am a fraud and it takes one to know one!'

If Valérie was going to ask for any further proof he might have, they were interrupted as Ian Connor stalked around the mezzanine before slamming closed the door to his bedroom behind him. A couple of seconds later Nevaeh appeared on the mezzanine too, wearing a silk dressing gown, her hair still wet from the pool.

She knocked on Connor's door. A door clearly marked Connor as opposed to the other entrepreneurial notaries.

'Oh, Ian,' Nevaeh spoke lightly. 'Can I come in?' She looked down over the balustrade and saw Richard, Valérie and Bernie staring back up at her. There was no answer and her face now carried a nervous look. She knocked again and this time the door to Ian Connor's room opened slowly. She looked down at her three onlookers again but this time with an air of triumph, before then walking calmly into the bedroom and closing the door softly behind her.

Chapter Eighteen

The lunchtime buffet looked very inviting, a real seafood and salad feast and for the first time that day Richard realised that he was ravenous. He was finding it hungry work being a pretend psychiatrist and some lobster rillettes, tuna *brochettes* and what Bruno proudly described as *saumon sauvage rôti sur salade des haricots et oeuf dur* – or roast wild salmon on a green bean and hard-boiled egg salad, as Richard translated for Pastor Gilbert – would go down nicely. Especially if there was a crisp white wine to accompany it.

'Do not eat too much, Richard,' Valérie warned him quietly. 'There is no time for one of your *sieste* this afternoon. We have work to do.'

Richard couldn't help feeling a little deflated by this; after all this was supposed to be his holiday, albeit a state-sponsored break to alleviate pressure on the head that wears the crown and so on. Frankly, he hadn't worked this hard in years.

'I really think I will need some kind of rest,' he replied, only narrowly avoiding saying it as a sulky whine.

'But we have no time!' Valérie retorted.

Richard's shoulders slumped and he went to pick up a glass, determined to at least fill up heartily on lunch and especially some of the local speciality that came in a bottle. He poured himself a large measure of wine and went to take a sip.

'Should you be drinking, Doctor?' Ian Connor asked loudly from his throne at the head of the table. 'I mean, it hasn't done you many favours in the past, has it? And you are on duty this afternoon. A whiskey in the evening is one thing, but…'

Richard flushed bright red, partly in anger and partly because he noticed that everyone else was now staring at him. Of course, he remembered, the real Doctor Ainsworth was somewhere on his uppers, penniless and a hopeless drunk by all accounts, and therefore quite probably having a better time of lunch than Richard was having.

'I just like to sniff it,' he said breezily, not fooling anyone. 'It's always good to remind oneself of one's weaknesses.' Then he muttered under his breath, 'If I wanted to be this bullied I'd have stayed married.'

'Good man!' Connor said, before taking a long sip from his own wine glass while eyeing Richard at the same time. 'That's lovely, perfect temperature,' he added. 'I mean, Doctor, you don't want to end up like Bernie now, do you?'

This comment sparked Bernie from his gentle background music into a feisty rendition of Dean Martin's 'Little Ole Wine Drinker Me…', complete with slurred chorus and deliberate bum notes.

'Are you not eating at all, Mr Webb?' Elise asked, a look of motherly concern on her face. 'You can't just drink wine all day, you need some solids.'

'I'll have a sandwich later,' Bernie replied, nodding an appreciative thanks towards Elise. 'Or, I might just sit on the patio, open my mouth and wait for a bird to fly in.'

'I was thinking about the whole bird thing.' The pastor interrupted his own closed-eyed intense iteration of Grace and forked some tuna into his mouth. 'I mean, it's not right, is it?' Nobody said anything. 'We are all God's creatures!' he thundered, causing everyone to agree immediately, fearing some divine retribution if they didn't.

'And what have you been thinking exactly?' It was Ian Connor who asked, his lips upturned slightly like the mouth of a basking reptile, his soft Irish accent easily sliding from hearty bonhomie to menacing.

'Well, it ain't right, that's all. It ain't just. Here we are, living in the lap of luxury, almost wickedly, like Sodom and Gomorrah. We have usurped their territorial land and they now die for our sins.'

Even Richard, not overly blessed with religious education or scripture knowledge, realised that this was a pretty confused argument and that if the pastor were to try and justify this chapter and verse they'd be here all day. Besides which, in the last few minutes, he had been banned from both drinking and napping, so in his eyes there was very little Sodom and certainly no Gomorrah going on at all.

'Are you suggesting that you would return the island to its original state?' It was Valérie who asked the question, getting a nod of approval from her boss for doing so.

The pastor swallowed his food. 'Not all of it,' he said slowly, 'but certainly enough of it to create a refuge for God's wonderful creatures.' This last sentence was delivered directly at Pascal and Lilibet Durand, who were standing either side of the double doors and it was as blatant a sales pitch as Richard could remember. Pastor Gilbert was offering if not the classical olive branch, then certainly what seemed to be a partnership. Richard raised his eyebrows at Valérie and she did the same back.

Pascal and Lilibet each produced their long-stemmed pipes at the same time, like some kind of Olympic synchronised piping team, and looked at each other with just a little less malevolence than usual. 'And what would become of the rest of the place?' Pascal asked quietly, not looking at the pastor, but at the end of his pipe stem.

'A place of worship and devotion,' the pastor said, a high ideal but one delivered with such lasciviousness that he made it sound like he was actually offering drugs and naked ladies.

'We'd have to think about that, wouldn't we, Skipper?' Lilibet said, a suspicious look in her eye.

'Pah!' her husband replied. 'I'd have to think about it, you'll do as I say, woman!'

Lilibet cuffed him around the head with her free hand. 'That contract will be in both our names, Pascal Durand, and don't you forget it!'

Elise must have heard them from the kitchen and ushered them back through the doors to continue their argument elsewhere. 'Anybody need more bread?' she asked with a harried expression.

Richard was the only one to respond. 'Yes, please,' he replied. He was trying to stock up on bread because in truth the meal was something of a let-down; it was remarkably tasteless. It looked amazing, but was almost cruelly bland and he noticed Valérie struggling as well. The eggs in particular were a crushing disappointment. As a very proud, some might say overly proud owner of a brood of Oscar-winning free-range hens, he knew his good eggs from his bad ones. And these eggs were so battery produced the recipe might well have been called Eggs à la Duracell. Where had Bruno foraged for these exactly, a late-night mini-mart at a petrol station?

His thoughts were interrupted by Connor, who was clearly taken by Pastor Gilbert's brazen attempt at negotiation. 'That's an interesting gamble, Pastor Gilbert. I wonder what we're to make of that? That you have the Durands' contract? Perhaps. I think maybe it was a wider statement, that's why it was done publicly. You're letting everyone know you are willing to make a deal.'

Bernie crashed in on the ensuing tension with a high-energy version of 'The Devil Went Down to Georgia', which caused the pastor's eyes to turn fiery at the mention of Satan's name and Connor to ask for peace, presumably because he'd had one of his guests cornered and now he was off the hook.

'Where's Nevaeh?' Lea asked, though clearly not from any concern, more of annoyance.

'She doesn't like to eat lunch,' Connor replied, sounding bored.

Richard stood up from the table. He'd had enough of the company and certainly of the food. 'I want to write up some notes,' he said, carefully avoiding Valérie's harsh gaze. 'You know, before I start again this afternoon.'

'I took some of the notes as well,' Valérie declared. 'I should come with you.'

'Really, Madame d'Orçay?' He returned with a steely look of his own. 'I'd prefer to collate my work on my own first and then perhaps we could add your contribution a bit later on. Shall we meet again in an hour? An hour and a half?'

Valérie stood up as well to fully illustrate that she wasn't backing down and Richard couldn't help snorting his annoyance like a fenced-in bull.

'That'll do!' Connor laughed at the pair of them and for a moment Richard saw a worried look cross Valérie's face suggesting that they had been rumbled, that they hadn't in fact met just the night before, but were as antagonistic an example of a tired marriage as the Durands.

'Whatever you say.' Richard nodded curtly to Valérie. 'And anyway, you're probably armed.'

'Do I need to be, monsieur?' She had cottoned on to what he was trying to do, but was overdoing it by actually taking a few steps forward and threatening him.

'Stop, stop, stop!' Connor cried. 'This is too much! Anyway, I've got a much better idea.' His face turned sour as if on the flip of a coin. 'I want you to analyse me, Doctor?'

'Erm…' Richard knew that this was a very bad idea indeed. He strongly suspected that Ian Connor had either spent an awful lot of his adult life on the couch as it were, or had rebelled strongly against the idea of it for good reason. Either way, it didn't bode well for someone pretending to be a psychiatrist with a few non sequitur film quotes at hand and a clumsy way with coffee. 'Well, I mean it's up to you obviously…' He was hoping that Valérie would step in at this point, but it didn't look like that was going to happen. 'I think perhaps I should interview you last, really? Work my way up the pyramid as it were.' He had no idea what he was talking about.

'Do you?' Connor said quietly.

'Yes, I do.' Richard stiffened.

'I don't. Now sit down and let's be having you.'

'Here?' Richard liked that even less. 'I think some privacy might be a good idea.' He looked around the group for some support and got none. They were obviously keen to see Connor brought down a peg or two and keener still to witness it first-hand.

Richard sat down trying not to look nervous.

'Where shall we start?' Connor asked, leaning forward. 'My dreams? My childhood? That's where you quacks usually kick off from, isn't it? My mother even? Well, she's dead, thank God.'

It was worse than Richard had imagined; the man knew more than he did and what was even worse than that, Richard suspected that he knew that as well. This was going to be like a game of chess. A tactical back and forth across the table. Richard hated chess. He also felt like this was a game that he shouldn't actually win. He should look like he wanted to, but not do so.

If had wanted to win, then he'd have started with the mother thing straight away because there was obviously something there.

'We can start where you like,' he said, hoping that he sounded calm and not just like a teenager whose voice was about to break. 'Very often dreams make things feel authentic, but more often than not they have no actual basis in reality.'

It was a good start and Connor was on the back foot, obviously expecting Richard to crumble under the pressure. The fact that Richard was once again leaning heavily on Fred Astaire wasn't important, he had moved forward.

'My only dream,' Connor replied, 'is to be rid of this place and that's one of the reasons why you are here.'

'And have you always hated this place?' Richard asked, gaining in confidence.

Connor thought carefully about this. 'No,' he said thoughtfully, 'no, I haven't. Not always. I loved it once,' he said, though not with any sentimentality.

Richard nodded sagely and reached for another quote. This time a variant of Cary Grant in *Bringing Up Baby*. 'Ah, you know what it's like – love, man, impulse, conflict. A story as old as time,' he added, fiddling with his wine glass and wondering if he could go for a victory sip without getting told off.

The next person to speak and rather interrupting Richard's concentration as well as irritating Connor, was Passepartout, who was yelping as he chased shadows around the floor of the lounge area.

'Isn't conflict normal, Doctor?' Connor wasn't comfortable anymore and Passepartout's noise was getting to him more than he wanted to let on.

'Madame d'Orçay.' Richard turned towards Valérie. 'Would you mind comforting my dog for a moment. I fear he's interrupting our session, just as we might be getting somewhere.'

Valérie gave him a look that he had never seen from her before, nor could he recall seeing it from any other woman. Or man, either, come to that. It was immense admiration bordering on possible hero worship. Either that or she needed to go to the toilet.

'I was saying, Doctor,' Connor continued irritably. 'Love as a conflict, surely that's just normal behaviour, is it not?'

Richard was fast running out of quotes. It was becoming clear that most cinema psychiatrists were either impeccable dancers, victims in a screwball comedy or mother-fixated knife-wielding shower maniacs. It didn't help that Valérie was getting nowhere with a near frenzied Passepartout as he barked now at the ceiling and the swimming pool. 'Normal, heh?' Richard nodded as though mulling over the entire concept of normal, which is after all what psychiatrists actually do. Then it came to him in a flash, a wonderful soliloquy from his namesake Richard Burton in the film *Equus*, which he immediately dismissed as he couldn't pull it off with the required weight. 'And what exactly is normal?' he asked instead. 'A child's smile?' He slammed his fist down on the table to underline his point and hide the fact it made no sense. Thankfully, Lea

Boudon screamed, interrupting his blather. Then she got up, pointed at the ceiling and screamed again, this time falling into the waiting Bruno's arms.

Everyone followed her finger, which was still pointing up to the see-through rooftop pool. Nevaeh lay there under the water, floating face down, her eyes wide open looking on all of them, yet seeing nothing.

Chapter Nineteen

'Touch nothing,' Valérie said needlessly, as they all gathered around the edge of the pool. Nevaeh was four feet underwater, so it was unlikely that anybody would, and then Valérie jumped in and swam urgently down to the prone body of the young woman.

'That's what comes from messing with the name of Heaven,' Pastor Gilbert said distastefully, before uttering a short – very short – prayer. Ian Connor sat at a table a little away from everyone else and Richard watched him. He looked deep in thought, which didn't surprise Richard at all because as far as he was concerned now – and he was sure Valérie would be in agreement – Ian Connor was suspect number one.

Valérie resurfaced and took a big gulp of oxygen.

'Is she dead?' Lilibet asked redundantly, before turning towards her husband who put a consoling arm around her shoulder. 'Drowned?' she added in a wail.

'She has been weighed down by something,' Valérie said after further gulps of air. 'It is a belt of some kind, I think.'

'More likely the weight of her own godlessness.' If Pastor Gilbert was looking for new members for his flock, he was going the wrong way about it.

'Oh do shut up!' Lea pounced on him angrily. 'A young woman is dead, what kind of humane response is that?'

The pastor merely closed his eyes, shutting himself off.

'Bruno?' Valérie called from the pool. 'Can you help me, please? I cannot lift her out on my own.'

Bruno removed his shirt, which proved a distraction for many around the pool as the man was what Richard had heard young people call 'buff' or 'ripped'. He didn't just look like he did weights, he looked like he'd swallowed a few as well. In fact, Richard hadn't seen a six-pack that good since Clare had decided one Christmas that all Richard needed as a gift was some IPA brews from the old country.

Bruno dived in, making barely a ripple as he entered the water, and resurfaced alarmingly close to Valérie. Richard saw Lea Boudon's eyes flash with jealousy, which was ironic because his were doing precisely the same.

Together Valérie and Bruno dived down and emerged shortly after with the body of Nevaeh. Valérie swam to the side and got out, where Elise handed her one of the towels that she had gathered, while Bruno, having reached the shallow end, held the prostrate body of the young woman flat in his arms, carrying her up the steps of the pool as though offering her to the gods.

'Lay her here,' Elise commanded, as she put some more towels on a sun lounger. Everybody then stared at the lifeless body of Nevaeh. *Something she had maybe sought in real life as an influencer, she now has in death, everyone's rapt attention*, Richard thought. Then he shook his head, wondering where on earth that thought had come from and that maybe he was going a little too undercover as a psychiatrist. Everyone stayed silent though, even Bernie who was sitting inevitably at his piano, drink in hand.

The truth was that the young woman looked calm, maybe calmer than in life, and beautiful too; not the exaggerated beauty that she had carried but almost an inner beauty of peace. At least, she would have if the belt from her dressing robe wasn't tied tight around her neck, in an awful symmetry of the belt that had weighed her down. It was the same belt from the robe Richard and Valérie had seen her wearing when she entered Connor's room just before lunch.

'She cannot stay up here,' Valérie said, taking charge. 'Bruno and Richard can help me take her to her room.'

'That'll be the Zuckerberg room.' Elise's voice sounded distant, shocked.

'Oh, please!' Lea was reacting differently. 'Would it kill you to name some of the rooms after women?' Richard felt that she might have phrased that better.

'What? Like after all the women entrepreneurs?' Connor rolled his eyes.

'Radhika Aggarwal,' Lea replied instantly. 'Arianna Huffington.'

'Chanel,' Valérie joined in.

'Yes, but…' Connor was fighting a losing battle and he should have known it.

'Oprah Winfrey?' Richard added.

'I think Zuckerberg probably works here!' Connor snapped. 'She was one of his best customers.'

He looked pleased with his defence but was suddenly attacked again from an unlikely source.

'Aren't you going to do something?' Elise snapped at him. 'Just sit there, is that it? This poor young woman is dead, you can't wrap this up in your "natural causes".' She said the words 'natural causes' in not just a perfect Irish accent, but very much with Connor's voice. She was publicly mocking her boss, which at least finally seemed to wake him out of his torpor or shock.

'This is still my island,' he said with a quiet menace. 'So we will, for now, do things my way and my way only. Is that clear?' He addressed the question directly at Elise, but it was clear that it applied to everyone and nobody argued, even Valérie who, Richard assumed, had already in her mind taken charge.

'We will take her body downstairs,' she said authoritatively, confirming Richard's view. 'But can we remove this belt first, please?'

Bruno bent down and gently unclipped the black weighted belt around her stomach, before placing it on the floor. 'What's that?' Lea Boudon pointed at an envelope that was stuck, soaked to the inside of the belt.

'It looks like one of the contracts.' Connor was straight away back in game mode, prodding the ambitions of those around in the same way a cat toys with a half-dead mouse.

Valérie prised it carefully off the belt and opened the sodden envelope. She laid it down in front of Ian Connor, who with equal care unfolded the piece of soggy paper. Very little remained legible, the heavy bold type of Lane Bridge Holdings was just about there, but the rest was a mix of black and blue smudges. Black for print, blue for the name of whoever the contract was made out to.

'Can you read it?' the Pastor begged.

'No,' Connor replied salaciously, clearly getting more excitement from this latest twist. 'Now, that leaves, oh, how many? Only six I believe.'

It wasn't much later that Richard let out a huge sigh of relief as Bruno closed the bedroom door marked Zuckerberg behind him and Richard sat at Nevaeh's desk in the dead girl's room. This was all getting far too much, but he welcomed the opportunity to thrash out with Valérie just what was happening, and in semi-private too, the dead body of Nevaeh lying on her bed, now in a demure towelling robe, notwithstanding. Valérie, who had quickly changed her clothes, had her back to him, and she was staring out to sea, her arms half folded with one hand resting on her chin, feet apart. He recognised that stance, it was her frustration stance.

'A penny for them?' Richard asked, not really wanting to disturb her, but preferring that to the morbid silence that surrounded them.

She turned around, but her eyes didn't seem focussed, so concentrated was she in her thoughts; then she looked at Nevaeh and shook her head. 'I do not like this, Richard,' she said quietly but with a furious undertone. 'This young woman has been strangled, but by whom do you think?'

Richard raised his eyebrows. 'Well, my money's on our host. The last time either of us saw her alive, she was going into his room. It's not conclusive, but it's pretty damning.'

She nodded. 'Exactly,' she replied softly. 'My employer.'

Richard half-wondered if what she was now suffering from was some sort of ethical crisis. That she really was there to protect Ian Connor, but that the man might actually be using her as a shield, a diversion from his own murderous plans. If so, knowing her as well as he did – and he'd freely admit, he didn't know how much that actually amounted to – that wouldn't necessarily lead to an equal crisis of confidence, but it would surely make her take stock and think. He was even more taken aback by her next question.

'What do you think, Richard?' she asked, now looking at him intently.

It was not, he didn't think, the first time she had asked him this question. She had, in their previous investigations sought his opinion and, on infrequent occasions, even advice. But only when she had already made her mind up about something, so either to underline the decision she had already taken or as an opportunity to explain her thought processes. This was entirely different and the look on her face even suggested that she needed him. It was a situation that in some ways he had dreamt of, certainly hoped for and for which, he now realised, he was entirely ill-prepared.

'What do I think?' He puffed out his cheeks. 'I think your employer is either stupid or a genius and whichever it is, he is certainly dangerous.' She looked at him questioningly. 'I mean, he either knew his so-called game would produce murder, or he not only didn't think things through, he has no real awareness of human nature.'

'Like a child?'

'Yes, like a child,' he repeated. 'Hence the mood swings, the tantrums, writing his name on the window. I'd say emotionally he's still a little boy.'

She smiled at him, though not mockingly. 'Maybe you could have been a real psychiatrist, Richard,' she said warmly and he blushed.

'Anybody can if they watch enough films,' he replied. 'All of life is there.'

Whatever that moment was, it was over pretty quickly and Valérie jolted herself into action. 'We must search the room,' she commanded, albeit rhetorically.

'What are we looking for?' Richard stood up.

'Anything, really. Some papers I suppose. Can her real name be Nevaeh, Heaven backwards? It seems unlikely.'

'And her mobile phone,' he offered. 'She may not have been connected, but that didn't stop her filming everything. She may have even filmed her killer.'

'Undoubtedly she did at some point, Richard, because it is one of us!'

'Us?'

'Well, them then.'

'No, hang on. Are you seriously thinking of me as a suspect?' It was remarkable how quickly the mood in the room had changed.

She approached him and put her hand on his arm, and for a moment he thought she might slap some handcuffs on him. 'No, *cher* Richard,' she said. 'I do not think of you as a suspect, but for now we must let everyone else still believe that, because one of *them* has a contract with your name on it.' She made it sound like a contract for a hit, an assassination, a rub-out by a rival, which of course is just what it amounted to.

'I might just stay in my room from now on,' he said and he didn't care that his voice betrayed his nervousness. 'You don't really need me, do you?'

She snorted. 'I very much do need you, Richard.' It bolstered him a little. 'Now, you look for the phone and I will look for anything else.'

'And then I can just go to my room?' he asked.

'Then we go back to Herr Schmid's room – we need to look over that place again.'

Richard stumbled around the room looking for Nevaeh's phone while Valérie searched her luggage. He did his work trying not to look at the body of the poor young woman on the bed, though it was obviously quite off-putting. He searched through drawers, in wardrobes, under the bed, in the bathroom, in pockets, but her phone – and he remembered it being quite a large one, almost the size of a tablet – wasn't to be found anywhere. His search was interrupted by an exclamation from Valérie, who had found a *pochette* of paperwork hidden in the young woman's suitcase. She tipped it out on to the desk and started to sift through. There was an English passport, which Richard felt was quite odd as she definitely had an accent. It even showed her birthplace as Oldham, Greater Manchester. She was born on 14 March, 2006, he read and her real name was…

'Nevaeh Ormorod!' Richard and Valérie said at the same time.

'So it is her real name!' Richard, not normally a fan of made-up names while admitting they had to come from somewhere, nevertheless thought that it actually suited the young woman. It would certainly have been a rare name in Oldham though.

'I have her birth certificate here, Richard,' Valérie said with some excitement. 'Her mother was called Patricia Ormorod.' She paused.

'And her father?' he asked impatiently, suspecting she was milking the drama of the moment.

'Her father, it just says, UNKNOWN.' She looked at him.

He returned her gaze. 'Or, *inconnu*, as you French say.'

Chapter Twenty

Having made their way surreptitiously to Herr Schmid's room unnoticed, as no one appeared to be downstairs in the lounge anyway, they both stood shivering as Valérie closed the door behind them. The discomfort of the room temperature was offset, however, by the relief that Albrecht Schmid hadn't gone walkabout again and he was still sat there in his wheelchair, silhouetted against the Atlantic Ocean.

'What are we looking for here?' Richard whispered, unsure of just how thick the walls were and conscious that Pastor Gilbert was on one side and Bernie Webb on the other.

'Something,' Valérie returned unhelpfully.

'Well, I'm glad we've narrowed that down.' Richard shook his head. 'We've searched this room before,' he added. 'And we didn't turn up much, only the contract in Elise's name.'

'We also didn't find his body here last time, Richard, so obviously someone has been back.'

Richard had to concede that was a pretty fair point. 'They could have left something incriminating, you mean?'

'Precisely, Richard, or even the murder weapon.'

Ridiculously, and he had to admit to a high level of naivety here, he hadn't really considered that. 'Are you saying that Schmid may have been first drugged or something and then killed later on – that's why I couldn't find a pulse? But why take the body away to do that? The murderer had the perfect opportunity to do it here and in private.'

'That's the point, Richard, why remove the body?'

Richard sat on the bed and then realised that Herr Schmid, with his eyes open, was giving him a rather uncomfortable stare, as if Richard was trespassing on his time. 'Well, someone's removed his glasses, that's for sure,' he said, finding it hard to take his eyes off the dead man's mesmeric glare. Richard could have done with his own sunglasses too as the sun was beginning to come round and hit the window of Schmid's room.

'So we have no phone from poor Nevaeh and no sunglasses from Herr Schmid…' Valérie was thinking aloud, but Richard couldn't see what she was driving at, unless she was thinking of setting up an eBay account. A thought he wisely kept to himself.

'Obviously the connection between the two is the island,' he said instead. 'They were both potential winners and therefore enemies of each other and everybody else in the game. And before you say it, yes, I know that includes me.'

'It is like a sport for Ian Connor, I think,' Valérie answered angrily. 'A dangerous blood sport.'

Richard nodded. 'Do you think he could really have been Nevaeh's father? He'd only just be old enough and he certainly doesn't seem mature enough if you know what I mean, nor, you know, dad material…'

Richard had learnt from painful experience that Valérie simply didn't comprehend the use of euphemisms, but seeing as Richard equally couldn't bring himself to be more detailed or specific, or even know what he was driving at, it meant for something of a conversational lull.

'Do you mean, is Ian Connor a homosexual?' she said, after a moment's silence.

'Not necessarily that.' Richard was relieved that she had at least bridged that particular impasse.

'Well, he is not,' she said definitely. 'I have a very good nose for these things, Richard. Could you get me a towel please?'

'A gaydar, you mean?' Richard handed her a towel from the bathroom. He had read about 'gaydars' in a magazine supplement and it had made him feel under-equipped as a result as, like most men, he loved a gadget.

'I think that Ian Connor is interested in neither women nor men.'

'Right, a sort of asexual, you mean?'

'A child, Richard, an emotional child, just as you said before.' She was vigorously going through the dead man's pockets and then wiping her hands after each fruitless search. 'Though some very emotionally mature men I know show no interest in sex also. It is an individual thing.' She rummaged about in the inside jacket pocket. 'You, for instance Richard. I consider you to be an intelligent man and in fact surprisingly sensitive for an Englishman, but you appear to show no real interest at all in women.'

Richard sat down on the bed, crushed, he had to admit. If the woman really did think she had a sixth sense for detecting homosexuality she was way, way off the mark on reading heterosexual signals. OK, it was fair to say that Richard's signals, such as they were, were shrouded in diffidence and, as she'd pointed out, his English DNA, but seriously, was the woman blind? Did she see nothing at all? Should he be more demonstrative in future? Just walk up to her, take her in his arms and kiss her? That would be the strong cinematic way to do it obviously, but in reality he knew she'd think she was being attacked and instead of spending the next few hours in a romantic tryst, he'd more likely be in Accident and Emergency having various limbs rebuilt.

'I wouldn't say I have *no* interest,' he eventually said, somewhat morosely.

'And that is a good thing,' she beamed, drying her hands. 'Men should have interests. Your interests are clearly passive,' she continued, in what Richard was now feeling was 'Kick Richard Day', 'but it means that you deal so well with people. Look at the way that you interviewed Lea Boudon and Bernie Webb earlier? Richard, that was *brilliant*!'

'Well, thank God that's over!' he harrumphed, feeling sorry for himself.

'But why?' she asked genuinely. 'You must continue! We learnt so much. Lea Boudon is a strong, successful woman – ambitious, undoubtedly resentful about male financiers and has an adopted daughter.'

'Like Herr Schmid, male financiers I mean?' he agreed, recognising the possible motive that Valérie was hinting at.

'Exactly, like Herr Schmid. And Bernie Webb is a frightened little man, hiding here from himself.' She sat down next to him. 'That took a lot of skill, Richard, and you must continue with these sessions.'

He appreciated the compliment, not just for the fact of it but that it had come from Valérie, a woman notoriously stingy with praise. The hurtful truth was though, that it in no way made up for the fact that she didn't see him *that* way. In short, as a potential lover. But then, if he were to give a brutally honest self-assessment, he didn't see himself as a lover either.

Valérie continued to rummage ungraciously around Herr Schmid, who was getting quite a going-over, like he'd been stopped under suspicion by airport security. 'Ah!' she cried triumphantly and produced the dead man's glasses from under his backside. She handed the glasses to Richard, who examined them gingerly. Not actually wanting to touch them, even less so because the inside of the temples were sticky. 'How come he was sitting on them?' he asked, but Valérie ignored the question.

'I would like to see you interview Ian Connor again, Richard, I think you need to regress him.'

'He seems pretty regressed to me already.' Richard, putting the glasses to one side and wiping his hands, was feeling pretty regressed himself.

'Could you not hypnotise him or something?' she asked as if it was easy as buttering toast.

'Yeah, OK,' he muttered, laying the sarcasm on extra thick. 'I'll just dangle my Victorian pocket watch and have him running around thinking he's a rutting llama within minutes. That should do the trick. Or, failing that, how about just a direct question. "Ian, old chap. Was Nevaeh your daughter and did you strangle her?"'

She stood up and stared at him. 'You are being facetious, yes?'

'Yes.'

She looked very, very disappointed in him.

'What about some triggers, some word association, something like that?'

'On the face of it good suggestions, all of them. But you're forgetting one thing. I am not a bloody psychiatrist!'

'You might be if you put your mind to it!' She took a deep breath. 'It is very annoying that we do not have any internet to use. I would like to know more about everybody here, not just Ian Connor.'

Richard wasn't as hooked on the internet as most other people, largely because he still resented the fact that it had cost him his job, but he did recognise that it would help in their current situation.

'I thought you had done your due diligence?' he asked.

'It was a late booking,' she shrugged. 'What is *intranet* anyway?' Valérie asked, making it sound like it was a fictional concept.

'Well, it's a locked internet. Like a company would have an intranet that only its employees could sign into. It's mainly for security. I imagine here they use it to keep the executive burn-outs from doom-scrolling the market or something.'

'But does that mean that, for instance, Elise has no outside access either, nor Bruno and the others?'

'Possibly. Bernie doesn't want outside access and the Durands don't strike me as massive internet users anyway, nor Bruno. Elise most likely has access to intranets, you know private networks, from other companies, booking agencies and so on…' Suddenly Richard's demeanour changed. 'Actually,' he said excitedly. 'I probably have access to the same sites with the log-in details from my own bed and breakfast!'

Valérie didn't share his enthusiasm. 'So, what would that do?'

'It means I could contact Madame Tablier or, probably more helpfully, Martin and Gennie through a booking system. They could do the research for us!'

'Martin and Gennie?' she repeated, with some distaste.

Martin and Gennie Thompson, who lived in Saint-Sauver as well, also ran a bed and breakfast. Shamelessly, however, and you certainly wouldn't think it to look at them, Martin and Gennie's establishment was aimed at a racier clientele: the sort seeking more shared, intimate experiences that were said to spice up moribund marriages. In short, swingers. Richard liked to steer clear of them whenever possible but he also recognised that this was an emergency and it would do the couple some good to maybe dilute their Google history for a good cause.

Valérie pursed her lips, which meant she agreed with the suggestion but wished to have nothing to do with it, having resisted Martin's lewd suggestions for as long as she could stand.

Richard was about to ask her to remind him to try and contact them later, but was rudely interrupted by a crashing thud which caused both of them to fall to the ground in fright. It was another tragic bird crash, a duck this time and he looked like he'd been spatchcocked across the window. Richard shook his head sadly; it really was the most awful sight, though he could also see that the duck miraculously wasn't dead. It was blinking as it stuck to the window. The other thing he noticed – and this could only happen after a conversation about Martin and Gennie – was that for a duck he was remarkably well endowed. Ducks are one of the few species of bird that don't have internal genitalia; they have what looks like a corkscrew instead and on the outside. This little fella, however, and Richard was not usually one for such observations, was hung like a swan. The bird, having slid to the ground, shook his body and wings and waddled about a bit on the thin ledge. Through the imprint he'd left on the window, the sun now pierced into the room with some force, almost like a laser beam. Richard wasn't at all sure what he'd just witnessed and decided not to ask Valérie if she'd seen it too. She was engrossed anyway, searching more of Schmid's pockets.

'I don't understand why everything is so wet,' she complained, drying her hands once more. Before Richard could offer any form of explanation, she spoke again. 'Ah, what is this?' From the dead man's jacket pocket she produced what looked like a train ticket in a damp plastic wallet. Fortunately the ink was still visible. It was a return ticket from Nantes to Pornic, the closest open railway station to the harbour and the Durands' taxi boat. 'The date, Richard,' Valérie cried, gripping his arm. 'It is for two days *before* he arrived with you!'

'Before you had me hornswoggled, you mean?' he said, never one to let things go.

'Hornswoggled?'

'Kidnapped, pressganged, abducted…'

'Oh, Richard, please do not be small-minded, do you see what this means?' She was at fever pitch.

He wanted to see what it meant, he really did. He just couldn't.

'No,' he replied apologetically.

'Neither do I,' she said, her excitement not dipping at all. 'But it is something!'

Suddenly and with a tinny bang, the battery on Schmid's wheelchair burst into flames, the sun having heated the machinery to an explosive level. In their panic Richard and Valérie crashed into one another before Valérie remembered seeing a fire extinguisher in her own bathroom and guessed that this room would be similarly equipped. She grabbed it just as the sprinklers came on and an alarm went around the building. 'Evacuate!' came the metallic instruction. 'Evacuate!'

Richard picked up Passepartout and made urgently for the door before realising that Valérie hadn't moved and that she was still staring out of the window, rather than even using the extinguisher. He grabbed her arm and pulled her outside. 'Evacuate!' he shouted, and got a metallic echo of the same in reply.

Chapter Twenty-One

They hurriedly followed the 'Emergency Exit' signs to the roof where, far from the expected panic and brouhaha, they instead found almost everyone in a very relaxed fashion and being served cocktails by Bruno. Richard had often wondered if, in the last moments of the *Titanic*, some of the passengers had simply accepted their fate and nonchalantly ordered a pink gin or something, and this looked exactly like that image.

'Ah, you're safe!' Connor cried happily from the pool and pressed a button on his mobile phone which immediately put an end to the sirens and evacuation demands.

'We were searching Herr Schmid's room!' Valérie said breathlessly. 'His wheelchair burst into flames!'

'Really?' answered their disinterested host. 'And did you find anything?'

'No.' Valérie's reply came heavily wrapped in suspicion.

'Cocktail, monsieur?' Bruno held a small tray in front of Richard and Valérie, and while Valérie angrily shook her head to say no, Richard – somewhat guiltily, but nevertheless gratefully – accepted what looked like an ice-cold Piña Colada.

'Shouldn't someone put the fire out?' Valérie asked urgently, making Richard feel even more guilty for accepting the cocktail, knowing that part of the island hotel might be ablaze. 'I did what I could with an extinguisher, but…'

'There is no need to worry,' Connor said, his voice about as patronising as a voice can be. 'Each room is a sealed unit. The walls and door are fireproof, and the sprinklers automatic. It has already been dealt with. And I doubt Albrecht will complain.'

'And you're controlling all of this from your phone there?' Pastor Gilbert leant in on the conversation.

'Yes, I am,' Connor replied with pride.

'And it comes with the island, right?'

'Of course it does! If, *if*, you get the island that is.'

The whole scene was most surreal, causing even Richard to put his cocktail down and try to make some sense of the situation. Two people were dead, one strangled and one possibly by natural causes, though the smart money would be against that idea. The remaining guests, Lea and the pastor, were enjoying afternoon cocktails; Connor was on a lilo reading a book; Bruno was busy with his cocktail shaker for any refills while Bernie, even in the searing heat, was in an immaculate tuxedo and dress trousers playing a medley of songs about fire. *Fire!* he sang rather tastelessly, trying to ape Count Arthur Brown.

'I think they're all mad,' Richard whispered to Valérie, to which she nodded in agreement before moving away from the group and in the direction of a table and chairs under a parasol on the far wall, the mainland side.

'You are sure that everyone is safe, though?' Valérie asked Connor as she passed by. 'Because I do not see Elise or the Durands?'

'Ah, they're fine! They usually get a couple of hours off in the afternoon anyway, not even a fire alarm will interrupt that.'

'I also must ask, Monsieur Connor, in my capacity as your personal security, are you not concerned by these deaths?'

He didn't even look up from his book. 'Hell no! Without me the contracts aren't viable, so I'm not a target at all. Let the rats in the sack fight it out.'

It was a very concerned Valérie that joined Richard at the table, well out of earshot of the others. 'You are right, Richard, I think they are all mad.' She shook her head not just in anger, but a little in what he took to be shock too.

'That's greed, I suppose,' he said, giving it some thought. 'Fortunately I've never had any money, nor really come close to it either, so I guess I'm immune to it.'

She looked at him strangely. 'But you are close to it now, Richard; you could win this island, you know?'

'Not that again,' he mumbled. It was something he really didn't want to contemplate.

'But what if you win?' she asked seriously. 'What then?'

'I won't though, will I?' He was trying to be as nonchalant as possible, an effect that wasn't helped by him loudly slurping the remainder of his Piña Colada through his straw.

'Why do you say that? You have as much chance as the others, do you not?'

'As much chance as Albrecht Schmid and Nevaeh Ormorod, you mean?'

He put his glass down heavily in a way that he remembered his dad used to do at the family dinner table when he had decreed an end to a conversation he was not enjoying. His dad had never met Valérie d'Orçay though.

'What would you do if you won the island, Richard? I'd like to know.' Her question was asked softly, almost intimately.

'I honestly don't know,' he replied, after some thought. 'These kind of things don't happen to me.'

'You said that before, when I first met you,' she laughed. 'The first time we broke into a house together, you said that. The first time we solved a murder, you said it. The first time you were attacked, the first time I went over sixty kilometres per hour in a forty kilometres per hour zone...'

'Yes, yes,' he replied irritably. 'But this, this is different. Two people have died, more than likely because they stood in the way of someone else getting the prize.' He paused.

'Yes, and so?'

'Well, maybe I'm old-fashioned but no prize is worth that, so I wouldn't want it.' He stood up and went to the wall at the very edge of the fort, staring out at mainland France through the hazy sunshine and sea spray.

'You are a good man, Richard,' Valérie said, joining him. He hoped she didn't see him blush.

'What would you do if you had an island like this?' he asked, enjoying the sea breeze on his face.

She shrugged. 'I would be incredibly bored for one thing!' she answered. 'I like my life as it is, I do not need anything else really.'

'Nothing at all?' he asked, finding some confidence from somewhere.

'You, Richard,' was her simple reply. He started coughing violently. 'I want you Richard…'

'Yes?' he managed to interrupt.

'…to be safe. And right now you are in danger, I think.'

Richard managed to control his involuntary coughing fit and inside, despite the immense disappointment, couldn't help finding the funny side of the conversation. So close, yet so far away. As he had just said, 'These kind of things don't happen to me.'

Valérie suddenly grabbed his arm tightly. 'Did you see that poor duck though?' Her eyes were wide open again now, gone was the brief moment of closeness, it was back to work.

'I could hardly not see him!' he retorted.

'I know, that's my point!' she said and her face was deadly serious.

'More like his point.' Richard cursed himself that years of acquaintanceship with Martin 'innuendo' Thompson had finally rubbed off on him.

'Richard, it wasn't real!'

He had, in a few short years, navigated many an awkward conversation with Valérie. Sometimes, albeit rarely, the obstacle had been a language barrier, though Richard was nigh on fluent in French. Sometimes it had been because Valérie had been overexcited and was finishing her own sentences before she'd properly started them. Other times it was Richard who had trouble dealing with specifics, the aforementioned euphemisms. This seemed like a combination of all three and was dangerously close to descending into one of those parlour games that no right-minded person enjoys.

'It looked pretty real to me,' he said at last, hoping it would be her who mentioned specifics.

'No, Richard. It was a real duck but where it hit the window, you could see that bit was not real.' All sorts of images and questions ran through Richard's mind, none of which would make a healthy internet search history, so in the end he decided to lob up his reply and let Valérie deliver the winner.

'In what sense?' he asked, trying to keep a straight face.

'Its penis, Richard,' she said matter-of-factly like a bored biology teacher who's heard all the jokes before. 'It was magnified. The window at that point was magnified.'

It made perfect sense of course, though he felt it was a shame that the drake in question would never know how close he came to immortality.

'Maybe it was just a kink in the window?' he suggested, not unreasonably. 'That's some thick glass, there's bound to be bubbles or something.'

She wasn't having it. 'No, not here. Here, at the Fort de l'Esprit de l'Air everything has a purpose. You saw how the wheelchair battery sparked into flames?'

'Ye-es.' Richard was finding it difficult to believe her theory. 'The sun hit it.'

'The sun hit it directly, concentrated on it, like using a magnifying glass to start a fire!' She slammed a triumphant fist into the palm of her hand.

Still Richard was finding it difficult. 'Alright,' he said, thinking through her argument. 'But why? Why go to all that trouble just to set fire to the wheelchair of a man who is already dead. In fact, dead twice come to think of it!'

She stared at him, stunned. 'Dead twice! Brilliant, Richard! Dead twice.'

He had no idea what revelation he had just stumbled upon and nor was he going to refuse the accolade. Still, some explanation would ease his conscience. 'One thing at a time, please,' he said. 'Why set fire to the wheelchair?'

'It has nothing to do with the wheelchair,' she said, now making sure her back was to the rest of the group. 'The magnifying glass in the window creates an intense beam. That beam must hit something else in the room.'

'Like what?' If pushed he'd have admitted to being at a total loss, but he was determined to hang in there.

Fortunately, it seemed Valérie didn't have the answer to that and just shrugged instead. 'I wonder if all of the rooms have the same trigger?' She was thinking out loud now, which Richard always found easier. 'We must check.'

'And the "died twice" thing?' he asked, hoping it was maybe just a slip of the tongue.

'Oh that,' she sounded suddenly quite bored. 'Well, obviously, the first Herr Schmid, the one whose pulse you could not find, was not the real Herr Schmid.'

He gave this some thought. Of course, he had never met Albrecht Schmid before, but everybody else seemed convinced, certainly Ian Connor. His thoughts were interrupted by some singing wafting up from below the wall. It was a delightful soprano, almost childish in its light-ness. He looked down over the parapet and was surprised to see three large furnished balconies and another jetty where a small boat was bobbing up and down, tethered to the quay.

Pascal Durand was sitting at a table on the middle balcony, smoking his pipe and playing with some fishing hooks. The far left balcony had crab nets hanging off it: presumably, Richard thought, Bruno's outdoor space. The third had just a desk and chair, the desk covered in weighted-down paperwork. So this was the staff quarters, Richard surmised, and pointed them out to Valérie. Richard had learnt from various books and television programmes that 'staff' quarters, certainly in traditional mansions and manor houses, were connected by a series of hidden corridors and stairs, staff being valued even less than Victorian children in that they should be neither seen nor heard. But he saw the calm that was there on show and was actually rather jealous. He hadn't lied when he had told Valérie he didn't want the island, far from it, but suddenly he hankered after the life of an isolated troglodyte with a sea-adjacent balcony with only the waves for background noise.

Pascal Durand looked up and saw him, but there was no warmth at all in his paltry greeting and even less when Lilibet joined him and the singing stopped abruptly.

Chapter Twenty-Two

It had been another long day and quite frankly the last thing Richard needed in his life was more death. Somehow it felt inevitable though, either from murderously competitive fellow guests and staff or just kamikaze seabirds. He undressed in front of his large window, comfortable in the knowledge that he couldn't be seen from any other window and that there were no obvious passing fishing boats on the horizon. The only person who might possibly see his doughy middle-aged body was likely to be some pervert on the east coast of the United States with a criminally powerful telescope that should rightly be trained on the stars.

He caught himself in the mirror. He didn't look *that* bad for a man approaching his mid-fifties, did he? Things weren't as tight as they might once have been perhaps and shoulder hair was always an embarrassment, obviously. What was it about men's bodies of a certain age that the hair thinned on the head but sprouted on the ears and back like some pubescent werewolf? It couldn't be helped he kept telling himself, that's just age. And stress. And fatigue. Once again he felt a well of resentment that Valérie had diverted his much needed rest and recuperation time to help her sort out a collection of homicidal basket cases. He breathed out heavily. He knew, not too deep down, that that wasn't the real source of his indignation; it was Valérie's brutal assessment in describing him as a non-threatening 'friend' type man, the old 'I love you like a brother' stuff of painful playground memories. Obviously, he reminded himself, he didn't want to be a threat to women or anyone else, but he would have liked to have maybe an air of mystique, perhaps an element of the roguish cad about him. The kind of man who women didn't have to be wary of, but who they had to guard themselves against, lest they fall for his dark, handsome man-of-mystery charms.

He snorted out loud. This dark, handsome man of mystery with shoulders so hairy they looked like epaulettes.

'Better get ready for dinner, Passepartout old son, eh? What shall it be tonight? The black dinner jacket or the white tuxedo?' Passepartout buried himself in a pillow, equal part embarrassed and disgusted by Richard's nakedness. It was then that Richard noticed a dark shadow approaching his window at some speed. He ran to the window and started jumping up and down, waving his arms about trying to distract whatever flying creature was heading his way and to doom itself. From the outside he must have looked like an animated version of Da Vinci's *Vitruvian Man*, throwing his arms and legs akimbo in star-jump fashion. It also struck Richard that if there was a pervert somewhere on the east coast of America with a criminally powerful telescope, he was getting quite the eyeful, especially if Richard's window had a magnifying kink the same as Herr Schmid's. Then it struck him that if indeed his window did have such a design fault, he was on the other side of it and therefore not magnified, but minimised. Understated at best. He stopped jumping and the gull managed to abort its crash-landing just in time and with what Richard would swear was a rather shocked look in its eye.

Out of breath and with the sun veering in at a dangerous angle for his nether regions, he made his way to the bathroom and the walk-in shower, relaxing under the warm, soapy water with the window blind down so that the sun didn't penetrate his ablutions.

Thirty minutes later and feeling not only refreshed and ready to face the world again, but also quite upbeat, Richard tied his bowtie with a flourish, and retrieved his cuff-links from next to the pot pourri. 'When all is said and done,' he said to the now sleeping Passepartout, 'there really is something about the high life that is, I don't know, invigorating? Intoxicating?' Whatever it was and despite the chaos that was unfolding around him, he now felt pretty relaxed about things. Obviously his role in preventing the death of yet another seabird had cheered him, but apart from that he couldn't honestly explain his jump in mood; was it the Bogart-esque tuxedo, the refreshing shower, Valérie's compliments about his fake psychiatry? Whatever it was, he left his room with a spring in his step and even fiddled jauntily with his cuff-links while waiting for the lift.

Would it be too much, he thought to himself, *to order a dry martini, shaken, not stirred?*

The lift door breezed open on the ground floor and while he still didn't exactly feel like a threat to anyone, nor certainly a ladies' man, he did notice heads turn in his direction. For one confidence-sapping moment he thought he might be flying at half-mast, as his grandad used to say, or have a piece of toilet tissue stuck to his shoe, but he strode confidently to the centre of the room and ordered a whiskey and soda – he had no idea why – from Bruno while Bernie cheekily played 'Nobody Does it Better', one of the better Bond themes.

Valérie sidled up to him, a look of concern on her face. 'Are you feeling quite alright, Richard?' she asked earnestly.

It wasn't the question he had expected to hear. 'Of course I'm alright,' he snapped irritably. 'Why wouldn't I be alright?'

'I don't know, you look a little different that is all.'

'Oh, really, how so?' His voice was smooth and he nodded a thank you at Bruno as he spoke. *Different, eh?* he thought. *Debonair, rakish, lothario-like?*

'I think that maybe the cocktail you had this afternoon did not agree with you!'

Any other time and this innocently delivered bubble-bursting sentiment might have got to him, but instead he smiled raffishly and sipped his drink. 'Valérie,' he answered eventually, 'you really must learn to relax, enjoy these glorious surroundings while you can.'

She gave him a very worried look.

Ian Connor came skipping down the stairs, wearing the same white tuxedo ensemble that Richard had on and not looking hugely impressed by the fact either. He removed his glasses. 'Everybody here?' he asked unsmilingly. 'No other dropouts to record? Good. I'll have a dry martini,

Bruno,' he demanded, giving Richard the skunk eye, 'shaken, not stirred.'

Dinner was an unsurprisingly quiet affair, which seemed to annoy the host even more. Even Bernie was asleep at his piano, so temporarily unable to provide ambient accompaniment. In its absence, Connor filled the silence talking endlessly about his pet love of science and the power of the human mind.

'The potential for the human race is infinite,' he said at one point, sounding genuinely enthusiastic about the possibilities that were within mankind's grasp. All of which struck Richard as rather odd considering that Ian Connor seemed to carry around a loathing for his fellow man the way hod carriers transport bricks – that is, as a burdensome necessity. 'I suppose you're not a fan, Pastor, of science, I mean?'

Pastor Gilbert answered without hesitation. 'It has its uses,' he mused. 'But God created everything and therefore he created science. The good bits obviously.'

'Spoken like a true creationist!' Connor clapped heartily. 'Good for you!'

Lea Boudon wasn't impressed, however. 'Ironically,' she said, rubbing a finger around the rim of her wine glass, 'you sound like a dinosaur.'

Connor found this hilarious while the pastor surprisingly just smiled benignly, not rising to the bait.

'I think there's a case for both,' Connor replied. 'What did Voltaire say? "If God didn't exist, it would be necessary for man to invent him."'

Richard watched all of this with a nervous disposition. He wasn't religious himself, but live and let live was his motto. Of course, there was relatively little of that sentiment at Le Fort Esprit de l'Air, two dead bodies were proof of that. He was just about to intervene with something about the natural beauty of their location in the Atlantic Ocean, when Valérie beat him to it with an observation of her own.

'Are you applying for the job?' she asked, referring to Voltaire's famous quote. She was trying to sound playful, but it wasn't really in her capacity to do so, and Connor looked hurt at what he perceived to be a sarcastic attack. Elise saw it too and tried to head it off.

'Shall I just collect your plate, Madame d'Orçay?' she interrupted, leaning over. 'Did you enjoy the *langoustines au beurre à l'ail*? It's one of Bruno's specialities, isn't it, Bruno?'

Bruno didn't look too interested in chatting breezily about his kitchen skills, but nodded graciously at the compliment while refilling Lea's wine glass.

'There's not so many as there used to be,' Pascal Durand said. He and his wife Lilibet were sitting in the corner, each with a pipe in one hand and a small glass of what looked like fierce homemade *eau de vie* in the other.

Connor affected boredom. 'Oh really,' he drawled. 'What are we talking about now, gods, langoustines or guests?'

'A bit of everything if you ask us!' Madame Durand spat.

'There's certainly fewer langoustines than there were,' Pascal continued. 'And they're smaller. They look more like shrimps these days.' Richard saw Connor's shoulders slump.

'Fewer birds, see?' Lilibet added.

'That's right!' Pascal replied. 'That's what you get for messing with the natural order of things.'

'Yes!' his wife confirmed. 'The natural order of things!'

'I just said that, woman!'

'So what?' she barked.

Connor rolled his eyes, the pastor looked grateful for their indirect support and Richard was quietly in admiration of the couple who certainly didn't hold back on their views to Connor, even perhaps at the cost of their home. Valérie seemed to have missed it all.

'If you have such a high opinion of *man*kind,' she began, stressing the 'man' bit, 'why do you persist with this silly game? It can only bring out the worst in people and it has been the cause of one, possibly two deaths.'

'So far,' Lea Boudon added, though it wasn't clear in her voice if she was concerned for the next death or planning one.

'Because stress management is how you win at life.' Connor smiled and for the first time it looked genuine: chilling, but genuine.

'But this is artificial stress,' Lea argued, 'and probably did for Herr Schmid.' Richard felt that that was exactly the kind of argument he should have been putting across in his capacity as group psychiatrist.

'Ah.' Connor was enjoying himself. 'All stress is artificial.' Richard was minded to say that if you grew up with the wealth Connor had then that was possibly an understandable viewpoint, but only if you'd grown up with the wealth Connor had.

'I thought this place was supposed to reduce stress, though?' he asked instead. 'Cleanse the soul as it were.'

'It was, initially.' Connor shrugged. 'Then I realised that most people are lost causes, so why cure something like stress, when the people you are trying to help don't really want to be helped. They glorify stress, wear it like a medal. No, Doctor, you are doing things wrong, don't fix it, use it.' He stood up and began to walk around the table, all eyes on him. 'You see, harnessing the thought processes, the latent power and insight of pressure, trauma, even grief, that's how the human race moves forward, not cowering in the face of fatigue or strain.'

Silence followed this monologue, the dawning realisation that they weren't just in a game, a competition to 'win' the island, but lab guinea pigs running around for Ian Connor's personal pleasure and slightly lunatic ideas of progress.

'Mad as a drunk jellyfish!' Lilibet Durand said loudly.

'I told you that!' her husband inevitably retorted.

Richard's good mood of earlier in the evening had evaporated completely and he suddenly realised with a crushing thump how much he missed his hens and some semblance of sanity.

Chapter Twenty-Three

It was no surprise that the group dispersed shortly after dinner. The mood had reached rock bottom for one thing and Richard had the feeling that people preferred their own company anyway. He also felt that, if that was the case, then for some of them that was a wildly optimistic view of their own personalities. There was probably the sense too that they might actually be safer locked in their own rooms. Besides, the only conversationalist had been Connor, something he was obviously totally at ease with, though even he appeared to get bored with the one-sided nature of it all.

Richard was one of the first to make his way to his room, whiskey tumbler in hand, but this time he didn't get ready for bed. Instead, with a still drowsy Passepartout, he waited for Valérie, who he knew would come calling as soon as Connor was safely in his own room for the night.

The wait wasn't a long one and he opened the door when he heard her quiet knock. 'Oh, my poor darling,' she cried on entering the room, 'it has been so long since I saw you!'

Richard wasn't in the mood for day-dreaming so he stepped smartly to one side and allowed Valérie to scoop Passepartout up into her arms.

'He's sleeping a lot actually,' Richard said as though it were his fault, 'it must be the sea air.'

'Perhaps.' Valérie's voice was full of concern and she unclipped her shoulder gun holster and laid it on the bed. 'There is no real air in these rooms though; I find them stifling.' She gave Passepartout a few loud kisses to the top of his head, before turning back to Richard. 'I want you to come to my room, Richard, I have something that I want to show you.'

If Richard had indeed been a cad or a ladies' man, this was probably the time to say something. Possibly arch a Roger Moore-like eyebrow and in a sonorous playful tone say something like, 'And what gentleman could refuse such an invitation,' but inject the words with mischief like you inject jam into a doughnut. He wasn't though nor, he realised, would he ever be, so instead he just asked if he would need his glasses, to which the answer was yes.

The blinds were closed in Valérie's identical room, a shame he thought as, even when it was pitch black outside, the view, such as it was, held mystery and promise, especially with the lighthouse wheeling away from the rooftop. He went for the minibar and was relieved again to see it stocked in the way all right-thinking minibars should be, except his.

'Close your eyes, Richard, I have a surprise for you!'

Valérie was obviously very pleased with herself about something and though he had always been taught never to close your eyes in the proximity of a gun-wielding bounty hunter who was also holding a Chihuahua, he did as he was told.

'Can I open them yet?' he asked, aware that she was struggling with some kind of material, which was making a swishing sound.

'Count to three!' she ordered.

'One, two, three!' Richard raced through the numbers and opened his eyes. The swishing sound had been the window blind, which she'd pulled back to reveal not only the window, but a series of arrows, names, underlinings and question marks which she had scrawled on to the window itself in various colours.

'Ta da!' She was very pleased with herself. 'I have created an incident board,' she said, stating the obvious.

Richard took a few steps closer. 'I hope you haven't used permanent markers,' he tutted. 'That'll be hell to shift.'

She looked at him in confusion. 'What do you mean?'

'Nothing,' he said. 'It's very impressive.' And then he took a step back again and tried to make sense of it all.

At the centre and written in red capital letters was the name IAN CONNOR and in brackets Le Fort Esprit de l'Air and Lane Bridge, the name of his holding company. Arranged around his name like satellite moons were the names of everyone involved in his so-called game. She had started with the two dead people, Albrecht Schmid and Nevaeh, though she had crossed them out. She had then added Richard's name below – he was unsure if this was an unfortunate portent or billing order – followed by Pastor Gilbert and Lea Boudon. On the opposite side were Elise, Bruno, Bernie and the Durands, Pascal and Lilibet. Below, and attached with what looked like Blu-tack, were the two contracts given to each of the deceased and under the word MISSING was written MOBILE PHONE.

'It's a big help don't you think?' She beamed. He'd rarely seen her so impressed with her own abilities.

'It really is,' he replied, though he wasn't sure what the arrows between each person meant. 'Could you explain the arrows for me?'

'Ah, yes, of course.' She took a pen from what Richard could only describe as an incredibly girlish pencil case and he marvelled again at the mundane world, the everyman ordinariness of the bounty hunter, possible assassin. For example, he would never have guessed that they might have to supply their own stationery. 'Well, we have Ian Connor at the centre of the web here,' she began.

'Is it a web?' He couldn't help himself. 'It looks a bit too square to be a web.' She gave him a look that suggested should he wish to continue down such a pedantic route, his name may very well be crossed out next. 'He has invited all of the people on the left. On the right, are the staff, permanent inhabitants if you will. Lea has a green arrow pointing at Herr Schmid because she hates male financial investors. She also has a green arrow pointing at Bernie Webb, because she suggested he might be hiding something.'

'Right, so green is motive?'

'Yes. And you see Bernie Webb has a green arrow pointing at Pastor Gilbert for the same reason.'

'But you've put a green arrow from Lea to Nevaeh as well?'

'Yes. Jealousy, age, beauty and so on.'

It seemed a bit thin to Richard, but he went with it. 'Ian Connor also has green arrows pointing at Schmid and Nevaeh,' he said questioningly. 'I can see the Schmid motive – he was going to pull funding – but Nevaeh?'

'Well, she might be his daughter.'

'Why on earth would he want to kill his daughter?'

'Maybe the mother died and she was a part owner of his company?'

Again, Richard doubted that would stand up in any court of law, but it was a start.

'And the staff?'

'They must all want ownership of the island for themselves, so it's as simple as just removing your opposition.'

'Just as simple as that?' he asked, a little confused.

'Yes!' she beamed.

He took a deep breath. 'But what you're saying, and don't get me wrong, with this web, it's very useful. It really helps to clarify the current position, but what you're actually saying is that they are *all* potential killers and *all* potential victims?'

'Precisely!'

'I really think we need to narrow it down, don't you?'

'Of course,' she answered as though he was wearing a dunce cap. 'I will come to that shortly, but for now, let us recap what has happened so far.'

'OK, I'll start,' he said stiffly. 'You had me kidnapped.'

She looked hurt. 'Oh, Richard, it is not all about you all of the time! Please concentrate. What happened first?'

He had always been led to believe that kidnapping was a very serious offence. Just because everyone seemed to have been at it in the seventies and eighties didn't make it any the less serious either, and he was determined to return to the issue at a later date with some choice words. For now though, he did as he was told.

'I arrived at the quay. Everybody, the invitees, were already there waiting with the Durands. Nobody was talking to each other and Schmid was just staring at the fort in the distance.' Valérie nodded in encouragement. 'That was it really. Nevaeh was talking into her phone, oh and Lea Boudon was flapping about because she was being bothered by a wasp.'

'And was she stung?'

Richard didn't see what difference that made at all. 'No, in fact she batted it very hard with the back of her hand and it landed on Schmid's neck. He was lucky he wasn't stung.'

'And did it bother him?'

'No, not at all. He didn't move.'

'An angry wasp lands on his neck and he does not move?'

Richard thought about this for a second. 'No. That's quite odd, isn't it?'

Valérie tapped the pen against her teeth, a serious look on her face. 'You don't think that he was already dead, do you?'

Richard shook his head immediately. 'Earlier you were convinced he'd died twice. It can't be three times! No, he had a short conversation with Elise when we arrived and drove himself to his room. He was definitely alive.'

She seemed disappointed. 'So then you checked in?'

'Yes, again, I was last to check in. I just couldn't believe the place so I sat down with Passepartout and tried to take it all in. Of course Elise thought I was just spying, as a psychiatrist, on the other guests and she warned me to be careful; they have "far too many skeletons in their closets," she said.' He smiled widely at the memory.

'Why are you smiling, Richard?'

'Well,' he began, not realising that he was smiling but knowing that he was about to go down a long, winding road that had no bearing on their current conversation or predicament, but one he felt oddly compelled to go down anyway. '"Far too many skeletons in their closets." That's what Daphne says to Hercule Poirot when he checks in at her hotel in *Evil Under the Sun.*' Valérie gave him a strange look. 'I love that film. You see, it also has James Mason in it, who was in that other film I mentioned to you before called *The Last of Sheila* about a host who sets up a deadly game for his guests.'

This seemed to spark some interest in her. 'And what happens to the host?'

'He's murdered. Anyway, James Mason was also in a film called *A Touch of Larceny*, which was directed by a man called Guy Hamilton who directed five James Bond films, but not the one with Diana Rigg in it, though she was in *Evil Under the Sun*, which *was* directed by Guy Hamilton. Film family trees,' he added proudly. Valérie said nothing, just looked at him as if he had been speaking in a language of which she had no knowledge at all. 'Anyway, I checked into the room and then Passepartout ran out of the door and…' He clicked his fingers, snapping himself back into the real world. 'This is what I was going to ask you. You must have been here before! How did Passepartout know where to go if you hadn't already been at the fort with him?'

She nodded. 'It is a scent thing, Richard. One of Monsieur Connor's laboratories has been working on a scent that attracts dogs to a toilet area. He told me about it. He intends to sell it to towns and cities to clean their streets; he says that it will be worth billions. But, also he told me that there is a court case with another laboratory over the patent.'

'A dog-toilet homing scent? You wouldn't want to get that mixed up in your perfume bag, would you?' he joked, but the attention of his audience was elsewhere.

'And that is when you met Bernie Webb at the upstairs piano and you said that you saw a face at the gym window?'

'That's right, which of course must have been Connor because we saw his name written on the window after interviewing Lea Boudon.' Valérie was now deep in thought, staring at her incident board once more.

'Richard,' she said after a while. 'What if one of the guests, or even staff, is an imposter?'

'I think that covers all of them in one way or another,' he replied tartly. 'They're all bonkers.'

'No, but you gave me an idea. This court case for the, the er…'

'Eau de Dog Poo?'

She looked at him distastefully. 'What if someone is trying to win the patent case outside of the court by framing Ian Connor as a murderer?'

'So it's not about the island at all, you think?'

'It is a possibility, no? This game he has created, it is childish, yes. An experiment from a bored mind. He is not interested in Lane Bridge Holdings hotels, science is where he wants to be, I think.'

He had to agree that it was a possibility and that it also might be easier, quicker and certainly less messy to unmask an imposter of industrial espionage rather than just wait for the only remaining player in the fort game to reveal themselves by virtue of being still alive.

'Do you know who this other company is?' he asked. 'That might help.'

She shook her head. 'I wish I could look it up,' she said in extreme irritation.

'I can try and message Martin and Gennie through the booking website intranet,' he offered. 'This place is on the same booking system as mine. I'll have to go via Madame Tablier first, so that she can get hold of them, but it's worth a go.'

Valérie didn't look convinced. 'Your small *chambres d'hôte* is on the same website as Le Fort Esprit de l'Air?' She was unsurprisingly unable to hide her doubts, which offended Richard's pride.

'It may be small, Madame d'Orçay, but it is exclusive nonetheless and, I might add, has had fewer deaths to date!' He couldn't claim no deaths because of the circumstances in which he and Valérie had met, but it was certainly fewer.

She smiled warmly at him. 'Then you must go and do that, Richard,' she said with a slight hint of apology. 'Passepartout can stay here with me tonight.'

Richard, still smarting a little, finished his drink and left Valérie, her pooch in her arms, staring at her incident board in deep concentration.

Half an hour later he was lying in bed in the dark, feeling weary and his head throbbing. He'd sent a message to Madame Tablier and hoped that she might see it soon but even if she did, would she know what to do? There was no one in the world who could touch the redoubtable Madame Tablier in the world of broom manipulation, duster wielding or stain removal. Twenty-first-century internet communications, however, were not just merely an anathema, they were just plain wrong, which is why Martin and Gennie had to be involved.

His eyes began to droop heavily as sleep started to creep through his body and then he heard his door open softly, the dull mezzanine light briefly entering the room before the door closed again. 'Richard?' Valérie's heavily accented voice penetrated the room just as the light had done.

'Yes?' he said, totally unsure of himself.

She didn't say another word but slid into the bed beside him and did not leave until just before dawn.

Chapter Twenty-Four

He hadn't slept since she'd left. Plus, he'd ignored the morning alarm call too, deciding that some self-examination might be better for him than cereal and yoghurt. In truth, if asked how he felt, the answer would have been some variation of numb. He had no idea why what had happened, had happened. Only a few hours earlier Valérie, in her usual backhanded way, thought she had been complimenting him on his invisibility in the ladies' man stakes and then, without any warning whatsoever, had seduced him. *Was she in some way trying to prove her point?* he asked himself. *Had she taken notes on his performance and was due to report back later with conclusions on how he could be more assertive?*

Stupefied he might have been, but he was also aware that his face was aching wildly, almost cramping as his grin simply wouldn't subside. He was happy, he knew that; or did he, did he know that? He couldn't deny that what had occurred hadn't been something he had wished for almost since he'd first met her. In fact, such was his romantic view of life and yearning for Golden Age cinema fiction, it had been a yearning since before he had met her, if that made sense.

He realised of course that it really didn't make sense at all, but right now, nothing did. He tried to order his thoughts and come to some conclusions. Was it the start of a beautiful friendship or the beginning of the end of one? He couldn't believe that she had been hiding her feelings for him these past couple of years because if there was one thing Valérie d'Orçay couldn't do, it was hide her feelings.

Was it just a whim, then? Had he been so irresistible in her room earlier that evening, when they were going through the events at the fort, that she had been overcome with desire and emotion? It seemed unlikely. Richard had been his usual acquiescent self, making jokes that flew over her head and hit the wall behind as he always did and had even gone on at some length about Agatha Christie films, Dame Diana Rigg, James Bond and Guy Hamilton. In short, he had done nothing out of the ordinary at all and had never before been found to be even remotely alluring. In actual fact it was precisely that kind of diffident, self-absorbed docile behaviour that would, sooner rather than later, find him and Clare in the divorce courts.

If it had been just a whim on Valérie's part then – and she was certainly prone to impulsive, sometimes even reckless behaviour – was it now a regret? Is that why she had left before sun up? And if it was a regret, how did they behave with each other from now on? Would she move out? Would they disband their business partnership? Would she never speak to him again? Was he just another notch on her bedpost? And why was he asking himself so many questions?

'Good god, man!' he berated himself loudly. 'Just let yourself be happy for five minutes without overthinking everything!' He sipped some water from a glass he had on his bedside table. 'What happened, happened,' he continued. 'We are both consenting adults, no harm was done, we are mature enough to move on without one night of quite incredible passion becoming yet more baggage to be carried around or a cross to bear.' He felt better for that self-lecture, even if it did mean that his habitual lack of self-confidence had concluded the entire episode to be an error of judgement that would never happen again and should be roundly forgotten. Moreover, he had done so without canvassing the opinion of the other party.

While lying back in bed and mulling over the circus that was loudly crashing around in his mind, he was suddenly shocked to hear his phone ringing. For a moment he couldn't quite believe his ears. He hadn't heard any phones ringing, beeping or buzzing for a few days now and it was amazing to him how quickly that had become the norm. He grabbed the phone from his bag on the floor and lay back on his pillow before answering.

As usual he pressed 'ACCEPT' without realising it was a video call, this time through his own booking intranet system, and was shocked to find Martin and Gennie grinning at him through the small screen.

'Late night, old man?' Martin asked lasciviously, his military moustache testing the screen pixels on Richard's old phone.

'Oh, Richard,' Gennie joined in giggling. 'What *have* you been up to?'

'He looks like the cat that got the cream!'

'Yes, doesn't he? Look at that grin!'

Martin and Gennie Thompson on the face of it looked like a perfectly innocent couple. The sort of middle-aged pairing that came with an annual membership of the National Trust, matching cagoules and a ritual of afternoon tea and cakes. That they ran, to Richard's mind, a rather sordid, anything-goes holiday business 'with all the latest equipment' in rural France was at first glance then, highly implausible. They even talked innocently on occasion, but Martin had a strong line in lewd, not very subtle double entendres and Gennie was apparently a volcano of barely suppressed desires and specific proclivities that Martin would detail quite openly given half a chance. Richard now saw them returning his own grin with a look that said – and his heart sank at this – 'Welcome to the Club.'

Surely news of him and Valérie hadn't travelled that quickly?

'I don't know what you're talking about?' he said, though his aching smirk probably told a different story.

Martin and Gennie both laughed. Richard did not think that that was a good sign.

'You're an internet sensation, Richard!' Gennie was still giggling.

'A what?' he asked in reply, finally the grin starting to droop like one of Dali's clocks. Richard really didn't like being the centre of attention at all, even in small groups. The idea then of being 'an internet sensation', especially on the kind of internet that Martin and Gennie Thompson spent most of their time on was, to him, a very bad thing indeed.

'An internet sensation,' Martin repeated. 'And not just the internet either. All the news channels are showing it. I mean, they've blurred the offending parts of the images obviously.'

Unconsciously Richard pulled the bedsheets higher. 'But, but, it's only just happened.' His voice was that of a frightened little boy, about to be unmasked for fiddling the tuck shop books.

'Good on you, I say!' Gennie beamed. 'You went away to have a rest and you certainly looked like you were enjoying yourself!'

He pulled the sheets over his head, hiding himself entirely.

'Did you know the boat was there?' Martin asked. 'I've never thought of you as the exhibitionist kind… still, it takes all sorts.'

'Boat?' Richard's muffled question came from under his linen refuge.

'Yes, bunch of Japanese tourists had hired a boat to go fishing and got quite close to some island retreat, dangerously so apparently, and when one of them looked up there you were, old man. Doing some kind of naked yoga by the looks of things. Quite energetic.'

Richard groaned, while Gennie picked up the story.

'Well, of course, they were Japanese so they had all the latest cameras, lenses, close-up things and you appeared simultaneously on quite a few TikTok and Instagram feeds.'

'People wanted to know who this gloriously happy retreat hermit was…'

'Then they found out it was a town mayor and off on a taxpayer jolly and that he looked a little… well, too happy, and the news got hold of it. They've been in town all morning. Poor Noel has been inundated with reporters and news crews. Are you alright, Richard?'

Gennie asked the question just as Richard's forehead and eyes appeared over the top of the bedsheet, still politely holding his phone. The eyes screamed horror and panic.

'It was you, wasn't it, old man?' Even Martin seemed fazed by Richard's sudden dip in form.

'Er, possibly,' he replied.

'That's a relief, thought you had a doppelgänger! Still, the bits that were on show are pretty unique I'd imagine.'

'Yes,' Gennie confirmed, 'like fingerprints.'

Richard groaned again.

'Anyway, is that why you wanted to get in touch?'

Richard couldn't immediately remember why he'd wanted to get in touch and whatever reason he'd had for doing so had now been knocked way down the pecking order of priorities by this latest bombshell. He sincerely regretted getting in touch at all, having much preferred the bliss of ignorance that the fort's non-internet and non-telecommunications bubble had provided. Now, in fact, he'd never wanted to win the competition and the island more. In fact, he'd be quite happy with just this bed, these covers and the blinds closed for the rest of his existence.

'Do you want us to release a statement on your behalf, Richard?' Gennie asked seriously. 'They're saying that wherever you are is in some kind of communication lockdown and nobody can be reached.'

'Yes, that's right,' he confirmed weakly.

'That's why you had Madame Tablier contact us, is it?'

Richard hadn't thought of Madame Tablier. The old woman had a face that said she had seen everything in the world and that she didn't like it all. This was likely to be the clincher on that philosophy.

'Has she, erm…?' he began.

'Yes.' For once Martin's voice wasn't enthusiastic.

'Oh no.'

'She told one reporter that the social services should take your hens away from you for safekeeping.' At least Gennie now sounded like she had some sympathy. 'So what can we do, Richard? You don't want to release a statement, then?'

'No,' he replied, sighing in utter defeat. 'Don't tell anyone that you've spoken to me. What I do need though is some information.' He paused, trying to remember what information that was exactly. 'Can you find out who Ian Connor…'

'Ian Connor,' Gennie repeated, writing the name down.

'…who Ian Connor, he's a billionaire, has a patent lawsuit with? It's something to do with dog-scented toilets.' Both Martin and Gennie pulled a face.

'Are you sure you haven't been sniffing something yourself, Richard?' Martin asked nervously.

'I promise you. Now, also try and find out who Bernie Webb is – he's a singer, comedian or something. Anything you can find on him. Why Bruno "Mangetout" Leroux had his television show cancelled and some background on a Pastor Gilbert Rondeau.'

Gennie finished writing down her instructions and then looked up at the screen once more; she did not look happy.

'I'm going to ask you to be honest here, Richard. You know that Martin and I have always helped you out in the past, keeping suspects in our dungeon space, even spying for you. But,' she looked at Martin, 'and I think I speak for us both, Martin and I really draw the line at cheating in a pub quiz. If you need this information to cheat, I really cannot in good faith help you.'

In a sense Richard was relieved that there was indeed a limit to what he saw as the couple's wanton depravity and that the bar was set surprisingly low. Also, no matter what he thought of their professional and indeed personal lifestyle choices, there was still decency in the world. Something sorely lacking at Le Fort Esprit de l'Air.

'I promise, Gennie,' he said gratefully.

'It'll have to wait, old man,' Martin interrupted. 'We have new guests arriving shortly and well, er, we have to spruce the place up a bit, if you know what I mean?' He winked horribly and Richard closed the conversation down.

* * *

Some time later Richard sheepishly emerged downstairs, just as the breakfast plates were being cleared away. 'You're too late for any food,' Elise said coldly, giving him a filthy look. 'There might be some coffee left, if you want that.'

'Thanks,' he replied. 'I'd like that.'

'So, Doctor, why the lie-in this morning?' Ian Connor seemed alarmingly bright-eyed and bushy-tailed. 'Guests here aren't usually allowed to skip breakfast; it's part of the restorative process.'

'I was going over some notes,' he said weakly, catching Valérie's concerned eye before looking quickly away.

'Ah, now, I've been thinking about that.' The pastor's raised voice was most unwelcome. 'It strikes me that the doctor here has an advantage over us. He can use his wicked ways, his sorcery of the mind to extract information from any one of us to help him!'

Richard noticed uncomfortably that everybody's eyes were trained solely on him now. All of them – Lea and the pastor, the Durands. Bernie's were barely focussed but those of Bruno, Elise and especially Valérie's certainly were.

'I like your thinking, Pastor Gilbert,' Connor enthused. 'My advice would be not to give anything away when the doc here interviews you!' He bounded for the stairs. 'We start in five minutes!' he announced gleefully and once again everyone started to disperse. Valérie, in her role as Connor's security, made for the stairs as well, passing closely by Richard on the way.

'We must talk about last night, Richard,' she whispered urgently. 'We may have made a mistake.'

Richard slumped into a leather sofa. *This is turning out to be a really rotten day*, he thought.

Chapter Twenty-Five

Richard and Valérie found the Durands out on the front jetty. Pascal was inevitably sucking on his pipe, mending some fishing nets while Lilibet, equally inevitably, had her back to him and was mending a different set of nets while also sucking on her pipe. *If you were to create a postcard of old-time west-coast France*, Richard thought, *it would be these two.* No technology in sight, other than fid and twine. They wore traditional utilitarian clothes including Breton jumpers, heavy cotton blue trousers and matching peakless caps, all of which had now become ultra chic for visiting Parisian weekenders. On top of that they carried a distrust of outsiders matched only by their deep suspicions of each other. They were the perfect distraction from his internet sensation troubles, which he was determined to park for the moment.

'They could be my grandparents,' Valérie said with affection, for the first time revealing something about her family history that wasn't just another ex-husband.

'Really?' Richard replied, relieved that whatever Valérie thought of the previous evening's 'mistake' they were still on friendly terms. 'They were from the west coast too?'

'No, but they did hate each other.'

He knew that she wasn't trying to be funny, she actually seemed to be in something of a bad mood, but Richard accepted the observation that as you reach a certain point in your life even the things you disliked as a child are grounds for comforting sentimentality. He hoped that what had happened the previous night between them might become a similar memory. Then he admonished himself for bringing everything back to that.

'So it's our turn, is it? Our turn to be…' Pascal was saying, without removing his pipe or looking up from his work.

'I told you we'd be next,' Lilibet interrupted, in the same manner.

'I told *you* that!' was the inexorable repost, before adding what he'd obviously planned to say. 'Our turn to be given the once-over with your mind mumbo-jumbo?'

They slumped back into silence and Richard felt that it was going to be difficult to know how to approach the conversation. *Maybe trying to unify them first might help?* he thought.

'Why do you two stay together if you so dislike one another?' Valérie said, who clearly thought divide and conquer was the way forward instead.

The change in the old couple was remarkable, so much so that they actually turned their heads towards each other and some silent communication passed between them.

'Who says we dislike each other?' they said in unison.

If any proof were needed that Richard and Valérie were a good team then this was it. Richard had thought that bringing the Durands together was the best approach and Valérie, in her own startling pit-brother-against-brother way, had seemingly achieved it with stunning brutality. He didn't point this out though.

'That is certainly the impression that you give!' Valérie snorted, while Richard decided that maybe it was time the good cop, or at least psychiatrist, showed his hand. Maybe a joke was the thing; he'd seen medics in the past who opened up appointments almost like stand-up comedians.

'I had a schizophrenic patient once,' he said, giving the routine some oomph. 'And during a session he started laughing just for no reason. "What's so funny?" I asked. "Never you mind," he said. "It's a joke between me and me!"' He looked from one to the other and their faces remained impassive, almost like they hadn't heard him at all. Their expressions were only beaten in stony bad humour by Valérie's own, which looked like she'd sucked on an over-ripe grapefruit. Richard made a mental note never to tell jokes again, even if they were stolen directly from the great and sadly largely forgotten Ronald Colman playing a schizophrenic in *A Double Life*. 'What I mean is,' he continued quickly and dramatically breathing in the sea air to underline his point, 'it's a lovely life you two have out here.'

'It was!' Pascal retorted, returning to his nets.

'And you've been here all your life?' Richard pursued.

'No!' Lilibet scoffed. 'Sometimes he goes over there!' She pointed her large needle in the direction of the French mainland.

'That's not what he meant, woman!' Pascal settled back into normal ways.

'I know!' his wife chuckled. 'I'm just having a bit of fun with these mainlanders and their… their bellywash!'

Pascal chuckled back. It seemed Richard's diplomatic approach was going to take some time.

'Did you kill Albrecht Schmid?' Valérie clearly had an urgent appointment elsewhere and wasn't prepared to wait for Richard's tactics to take effect.

'No.' Again they answered as one. 'Why would we?'

'Well, he was a rival to own this island was he not?'

'You know who owns the island, lady? Mother Nature that's who. She'll decide who stays and who goes.'

'That's why the old gentleman snuffed it.' Lilibet said these words as if they were written in granite and a thousand years of intensive research had formed their creation. 'Mother Nature,' she added by way of further explanation.

'Natural causes, see?' Her husband underlined the point.

'Wouldn't you like to own the island though?' Richard asked. 'You could turn it back into the wildlife sanctuary it once was.'

'That we could.' This time Pascal pointed his needle directly at Richard. 'But see now, that would take time and money, wouldn't it? Two things we don't have. So how would we do it?'

His wife picked up his lead. 'We'd have to finance the change of direction for this resort by inviting lots of people like you here to come and see the birds close at hand, charging money for it. Same thing as now really when you look at it. This place is beyond rescue.'

Neither Richard nor Valérie sensed that Lilibet had used her own words in her explanation. 'Who told you that?' Valérie asked, trying to make it look like she wasn't actually circling for the kill.

'Old man Schmid did.' Pascal's voice was matter of fact.

'So we don't want to own the place,' his wife carried on. 'We just want to stay here, like we have for the last forty-odd year.'

'But what if the new owner has no need of your services?' Richard put the question as gently as he could.

'And they boot you off?' Valérie did the opposite.

'I'd like to see them try!' Pascal responded, though it didn't sound like a threat, more of an old man's last rallying cry.

'This place don't run itself, you know?' Lilibet admonished them. 'I've seen the television, places like this with hundreds of staff. There's only four of us!'

'Five if you include that drunk piano player,' Pascal noted.

'Four and a half then. But we know everything about this place and even when some are away — and sometimes you do need to get away…'

'Not worth it to my mind, went there last weekend.' Pascal shook his head and pointed his pipe in the direction of mainland France. 'Hellhole.'

'…the others can cover.' Lilibet bustled her shoulders in pride. 'No. Whoever gets this place, gets us too, stands to reason.'

Richard could see their argument. In their eyes they weren't in a competition at all because for them nothing would change. He hoped that would be the case, but he feared also that harsh twenty-first-century hedge fund economics wasn't as sentimental as that.

'Is that why you're mending the nets, then?' he asked, trying to lighten the air again. 'Helping Bruno out before he goes fishing?'

Pascal scoffed. 'No! Bruno has his own boat. Keeps himself to himself mostly; does his share mind, no complaints.'

'He goes away for two or three days up and down the coast there and comes back loaded with fresh stuff every time.' Lilibet was still beaming with pride. ''Course, nothing's what it was. Too polluted, the sea is now.'

Richard remembered the rather stringy langoustines and saw her point. He also remembered that the Durands had apparently rescued a half-dead Bruno and taken him in, begging the question how far would Bruno go to save them from any potential oncoming harsh reality?

'If you ask me,' Pascal mused, removing his pipe, 'you want to be talking to that God fella.'

'That's right!' Lilibet backed him up. 'Something odd about him.'

'And you could ask him what he was doing in that dead young lady's room just before she was done in.' He put his pipe back in his mouth and left his damning statement hanging in the salty air.

'Was he in her room just before she died?' Valérie quite rightly wasn't going to leave it there.

'We saw him, didn't we, Mrs? Coming out of her room just before he came down for lunch.' He nodded, then his expression changed. 'I don't say anything happened mind!'

'No!' Lilibet confirmed. 'He's not saying that.'

'Just telling you what I saw, that's all. Just telling you what I saw.'

'You said that twice!' His wife turned her back on him again.

'I know I said it twice, woman! It's called emphasis. I was making a point.'

'Use your point to fix that net, Pascal Durand, and stop your yapping!'

Before turning away Richard remembered something from the day before. 'I enjoyed your singing yesterday, Madame Durand, it was very pleasant.'

She downed her needle and looked at him suspiciously.

'Don't rise to it, Lilibet,' her husband barked. 'It'll be one of them mind games!'

'But I…' Richard tried.

'No singing,' Lilibet said quietly. 'That'll be the wind in the rocks you heard.'

'She's not sung for years.' Pascal made it sound like a threat.

Richard and Valérie walked back up to the orangery silently, at least while the wind was around them, mulling over these latest pieces of information. It was Richard who decided to sit down before going back inside, while Valérie belatedly followed suit, though her demeanour screamed that they really didn't have time to rest.

'What do you make of that?' He sighed, closing his eyes and letting the sea air wash over him.

'I think we must find out what Pastor Gilbert was doing in Nevaeh's room!' she replied, making it clear that the answer must be sought right away.

'Yes, obviously, there's that. But I meant about those two, the Durands.'

Valérie shrugged. 'I think that if one of those two is next to die, it will be quite obvious who the murderer is!'

'I didn't mean that either,' he said quietly, opening his eyes. 'I meant, and I know we only have their word for it, I meant about them thinking that whatever happens, for them it won't change.'

Valérie looked back towards the old couple. 'I hope they're right,' she said, matching Richard's soft tone. 'I don't think they could cope with the real world.'

'I'm not all that sure I can!' he retorted. 'Things change so quickly. And anyway, to them, this is the real world.'

'I would not get too sentimental, Richard.' Valérie's tone changed and he rolled his eyes awaiting the inevitable 'that's what couples become' lecture as an introduction to why the previous night had been a mistake. He was wrong. 'It takes a lot of strength to survive in a wild place like this, well, before it was a hotel thing. You need to be ruthless and cold, I think. They cannot be as innocent as they make themselves out to be or they would not have survived.'

'You think?' he asked, trying to hold on to his largely optimistic view of such people.

'Oh, yes. To survive in a wilderness you have to see what is coming and adapt before changes happen, make impulsive decisions right or wrong. They may be lucky, the new owner may keep them on, but maybe also they want to make sure that luck has no part to play in that, that the new owner is *their* choice, just to be sure.'

Richard sat up. 'You're right!' he said, throwing a filthy look in their direction. 'They could be manipulating the whole thing from below stairs as it were.' He stood up.

'Where are you going, Richard?'

'I'm going to tell them that if I win, they'll stay no matter what! I don't want to find myself strangled in a swimming pool for god's sakes!'

'Must you always take the Lord's name in vain?' Pastor Gilbert appeared at the orangery doors, before sitting down and eyeing Valérie almost like he was seeing her for the first time. 'You know, it took me a while because I've tried to forget that part of my life. But it came to me eventually,' he said mysteriously, but with enthusiasm and a pointed finger. 'Valérie d'Orçay, I always wanted to meet you. I was a big fan of yours.'

Chapter Twenty-Six

Richard decided that telling the Durands he would definitely keep them on could wait. He sat back down as Valérie and Pastor Gilbert stared at each other across the table. The pastor's look was one of triumph while Valérie's was at best circumspect, if not bordering on hostile. Richard guessed that being recognised or, possibly worse, remembered in her line of work was not necessarily a positive thing.

'You're like the goat,' the pastor enthused, which did nothing for Valérie's demeanour. Richard had seen often how she was unaffected by compliments or insults; she treated them mostly the same. However, she did react to what she didn't immediately understand and sometimes angrily. This was one of those moments. Richard couldn't really blame her either; sitting elegantly as she was on refined patio furniture in a simple blue jumper with matching Capri pants and a pashmina draped elegantly across her shoulders, didn't immediately call to mind a hardy, domesticated ruminant mammal.

'What do you mean "the goat"?' she answered with some force.

'Goat!' The pastor recoiled slightly. 'G O A T. The greatest of all time!'

'Ah.' She visibly calmed down but not by much. She narrowed her eyes instead and asked slowly, 'At what exactly, Monsieur *le Pasteur*?' Her voice sounded like the cocking of a pistol.

Pastor Gilbert leant forward conspiratorially and invited her to do the same, and without taking his eyes off her he pointed a finger in Richard's direction.

'Is it OK to talk in front of the doctor here?' he asked slowly.

Returning his stare Valérie nodded and said, 'I have nothing to hide.'

Richard doubted that very much, but he leant forward as well. 'I can hear you two, you do know that, right?' he interrupted with a stage whisper.

They both turned towards him, but didn't address him any further.

'Valérie d'Orçay!' The pastor said again and probably would have slapped his thigh if he hadn't been sitting down. He shook his head in admiration, however. 'You are a legend in our business, Valérie. It's such an honour to be sitting here with you.'

The look of confusion had gone from Valérie's face, but it had landed on Richard's. 'You were a minister of the Church?' he cried, unable to hide the disbelief in his voice. 'A Bible-bashing, give us your money evangelist? No offence,' he added turning to the pastor, whose eyes had fired up again.

'I do not bash the Bible!' he retorted angrily.

'And the give us your money bit?' Richard asked.

'That's a moot point!' he shouted, but in no way defensively. 'It's not cheap spreading God's word, you know?'

'No, Richard.' Valérie's voice was unnervingly calm. 'I think what the pastor means by our world, is my world, my job.'

Richard nodded. 'Ah right, I see. A bounty hunter. So you're a bounty hunter too?' He asked the question as though he were a minor royal greeting crowds.

'I prefer the term Nimrod,' the man said grandiosely.

'It is a very good disguise you have.' Valérie nodded approvingly.

Now the pastor smiled. 'It's not a disguise.' His voice was for once soft. 'I'm the real deal. I was on a case in Vegas, working for the mob, rounding up bad debtors and suddenly, in the middle of a strip joint at two in the morning, I had an epiphany. "What am I doing?" I asked myself. "This isn't right." I walked into the nearest church and prayed.' His voice became evangelical again. 'And I've been praying ever since.'

Richard as a rule was inclined towards cynicism, but he also felt he was a pretty good judge of character and unless this man really was a quite brilliant actor, he believed his story. He saw Valérie felt the same way too.

'Dogged Dan Gilbert,' she said eventually, a half-smile forming on her lips.

'At your service,' he replied. 'Or rather not, anymore. Dogged Dan, always gets his man.'

Richard felt this made him sound like a cartoon character, but also had to admit that it was a pretty catchy advertising line, the kind of advert seen at small local cinemas. 'Just fifty metres from this theatre, Dogged Dan…' He realised that Valérie was talking again.

'We never met, but everybody always wondered what had happened to you.' She now seemed a little more relaxed. 'There were rumours that you were skimming off the top from each job and the mob caught up with you.'

'And I ended up wearing concrete boots at the bottom of the Colorado River?' he asked. 'I kind of spread that rumour myself.' He shook his head with a smile. 'Valérie d'Orçay,' he repeated. 'So tell me, is this thing on the level? One of us really does get the island?'

She nodded. 'As far as I know, yes. Ian Connor wants to be rid of it for good.'

'I didn't kill either the old German guy or the young lady,' he said seriously. 'That's not me, that's really not God's way.'

Valérie looked as if she was coming to a decision. 'But you were seen coming out of Nevaeh's room just before lunch.'

'Just before she was found dead,' Richard added for good measure.

'Would you believe me if I said I was taking her a Bible?' It seemed like a pretty lame excuse to Richard, but the man's face was deadly serious. 'We got talking, Nevaeh and I. She was a lonely kid. Oh, she had all these followers on the internet, but no real friends. You know she was adopted right? She'd been lonely her whole life and I said I know what that's like, I'll give you a book that helped me.'

'And her door was open?' Valérie added a note of scepticism.

'Promise to God,' he replied solemnly.

'But you had a look around for the contract anyway?' Richard couldn't help himself and the pastor laughed.

'Of course! I'm not an idiot!' He laughed, before adding suspiciously, 'You really are a shrink, aren't you? But wait until you hear the voice of God.' Like Pascal and Lilibet, he made it sound almost like a threat. Richard was about to respond with a long quote about voices in the head from the classic film about schizophrenia, *The Three Faces of Eve*, but felt it might get the pastor's back up.

'Did you find it?' Valérie asked.

The pastor shook his head. 'And because it got wet, we won't know whose it was until the end of all this.'

Valérie leant forward. 'And whose contract do *you* have?' she asked with the smile of a serpent.

The pastor returned her smile. 'Now really, Valérie, I have the utmost respect for you, but I'll play my cards close to my chest for now.' She was about to interrupt. 'Watch your tongue and keep your mouth shut, and you will stay out of trouble. Proverbs 21:23.'

She smiled at him again, more genuinely this time. 'I think you might already be in trouble,' she said.

He nodded in return. 'That I am, but God will take care of me.' He looked up piously. 'Besides, I have my eye on that Bruno character,' he said with a wink. 'He ain't all he seems.'

'Really?' Richard interrupted. 'How do you mean?' He had his own suspicions.

The pastor tapped his nose. 'Valérie here will tell you, I'm sure. Information shared, means case impaired.' The man was full of bounty hunter, possible assassin, straplines. 'Boy, I could tell you some legendary tales about this great lady,' he said. 'You want to get her on your couch, Doctor!'

Richard blushed and started coughing involuntarily. 'I'd love to know more,' he struggled out eventually. 'Maybe we can swap notes!' He was aware out of the corner of his eye that Valérie was giving him a stern look, before turning her attention back to Pastor Gilbert.

'And if it is Bruno Leroux?' she asked, raising an eyebrow.

'Then God will deal with him,' was the solemn response. 'Or I will!' He winked again, though not playfully, leaving Richard unsure about which version of the man disturbed him most – the smiting zealot or the Valérie-style professional.

Their conversation was interrupted by Elise, who appeared at the door to the orangery and the pastor leant back in his chair, his manner changing from the cosy-ish conspirator to what seemed to be automatically a more judgemental pose, Pontius Pilate in a white suit.

'Mr Connor is ready for your eleven am appointment, Pastor Gilbert. He's waiting on the roof for you,' Elise said, even more harried than usual.

The pastor shook his head. 'You always have to go upstairs to speak to power,' he noted wryly and bade his farewells.

'Can I get you anything while I'm here?' Elise asked, breezily and unnecessarily dusting the back of a chair with a cloth. Richard wondered how she and Madame Tablier would get on? Probably not well was his swift conclusion, imagining that two great housekeepers were like female leopards whose territory overlapped on the Savannah plains.

'Would you mind joining us for a few minutes?' Valérie asked with a warm smile.

Elise looked at her watch and turned her fluster up to ten. 'Well, I really should get things set for lunch…'

'It won't take long,' Valérie said placatingly. 'We really would like your opinion.'

With a heavy, nervous smile Elise sat down in the seat just vacated by the pastor, while Richard felt a swift kick to his ankle indicating for him to press on as the psychiatrist.

'How are you bearing up?' he asked sympathetically, putting his head to one side like a Labrador puppy. 'This must be very stressful for you.'

The poor woman looked on the verge of tears and was pulling at her dust cloth as though it were a tissue. 'It's not easy,' she answered quietly. 'It's bad enough when Mr Connor isn't here, but while he is… and what with these deaths.'

'Lilibet Durand was saying how well the small team run the place. That must be satisfying… well, like you say, when people aren't dying or being murdered.' He didn't turn his head, but he knew Valérie was giving him a very strong glare.

'We do, I guess. But someone has to be in charge and someone always has to be here.' Richard recognised the subtle dig at her staff.

'Did you not like retirement, madame?' Valérie interrupted.

Elise pulled at the duster in her lap once more. 'That wasn't easy either,' she said, appearing to be on the verge of tears. 'I retired to take care of my mother, but she deteriorated very quickly and had to go into a home.' She shrugged sadly and looked across at the mainland. 'Unfortunately that's very expensive and I needed to sell my house.' She looked up stoically. 'Mr Connor kindly gave me my old job back.'

'I'm sorry to hear about your mother.' Richard's concern was genuine. 'Can I ask what the issue is?'

'She has an aggressive form of dementia.' Elise avoided their eyes as though she was embarrassed. 'She can be violent sometimes, especially towards me. I'm the target.' A tear dripped from her eye and Richard felt another kick under the table presumably reminding him that, in his capacity as a mental health expert, he should be saying something. He wracked his brain for a suitable quote.

He vaguely remembered something from *The Dark Mirror*, which he hadn't seen in years despite it being one of Olivia de Havilland's finest performances, but talking about all women fundamentally being rivals sounded a bit close to the bone, so he tried to edit it in his head. 'The successes and failures of others are all explained away by luck,' he said, hoping to sound enigmatic rather than potty. 'It's the discount of alibi,' he added, not having a clue what he meant by that but now that his thoughts had turned to Olivia de Havilland his hen, he become distracted. Fortunately, no one else knew quite what he was talking about, so the awkward silence that followed covered the fact that his mind had drifted elsewhere.

'She was a great singer, my mother.' Elise sobbed gently, but spoke with pride. 'She toured with Piaf in the fifties.'

'And you sing too, beautifully.' Richard was back in the room. 'I heard you yesterday.'

Elise blushed and shrugged off the compliment. 'I was advised to give up or lose my voice completely,' she replied sadly. 'Doctor's orders, though my mother thought I should have ignored the advice.'

'Ah.' Richard was now on something of a roll. 'Passion, doctors cannot create passion but they can destroy it,' he intoned, once again reaching for the Richard Burton character in *Equus*.

'You said that you would not like to win the fort…' Fortunately Valérie was still focussed. 'But surely, this would end your money problems, would it not?'

Elise shook her head strongly. 'Don't you believe it!' she said with some force. 'This place is losing money hand over fist. All Mr Connor is doing is passing over a liability.'

'Really?' Richard found that hard to believe as they sat there on the sun terrace, the gentle sea breeze cooling them.

'Oh, yes. It looks lovely now, idyllic. But most of the time between October and late March this place is battered by the sea, surrounded by fog. Barely accessible by boat, it's not a retreat then, it's back to being a prison. Really quite depressing and harsh.'

'So it does not make money, then?' Valérie asked.

'Barely, no.'

'And that's why Herr Schmid was pulling his funding, do you think?'

'Not wanting to throw good money after bad?' Richard added.

'Oh, I don't know about that.' Elise was adamant. 'I do my stuff and other people do theirs; that's none of my business.'

'And poor Nevaeh?' Valérie had an odd tone in her voice and then burst into an obviously fake giggle. 'You know what he thought?' She pointed at Richard. 'He thought that Nevaeh might be Ian Connor's long-lost daughter! Silly man!'

Elise joined in the laughter. 'Whatever gave you that idea?' she asked.

'Oh, just my silly psychiatrist brain.' Richard's voice dripped with hurt and bitterness at Valérie's untrue jibe. 'We were looking to interview Bruno,' he said, changing the subject. 'Is he around?'

Elise was still laughing, so at least Valérie had cheered the woman up. 'Oh, you won't see him before lunch. He locks himself in his kitchen downstairs and sends things up on a dumb waiter.'

'That is a good place for Richard to see him!' Valérie was now laughing so hard, she had genuine tears in her eyes too.

Chapter Twenty-Seven

'Was that strictly necessary?' Richard asked with some feeling as they made their way inside. 'I know you said we made a mistake last night, but steady on!'

'I do not want people thinking we are too close, Richard!' she hissed. 'You can still win the island remember, so if the others think that I am on your side that could be dangerous for you.'

He realised that that was a perfectly reasonable explanation, but also felt somewhat aggrieved that he hadn't been given at least some warning and anyway, if the only way to avert danger was to be humiliated, it was a toss-up whether it was actually worth it or not.

As people started to gather for lunch, it became obvious that Richard wasn't the only one in a bad mood. Ian Connor came slowly down the stairs with a face like the Berlin Wall, followed by the pastor who nodded a greeting to Valérie, though it was clear that whatever their meeting had been about it hadn't been resolved to anyone's satisfaction. Meanwhile Lea Boudon was sitting on the sofa angrily flicking through a magazine and vaping so hard she looked like the start of a forest fire. Only the staff seemed content as they solemnly went about their duties, laying the table and putting out the buffet. Even Bernie Webb, despite looking vaguely sober, was playing some downbeat tunes that did nothing for the ambience.

'Who wants a drink?' It was Ian Connor who offered, though he managed to make it sound like a threat and he angrily adjusted his loose cravat as he spoke.

'I'll have a pastis.' Richard answered first and made it clear he couldn't care less for his professional reputation.

'A drink, Madame Boudon?' Connor raised an eyebrow in Lea's direction. 'Or do you just want to suck on a fire extinguisher for a while?'

She ignored him. 'What are we all actually doing here?' she said, making it sound as though she was speaking for the room. 'I'm not too keen to just sit around and wait for my turn to be bumped off!'

Connor handed Richard a pastis, while Valérie and Pastor Gilbert refused a drink and Bernie, Richard now saw, already had one. It looked like white wine in a pint glass.

'It's in your power to change the dynamic.' Connor addressed Lea but was speaking to the room, staff included. 'Everybody here, there's a contract with your name on it, meaning you who has a contract still in their name, can do something about it. It's up to you what that is. Someone has obviously taken the initiative in one direction...' A nasty smile came across his face. 'Maybe it was you!' He handed Lea a large yellowish-looking cocktail.

'What is that?' she asked, though she didn't refuse it.

'It's called a Death in the Afternoon, sometimes also called a Hemingway's Champagne.'

She sniffed it cautiously. 'Is that absinthe in there?'

'It is!' Connor clapped. 'You do know your drink, don't you?'

Lea threw the glass violently on the floor. 'Stop playing games, Connor!' she shouted. 'There's been two deaths already, so if you think I'm going to drink a cocktail mixed by you, you're wrong.'

She stood up and poured herself a glass of champagne instead, but left out Hemingway's absinthe addition.

'You are free to go whenever you like.' Connor was visibly angry that Lea Boudon didn't want to play.

'Oh no!' she said, walking confidently towards her host. 'I want to see how this plays out.'

'*À table*,' Elise shouted in a panic, clearly hoping her interruption would stop the arguing. 'Bruno has made some lovely crab cakes as you can see!'

They looked overdone to Richard's eyes and Bruno's cooking history so far suggested that the crab would be less foraged from the briny deep and more dumped out of a tin of John West.

'Of course, if you do leave,' Connor was eager to continue goading Lea as he sat down, 'and the killing stops, we'll know who did it, won't we?' He looked around the room as if searching for a round of applause, which didn't come.

Lea Boudon lowered her voice to a menacing level. 'Let's be clear about something, Connor,' she said. 'If I were inclined to kill anyone, it would have been you first. Chop the head off the snake before everyone gets infected. It most certainly wouldn't have been some old cripple or some poor kid with collagen for brains.'

'God rest their souls!' the pastor chimed in.

'Whatever,' Lea replied. 'Make no mistake, Ian Connor, you'd have been my first.' She downed her champagne and walked to the table, followed by the others. Valérie in her role as security moved towards Connor. He saw her reaction and waved her away angrily, prodding a fork into his pasta salad. Slowly, he stood up and threw down his napkin.

'Who has been in my room?' he thundered. 'Who's been messing with my stuff?' He picked out a joke severed finger from his plate and threw that down too. A joke severed finger with a black fingernail, Richard noticed.

Receiving no answer Connor snorted in anger before turning and running up the stairs, as if fleeing, pushing open the door to the roof terrace violently and disappearing from view.

'*My little runaway, I run-run-run-run runaway...*' Bernie sang with plenty of vim.

The door at the top of the room opened. 'I heard that, Bernie Webb!' Connor cried and slammed it shut again.

'Does anyone want more salad with their crab cakes?' Elise asked brightly, removing the toy finger. Richard caught Valérie's worried eyes and puffed out his cheeks. Even if he had been a qualified psychiatrist, he told himself, he wasn't sure one psychiatrist alone would be enough to handle this lot.

The next interruption came from an unlikely source. ''Course, if he is the killer,' Pascal Durand said, grabbing himself a hunk of bread and sitting down at the table, 'we's in a bit of trouble. No one knows this place like Ian Connor, so none of us are safe.'

'He's right,' his wife added, before sitting next to him. 'No one.'

'Will you two kindly not sit at the guests' table?' Elise looked shocked and quite put out.

'Why?' Pascal asked. 'I might be your next boss for all you know!'

'We,' Lilibet contradicted and received a surprisingly gracious nod in return.

Elise sat down slowly and poured herself half a glass of wine. 'I hadn't thought of it like that,' she said, taking a small sip. 'Here, Bruno, you may as well sit down too.'

Bruno did so, next to Lea Boudon.

'Are you saying that you know who has the contract with your name on it?' The pastor leant forward eagerly and pointed a fork in the direction of the Durands.

'Not saying we do…' Pascal drawled.

'…And not saying we don't.' Lilibet finished.

'It seems to me that we might be much better off combining forces and splitting the profits.' Richard wasn't sure he had heard Bruno 'Mangetout' Leroux speak such a fulsome sentence before, but he had to admit that his idea of teamwork was certainly far better than his grasp of crab cakes, which were dry and tasteless. He felt one of Valérie's 'go on then' kicks under the dining table.

'That would suggest,' Richard began, thinking on his sore feet, 'from a purely hypothetical point of view that is, that you don't have any leverage yourself. That the contract you have was either Herr Schmid's or Nevaeh's.' He knew of course that it couldn't be Schmid's, he himself had had that.

Bruno was unmoved by the suggestion. 'Not necessarily.' His voice was deep and soothing but Richard noticed that the man had dead eyes. Deep pools of nothingness, like two inkwells. He had probably seen things in real life with the Foreign Legion that Richard couldn't have stomached even in a book.

'Are you talking about the *esprit de corps*, monsieur?' Valérie asked.

Bruno nodded. 'It is in my blood,' he said seriously. 'If we fight as one, we can own the island as one.'

It was a noble thought and while it made perfect sense to Richard, it was reliant on one vital element to make it work: honesty. Bruno's possibly simplistic view of what lay before them as a group was forgetting that basic human nature probably wouldn't allow it, certainly as exhibited by most of those present.

'I think it's a very Christian idea...' the pastor began slowly, the edge in his voice suggesting that in this instance Christian ideas weren't uppermost in his thinking.

'Let him speak!' Lea's mood still hadn't improved.

Bruno nodded gratefully. 'We all have different skills, skills that could be used to run this place successfully as a team. If anyone here were to win, they would need to employ those skills anyway. It makes sense to pool our resources. One for all and all for one,' he added, perhaps confusing his Foreign Legion with his musketeers.

Richard decided to step in as psychiatrist before Valérie aimed another kick at him. 'I'm interested.' He scratched his chin for added gravitas. 'Why did you join the French

Foreign Legion in the first place? Most people do so because they're running away from something.'

He couldn't have absolutely sworn to it, but Richard felt the temperature of the room drop as Bruno turned his empty-eyed gaze towards him.

'Why did you become a psychiatrist?' he answered flatly.

Richard knew he was leaning heavily on Fred Astaire's character in *Carefree* for his psychiatry subterfuge, but everybody else was playing games it seemed, so why shouldn't he?

'I wanted to be a dancer…' he said, about to launch into the full quote and say psychoanalysis showed him the true way.

'Oh, I wanted to be a dancer too!' Elise interrupted. 'Maybe we can put on a show later? Bernie can help.'

This was the last thing Richard had in mind and he was sure he saw a slight smirk come across Valérie's face. He thought quickly as Bernie inevitably – and uncomfortably for Richard – played Fred Astaire's 'Cheek to Cheek'.

'Perhaps.' He nodded graciously, more strangling than crumbling a bread roll in his tense state. 'I'd like to know why you did join the French Foreign Legion though?' He repeated his question to Bruno thinking he had more chance against a trained killer than actually performing a dance routine.

'I killed a man,' was Bruno's cold, simple statement.

'Then why did you leave?' Valérie followed up.

'I killed another man.'

Richard's bread roll never stood a chance.

Chapter Twenty-Eight

Richard, like the whole of France and most of the world, was well aware that the French Foreign Legion is a troop of highly trained crack killers, but the matter-of-fact tone that Bruno had adopted with his revelations was almost more shocking than the confession itself. Richard was reminded of the Lady Bracknell quote from *The Importance of Being Earnest*: 'to lose one may be regarded as misfortune, to lose two looks like carelessness.' Bruno indeed made it sound like the two killings were just that, carelessness. Or, at the very least, a minor blunder. It wasn't so much an awkward silence that followed, more complete shock.

'Well, I'm sure we've all done things in the past we're not proud of.' It was Lea Boudon who spoke first and while on the face of it she was being supportive, she also shifted just slightly away from Bruno as she spoke.

'I'm sure we all have,' the pastor agreed, though he had more past to hide than most. 'However, I think that under the circumstances, we should have a full explanation.' He may have been soliciting for lost souls, but there was also a salacious edge to his voice as well. He might very well now be a man of God, was Richard's view, but he clearly still liked anecdotes about violence.

'I'm sure that Doctor Ainsworth here would feel that to talk about these things would help you.' Valérie was being sympathetic with Bruno while at the same time suggesting that Richard was being remiss in his own duties.

'I think that kind of thing should come naturally,' he shot back. 'Best not to push it.'

'I think you should tell us, dear.' Elise stretched across the table and put her hand on Bruno's muscular forearm. 'At least just let people know that you're not a poisoner in the kitchen.'

Bruno looked slowly at each person in turn and Richard hoped that Bernie wouldn't ruin the moment by playing some more dun dun duuun music. Eventually Bruno shrugged. 'The first was my father,' he said coldly. 'I killed him in self-defence when I was seventeen and was exonerated by the courts. That is when my name was Brice Burckhalter.'

'I'd have changed my name anyway, I think,' Richard whispered to Valérie.

'And the second?' The pastor leant forward eagerly.

'A fallen comrade.' His voice dipped in sadness at the memory. 'I couldn't leave him to suffer and be caught by the enemy, so I killed him myself. I knew then that I wasn't the killer that the Légion needed me to be and that I could never kill again.'

'Well, that's convenient!' Pastor Gilbert's voice was doused in scepticism.

'So you started eating grubs off trees?' Pascal didn't exactly sound sympathetic either and even his wife ignored him this time. Lea edged her chair back towards Bruno.

'It can happen.' Richard nodded sagely, aware that eyes were beginning to turn to him for some sort of professional opinion. 'Think about the fear of being swallowed up and disappearing into secret depths. It comes from infant potty training.' He took a sip of wine. He had no idea what this last paraphrased quote meant and he may have missed out some explanatory chunk. He also had no idea if it was even relevant, but he'd sounded wise and was grateful for Robert Cummings' standout performance as a psychologist in *Promise Her Anything*. He heard Valérie whisper 'Brilliant!' under her breath too, but he was also keenly aware that he was fast running out of classic cinema psychiatry quotes.

Valérie stood up and started pacing the room, deep in thought. All eyes were on her as the group – aware that they were probably harbouring in their midst a ruthless killer and certainly a reluctant one – looked to her for some guidance, some plan of action.

'It seems to me,' she said eventually, picking up Passepartout from a leather armchair, 'that we all have something to hide.' She looked around the room and the eyes that had watched her before, now avoided her gaze guiltily. 'And what is more, I think our host, your host, he knows that.'

The pastor stood up. 'I don't get it,' he said. 'If Connor is paying you to protect him, why are you now undermining him? Whose side are you on?'

There was a murmur of support from the table.

'I work for the French police,' Valérie said confidently, quelling any rebellion. 'And we have suspected Ian Connor for some time of fraud and smuggling and various other assorted misdemeanours.' It was vague, Richard could see that, but as usual she sounded so certain of herself that it was also convincing.

The pastor sat down again. The look on his face suggested he didn't necessarily believe Valérie's story, but he also knew her history and decided to keep quiet, at least for now. 'My name is Commandant Valérie d'Orçay.' She slammed her heels together and nodded officiously; Richard meanwhile feigned outrage even as the others seemed genuinely put out by the news.

'Well, I never!' he said, joining the others in their collective grievance.

'And this is not Doctor Richard Ainsworth, psychiatrist,' she continued. 'But my sergeant, Richard Ainsworth.'

Richard went bright red but managed a mangled 'How do you do?' to the table.

'Show them your identification please, Sergeant!' Valérie ordered.

'It's in my room,' he replied, after a pause.

'So you're not a real doctor, then?' Elise looked hurt and clutched at the pearls around her neck.

'Not *that* kind of doctor.' Despite being unmasked and smarting also from the slight insult of his rank, Richard felt immensely relieved to have got that off his chest.

'So what have you actually found out, then?' Pascal puffed on his pipe.

'Apart from two dead people,' his wife added caustically.

She had a point.

'That you are here for a reason and that it goes beyond this game I think,' was Valérie's swift response.

'But the game is real?' Pastor Gilbert needed the confirmation.

'I think it is,' Valérie replied. 'But why? We know that the business is losing money and that he also has tragic memories of this place – why? What are they? And why you?' She pointed at the group.

'She's right.' Richard stood also, partly because he was getting cramp and partly because he felt he now had to somehow justify his new role as police sergeant. 'The staff are one thing, but why you specific guests? It can't be totally random, there must be something else behind it.' He sat down again, his cramp had dissipated and he knew he couldn't answer his own questions.

'Does this mean that you're not in the game, Sergeant?' Lea Boudon asked, wounding Richard slightly with her use of his fake position.

'Please, call me Richard, or Doctor. I think we really must keep up appearances.'

'OK, *Doctor*,' Lea emphasised and Richard thought he saw scepticism in her eyes but they were inevitably shrouded in vape fog. 'Do you, or do you not have a valid contract?'

It was a tricky one for Richard to answer. Presumably someone sitting around the table did have a contract with his name on it, unless it was the damaged one found on Nevaeh's body. 'I have a contract in someone else's name,' he acknowledged, hoping his poker face wasn't slipping.

'So someone here must have a contract in your name?' Elise finished the logic for the room.

'And you won't say whose contract you have?' Bruno may have admitted to an aversion to killing, but his eyes, if they said anything at all, looked like they weren't entirely on board with the whole pacifist idea.

'I don't think that's wise, no.' This was beginning to feel like a deadly Christmas parlour game to Richard.

'I agree with the sergeant,' said Pastor Gilbert, offering unlikely support.

'Please call me Richard, or Doctor.'

'This might be a game to some,' the little man continued. 'But I reckon I could still get this place cheap.'

'Especially if the killings continue.' Valérie raised an eyebrow in the pastor's direction, who shrank like a salted snail under the weight of her suggestion. 'I think it is obvious that you just offered to buy the fort in your meeting with Ian Connor,' she continued, 'and that he turned you down.'

'I only did it to save more unnecessary deaths,' the pastor pleaded.

'So what do you suggest, Val?' It was Bernie who broke the ensuing silence. 'That we confront our boss?' It was a pertinent question only slightly marred by his breaking into song with a bluesy version of 'Big Boss Man'.

'I don't recommend that if he is the killer,' Lea Boudon said, and grabbed Bruno's arm for support.

'Do you think he's the killer?' Richard asked genuinely.

Lilibet answered the question. 'He can't be! We've known him for years!'

'You've known Mangetout here for years as well.' Pascal snorted. 'And you didn't even know his real name!'

Lilibet laughed along with her husband. 'I might even be a killer for all you know!' she cackled and then her face dropped as all eyes turned on her. 'I'm not, just sayin'!' Pascal rolled his eyes and went back to his pipe.

Richard caught Valérie's eye and knew that she was asking for some kind of distraction while she got her thoughts in order and an idea came to him.

'I think it would be very interesting,' he began, carefully folding his napkin to give the impression of calm, 'if we had a vote on the subject.'

'A vote?' Bruno's response seemed to speak for everyone.

'Yes, a vote. Who do you think the killer is?' There was some murmuring in opposition to the idea, but Richard remembered it from all the film versions of *And Then There Were None*. He'd never got around to reading the actual book and while it may not have solved anything at all in the films, it might reveal something about the characters that surrounded him. 'Is there any paper here?' he asked, drowning out any opposition.

Elise found a pad of Le Fort Esprit de l'Air customised writing paper and some pencils also with the logo on. She distributed them to everyone excluding Valérie and Richard, who both demurred citing their official positions as incompatible with the vote.

'I'm not sure about this,' the pastor said as he thought about whose name to write. 'I mean what difference does it make? These two love hearts here,' he pointed at Lea and Bruno who were indeed not hiding their closeness, 'they might have each other's contract and have the whole thing all sewn up!'

'If that were the case,' Lea replied, 'why would we kill anyone?'

'No copying, woman!' Pascal covered his paper from his wife's eyes.

'You copied me first!' she retorted.

'I hate doing things like this,' Bernie said, though he'd finished writing and was folding his paper neatly. 'I was a judge on a talent contest once. I was supposed to fix it for a friend and I wrote the wrong name down. I mean, me? A judge?'

'What happens to the winner?' Elise asked, a worried look on her face. 'Are you going to arrest them?'

'Not without evidence, no,' Valérie replied. 'Someone might write down the name of a person that they just don't like or write their own name as a red herring.'

'The killer may even write their own name,' Richard added. 'Narcissistic tendencies. It's happened before.' He hoped no one asked for proof of that.

'Has everyone finished?' Valérie spoke sternly and passed around an empty ice bucket.

There may have been nothing concrete riding on the vote, but there was still a claustrophobic tension in the air. Valérie handed the bucket to Richard, who proceeded to shake it as though working on the tombola stall at a village fete. There were seven pieces of paper and he took the first one out, unfolded it and fought off the biting temptation to shout, 'Kelly's eye! Number one!' or more appropriately, 'No more filler! Here's your killer!'

'Pastor Gilbert,' he said instead and with a serious voice. The pastor looked oddly proud and gripped the lapels of his jacket like a preacher from an old Western.

'Ian Connor,' Richard read next and the next three times as well. 'Lilibet Durand,' he then added, as surprised as everyone and thus causing a stir. There was one piece of paper left. 'Pascal Durand,' he said, like a bored headmaster who knew exactly who his culprits were.

Valérie was not impressed. 'Do not think that just because you play your little games,' she rounded on the Durands, 'that I will discount your votes!'

'Wasting police time?' Richard ventured.

'Exactly, Sergeant,' she answered angrily. She managed to calm down a little before continuing. 'So, it appears that the majority believe that your host, Ian Connor…'

'Or *Inconnu*,' Richard interrupted, 'U. N. Owen!' He made it sound like vital information that nobody else was party to.

'The majority think that Ian Connor is the murderer!' Valérie finished with a flourish.

There was perhaps a beat before everyone around the table started talking at once. There were pleadings, attempted bargaining, vape smoke, pipe smoke, recriminations, disbelief and the sound of a background piano merrily working its way through 'I Will Survive'. In short, it was pandemonium, getting louder and louder as it became more chaotic and as a result becoming more chaotic as it got louder.

A gunshot rang through the air putting a halt to the verbal mêlée in an instant. 'That is enough!' Valérie shouted, her gun pointing in the air, but before she could continue a terrible, blood-curdling scream came from the roof terrace.

Chapter Twenty-Nine

For a moment nobody moved, then Elise sprang up from the table, knocking her chair on its back in the process. 'Who was that?' she screamed, holding the sides of her head in blind panic.

'You must all stay exactly where you are!' Valérie shouted, though to everyone's relief she put her gun back in its holster. 'Richard and I will search the pool area. Please, none of you must move!' She ran towards the stairs and Richard followed suit, aware that despite being armed everyone had ignored Valérie's instructions and none of the group remained behind. She stopped on the first floor. 'I asked you to stay down there!' she remonstrated.

'Yes, but you're the one with the gun,' Lea argued defiantly. 'We'll stick with the protection if that's OK with you.'

Richard thought it was a good point well made as, fortunately, did Valérie who just shrugged and continued up the stairs. She held her arm up as she approached the closed roof terrace door, knowing that she was just out of reach of its automatic sensor, she then put a finger to her lips demanding silence. She took one step closer, the door slid open and she dived through the partial opening doing a forward roll towards the nearest table, which she kicked over in one movement forming a barricade. Valérie proceeded to wheel the round table around the pool area until it was facing the group on the stairwell, then as it rolled further it fell forward revealing nothing behind it. Valérie, wherever she was now, had used it as a decoy.

Richard felt a tug on his sleeve. 'GOAT,' the pastor said with pride.

For the next few minutes nothing happened and Richard, along with the others, worried that she might have been taken hostage. Nervously he leant through the door opening, hoping to catch a glimpse of her somewhere on the terrace. He could see nothing at all other than the upturned table, the fabric on the parasols blowing innocently in the breeze.

He began to whisper to the group behind him, 'I'm going to… Argh!' Suddenly he jumped out of his skin as Valérie landed next to him having leapt from above the doorway. Everyone else reacted the same way too, even Bruno, who at least should have been trained for such an attack.

'The coast is clear,' Valérie said as though she were just helping someone to reverse a car. 'There's no one here.' Once again she re-holstered her gun and then strode back into the sunlight followed more warily by the others.

'Where's Connor?' the pastor asked, crouching down, watchful of more gunfire or more screams.

'Do you think he jumped?' Elise was more panicked than most and it showed in her voice.

'We'd be able to see if he did.' Pascal Durand sounded like he was mulling it all over. 'He'd have hit rock below first,' he added ghoulishly.

Silently and separately everyone made their way to a different part of the outer wall and nervously peered over the edge. Moving to the right or left, they would occasionally and literally bump into another member of the party before apologising awkwardly and moving around the other person. No one though, much to their collective relief, saw any evidence of Ian Connor having jumped over the side.

'Is there another way to get downstairs?' Valérie asked, moving everyone's attention away from the wall's steep descent.

'There's a metal fire escape ladder built into the outer wall,' Bruno replied. 'It's very old, very rusty, I doubt it's even that safe. It leads to our rooms.' He pointed at Elise and the Durands.

'Also there's the dumb waiter that stops on every floor from the kitchen to the serving and dining level upwards.' Elise had calmed down slightly, but was now clinging to Lilibet for support.

'Could a man fit into that space?' Valérie asked.

'Well, it wouldn't be comfortable but yes, I think so.'

'And it can be self-operated?' Richard joined in.

'Yes, the ropes are all visible.'

'Where is this dumb waiter, Elise?' Valérie was having no truck with her obvious trauma.

Elise walked unsteadily to the pool bar and stepped down into the serving area. She pointed to a large wooden door under the bar top and Valérie opened it. The shelf part of the mechanism wasn't there, suggesting it was on a lower floor. She asked Bruno to raise the shelf to their level, which he did with a few muscle-rippling drags on the pulley ropes. The shelf was empty except for Ian Connor's blazer jacket that he had been wearing before storming out of lunch. Valérie grabbed the jacket and checked it thoroughly.

'What are you looking for?' It was Bernie who asked the question, for once not delivering it in the style of a hackneyed operetta.

'Blood,' was Valérie's simple reply.

Elise buckled again but this time fell into Lea's arms, which was quite obviously an inconvenience to the businesswoman as she looked like she had been planning the same fall into Bruno's arms. The whole thing looked like one of those world record domino trail attempts, but one that had fallen at the first.

'Why would he leave his jacket in the dumb waiter?' Pastor Gilbert spoke, but was either speaking rhetorically or asking God, it was difficult to tell.

'That is a very good question,' Valérie replied filling in the role anyway.

'It must be roasting in there though!' Lilibet offered some practical advice.

Valérie looked far from convinced that that was the reason for the blazer's presence.

Lea passed Elise on to the stouter figure of Pascal, who didn't look at all pleased by the move, and stepped forward. 'If Connor didn't throw himself off the side,' she began without her usual confidence, 'but something's happened to him anyway, who did it?'

'That's right!' The pastor slammed a fist into the opposing palm. 'We were all downstairs, all in plain sight of each other.'

'You mean there's somebody else on the island?' Elise looked like she might go again, but just in time noticed Pascal move slightly away and managed to steady herself.

Richard caught Valérie's eye and saw that she was extremely worried by this turn of events.

'I need some time to think,' she said quietly. 'Everybody must stay here, in sight of one another for the moment, please.' She wandered off leaving Richard in his new role as an official to make sure that people did as they were told.

'I could do with a drink.' Lea Boudon spoke for most people and Bruno moved smartly into cocktail mode. This lent the whole proceedings a totally surreal air again as if they weren't actually hunting for a corpse or a murderer but at a country house tea party and some scallywag had run off with one of the croquet hoops. Richard and Bernie were the only English people present, but the stiff upper lip mode of reaction was clearly quite contagious. Bernie even going so far as to play a gentle version of Noël Coward's 'Mad Dogs and Englishmen…'

For the first time since they had arrived, the whole party chose to sit at the same table without being directed to do so, meaning that a survival instinct had taken over, governed by fear. When they had been downstairs there had been a feeling that a killer was among them, but now that there could possibly be an unknown – a violent and murderous outside presence – they had come together like a pack. Richard felt that was almost heartening. If it wasn't for the dark cloud of a homicidal maniac travelling about the place on a food trolley.

He noticed Valérie come out of the gym and beckon him over. He walked as nervelessly as he could, aware that everyone's eyes were on him as he travelled the distance of the roof terrace. 'I want you to come inside, Richard.' Her voice was calm and she shut the door behind her. 'Sit down, please.' It felt awkwardly like a job interview, more so when she sat opposite him and put her hands on the table.

'What do you think of those people?' she asked, looking hard into his eyes. It may not actually have been a job interview, but it was certainly a test of some kind.

'A very odd bunch,' he replied. 'I can't get a handle on them. One minute they're terrified, the next they're completely relaxed.' He knew it was quite a vague answer, but he didn't really have much more to add than that. He turned to look at them through the gym window, but it was difficult to get a clear view of where they were sitting because of how grubby the window actually was. He tried refocussing to make it clearer, but like a camera that stubbornly refuses to focus on the desired object, the window and its attendant dirt remained front and centre.

'Well I never!' he exclaimed after a few more seconds and turned to face her with a smile. It wasn't dirt on the window at all, it was the imprint of a face, almost Turin Shroud-like in its wispiness; it had an ephemeral ghostly quality to it, but it was clearly a face. Not Christ-like though, there was no beard and this was definitely a young face.

Valérie raised her eyebrows at him, seeking his opinion and he looked again at the window, this time focussing his eyes on the glass itself. It was now he noticed that there wasn't just the one ghostly imprint, but several and all with a slightly different expression. Some were smiling, some frowning, one was laughing and a couple were screaming, open mouthed in anger or pain. As a collection they could have adorned the side of a theatre, a range of emotions displayed for a drama-hungry public, but they had a more haunting quality, they were sinister like gargoyles, a menacing, baleful presence.

'What do you think they're for?' Richard's voice was low as he asked the question, as though the faces on the window might hear him.

'I think they are a reminder,' Valérie replied with equal caution. 'A warning maybe. Ian Connor was an only child here, was he not?'

Richard nodded. 'As far as we know.'

'We must find him, Richard,' she said urgently. 'I think he is in danger.'

'You mean there really might be someone else hiding on the island.'

She shook her head and looked at him with concern. 'Not necessarily,' she said worriedly, 'I think he is in danger from himself.'

Having left strict instructions for the group to remain where they were – not, Richard noticed, that they looked in any hurry to be anywhere else – he and Valérie made their way back downstairs.

'Can you trust them?' Richard asked quietly.

'Passepartout will look after them for us,' was her odd reply, before she stopped and showed him her watch. It was a live video of the group upstairs and then it moved and before long showed the gate of the dog toilet area.

'You have a camera on Passepartout's collar?' he asked, impressed.

She winked at him, totally confident now in her working environment and he realised that the slightly dotty Valérie that he knew from Saint-Sauver, was fish-out-of-water Valérie. She didn't cope entirely easily with the real ordinary world at all, even one as unreal as Saint-Sauver had become since she had arrived there. She thrived in her heightened work world though, that was obvious.

'So where are we going?' he asked, this time in a loud whisper, remembering the faces at the window, which had made him quite nervous.

'We are going to search his room,' Valérie replied in a louder voice. 'Elise told me that he always keeps the same room, always has done since he was a child here.'

'You think he may have gone there? His own private sanctuary within a larger commercial sanctuary, you mean?'

She shrugged. 'I don't know if he will be there, but we might learn something anyway.'

The door to Ian Connor's room swung open silently revealing an inner sanctum completely different in feel to Richard's, Valérie's or any other room they had been in. The general shape was the same, a large rectangular space with an en-suite bathroom, but there was a much smaller, more traditional window. There were few similarities beyond that. The bed was a single bed, not the huge piece of furniture that every other room enjoyed; there was a babyfoot table gathering dust, an adult-sized desk but covered in school books, old comics, puzzle books and joke toys like the finger found in the pasta salad. On the wall were posters, but posters of rock bands from the late nineties and a picture of the Republic of Ireland football team at the 2002 World Cup. The whole place was a museum piece, a teenage boy's bedroom from over twenty years ago; but rather than inviting nostalgia, the set-up gave Richard a shiver up his spine. The room didn't feel like it had been left untouched out of joy or happy childhood memories; it felt like one of those macabre recreations in a waxworks museum.

'What do you think, Richard?' This time Valérie was whispering, the sheer oddness of their surroundings almost insisted on it.

'Miss Havisham,' was his reply. 'Time stopped still here for a very unhappy person,' he continued sadly.

'A very unhappy boy,' Valérie added.

Chapter Thirty

As they made their way back up the stairs, Valérie grabbed Richard's arm. 'We need to search the entire island from top to bottom,' she said, a look of fierce determination on her face.

'We can't do the whole place by ourselves though,' he replied. 'Remember what Pascal said, Connor knows this place better than anyone else, every nook, cranny, secret passage…'

'You think that there are secret passages?' Her eyes lit up at the thought, whereas Richard saw secret passages as an immense hurdle to their goal of finding Ian Connor or the murderer, or both – or maybe they were one and the same person.

'I think it's highly likely.' He made it sound like the bad news he thought it was.

'You are right,' she said after a pause, 'I do not think that we can do this alone. But do we trust anyone else to help us?'

Richard gave this some thought. 'You mean one of them might even be the killer?'

'Yes, but more than that, would they do a good job, a thorough job, Richard?'

It was a good point. Bruno would be capable and Lea was clearly a determined and successful individual. On the other hand, Bernie was a drunk; the pastor, because of his background, not entirely trustworthy; Elise permanently on the edge of a nervous breakdown; and the Durands incapable of working with each other let alone anyone else. It was not promising, but what other choice did they have?

'My old maths teacher,' Richard began, verging on the whimsical so he naturally avoided Valérie's impatient eye, 'he always said that if you give people responsibility, by and large even the weakest of individuals, the most chaotic even, will rise to the challenge. It's human nature, he said.'

Valérie nodded, apparently impressed by the thought. 'And was he right?' she asked.

'Difficult to say really. Some of the boys locked him in the stationery cupboard over the weekend and we never saw him again.'

Valérie looked sorely disappointed by that outcome. 'Boys,' she said distastefully, a look on her face like she had just found a rogue hair in her prawn cocktail. 'Girls would never have done that.'

Richard shrugged. 'I wouldn't know. I went to an all-boys comprehensive school, so I can't make any comparison.'

Valérie looked shocked by this information. 'You went to an all-boys school?' she asked, stunned at a concept quite alien to the French.

'Yes.' He knew he sounded defensive even though he'd hated the place.

'You mean, that there were no girls at your school at all?'

'No,' he confirmed. 'It was a boys' school.'

She shook her head and tutted sadly. 'That explains so much,' she said, coming to a conclusion that Richard wasn't party to but which he knew wasn't positive. She turned and the automatic door to the roof terrace opened, letting in the light and ironically leaving Richard exactly as he had been for most of his school life: ill-prepared and wishing he'd had a more exotic upbringing. There was a reason he had found solace in the beauty, romance and drama of Golden Age Hollywood and an all-boys school played a large part in that. It could have been worse of course; rumours abounded that Lee Spurling had become a notorious armed robber, yet was still regarded as the most successful former pupil of their year group.

He and Valérie rejoined the others on the roof and whatever discussion had been taking place stopped immediately on their arrival.

'Any sign of him?' the pastor asked, plainly interrupting himself mid-sentence.

'We're all terribly worried,' Elise added and at least had the good grace to look worried, whereas the others made it all seem like a minor inconvenience.

'Well, he's not in his room,' Richard replied. 'We really need to search the whole place.'

As a group they made it clear that they didn't like that idea at all.

'Isn't that a bit dangerous?' Lea asked.

'It might be!' Valérie answered with excitement, misreading Lea's feelings on the matter.

'Right,' came the curt response through a veil of strawberry-smelling vape. 'I don't want to sound lazy or anything, but isn't that your job?'

'We think everyone would be safer if we were a bit more proactive,' Richard interjected. 'It might be better than just staying here and maybe becoming sitting ducks.'

Everyone rose quickly out of their chairs, all except Bernie who felt compelled to get in one quick verse of 'I Fought the Law'.

'We need to split into groups.' Valérie raised her voice but also gave Richard a grateful look. 'We are nine I think, so please split into three groups of three and each group will take one floor.'

It was a nice plan, but seeing as Bruno – the trained, yet reluctant killer – seemed to have collected everyone except Bernie it was initially quite unworkable.

'I don't think that's going to work,' Richard helpfully pointed out.

'OK, I see I am going to have to pick the teams myself,' Valérie said gruffly, leaving Richard feeling as though he was back at school again and about to be left until the penultimate pick. Lee Spurling was always first pick or he'd hit the captain and the 'big-boned' – at least according to his equally large parents – Gordon Wittle was last.

'Monsieur and Madame Durand can stay here with the pastor and keep watch. Bruno, Madame Boudon and Elise can search the bedroom level. I will give you the master key and Richard, myself and Monsieur Webb will search the lower ground, staff quarters and the kitchens. I am assuming everyone has their contract with them and has not left it under their pillows.'

Everyone nodded, except Bruno.

'No one goes in my kitchen,' he said quietly and though there was no menace in his voice, it sounded menacing anyway.

'Why not?' Valérie wasn't one to back down. 'Is dinner a surprise, Monsieur Mangetout? Or are you hiding something?' Bruno didn't reply. 'It is not an ideal situation for any of us,' Valérie continued. 'But we must trust each other, it is for the greater good, Monsieur Mangetout!' There was still a little grumbling. 'We must rise to the occasion,' she added cryptically, 'unlike English boys in their teenage prison bubbles!'

In the end Richard reckoned it was the confusion of her statement that, if not exactly winning them over, at least got them to reluctantly agree on the exercise. They left the Durands on the roof with Pastor Gilbert, each eyeing the other suspiciously; then they deposited the next group on the mezzanine, before Richard, Valérie and a decidedly edgy Bernie Webb made their way through the double doors to the staff and food preparation areas.

'I can't remember the last time I came through here,' Bernie said anxiously. 'Actually, I'm not sure that I have. The others don't really see me as staff, you see?'

He was talking to fill the silence of the first room, covering his nerves too in reality, but he hadn't reckoned on the less than sympathetic Valérie.

'Sshh!' she hissed like an aggressive librarian. 'Please be quiet, Monsieur Webb, we don't want to let anyone know that we are coming.'

The room they found themselves in was a large, well-equipped and gleaming kitchen. High-standard catering sinks, ovens and chiller cabinets lined the walls while ovens, hobs and preparation areas made up a central island. To the right was a small office which had no door and showed a large calendar hung on the wall detailing each room and the names of the guests staying there.

Richard opened one of the large chillers and found it empty.

'I thought that Monsieur Mangetout had a locked kitchen?' Valérie asked.

'As I understand it,' Bernie answered in a low whisper, 'he prepares the main part of the meal in his own kitchen downstairs, sends that up and then preps the veg and stuff up here. He must have fridges and stuff there.'

'Why?' Richard was confused.

'His recipes are secret,' Bernie replied. 'That's what he says anyway.'

Richard rolled his eyes. He and Valérie had had experience with precious chefs before; they could be as secretive as spies. Valérie made her way to the office area and began rifling through a pile of papers on Elise's desk. There was paperwork everywhere, mounds and mounds of it and what computer there was was an old desktop machine. It was a very old-fashioned way of working, a bit like Connor's bedroom in fact – time had stopped. Next to the computer was a retro-style dot matrix printer that was at that moment zipping from side to side with a message from the booking website about potential future reservations. It was obvious from the wall calendar, however, that there were no future reservations, not after the end of the current week anyway. Valérie lifted the top sheet of the calendar and found the previous months underneath and one name stood out in April. 'BOUDON' it read in red ink. She had arrived to stay for the week but had left early. There was a Post-it note on the monitor which was also covered in red ink, 'BOUDON IS TRYING TO BOOK AGAIN. NO MORE BOOKINGS FOR BOUDON OR DUBLOON ENGINEERING.'

'Why would she try to rebook if she'd left the place early?' Richard asked, while out of the corner of his eye he noticed that Bernie had found an open bottle of wine in a chiller.

Valérie shook her head in thought. 'That is a good question, Richard. I do not know.'

'Maybe she worked out that something was wrong and wanted to come back to prove it? And maybe,' he clicked his fingers because he'd seen Bogart do the same, 'maybe, Dubloon Engineering is the company taking Connor to court! You see? Dubloon Engineering is fighting Connor for the doggy toilet patent!'

Valérie gave him a look that said she was impressed. 'Brilliant, Richard!' she said enthusiastically. 'Dubloon is obviously an anagram of L. Boudon.'

'Hopefully Martin and Gennie can confirm that when I speak to them again this evening.'

'You have spoken to them?' she asked, slightly put out that he hadn't mentioned it.

'Yes,' he replied diffidently. 'Didn't I say?'

'No.' She seemed almost hurt. 'I miss the outside world,' she added. 'Is there anything going on, anything interesting?'

She didn't see him blush. 'Oh, you know, just the usual. Some political scandal.'

'Tch!' She snorted. 'Those politicians, they are all the same. A man?'

He nodded. 'Probably! Anyway, where to next?'

'The living quarters.' She strode out of the office and into the kitchen itself, where she snatched Bernie's bottle and told him to behave himself.

The staircase leading down from the back of the kitchen was windowless but well lit. There was a small landing halfway down that gave on to a cave, possibly an old cell, containing cleaning products, piles of bed linen and washing machines, but nowhere for Ian Connor to hide. If indeed he was hiding.

The stairs gave out on to a long corridor, again well lit with the latest LED strip lighting as opposed to the technology museum pieces in the kitchen office. Along the corridor were three doors, two on the right-hand side separated by a distance of about ten metres and the third facing them at the end of the corridor.

'I think Bruno's rooms are at the end,' Richard said, remembering he had seen the balconies from the roof terrace.

'Let us start with that one then, Richard.' Valérie spoke quietly and put her hand out to say that he should go first. She had never done that before, he noted. Was this a change in their dynamic?

She turned to Bernie. 'I would like you to stay here, Monsieur Webb. Sit on the bottom step if you must. If anybody comes, you must shout for us.'

Bernie sat down. 'What do I shout?'

'Anything at all, just shout.' Valérie, never one to hide her impatience anyway, shook her head in annoyance.

Richard felt a little sorry for the man. He looked completely lost without either a piano or a bottle to hand, devoid of inspiration and running his fingers through his curly hair. '*You know you make me wanna…*' he suggested quietly and Bernie beamed at the idea.

'*…Shout!*'

'*…Kick my heels up and…*'

'*…Shout!*'

'*…Throw my hands up and…*'

'*…Shout!*'

'Brilliant, Richard!' Valérie hissed for the second time in ten minutes. With all that was going on it was a balm to his confidence.

They opened the door to Bruno's rooms and the first thing that hit them was the smell. It wasn't unpleasant exactly; Richard even liked it at first, unable to place the aroma. It's just that it was unexpected in what was essentially a cave. The lounge area which led out on to a balcony was sparse. There was a table with two chairs, though one chair had a pile of books on it, cookery books Richard noticed and pointed it out to Valérie. It wouldn't be unusual for a chef to have a collection of cookery books, far from it, but these were basic starter books, not refined cuisine from top chefs.

The bedroom was even more sparse than the lounge. There was a double bed and a lamp on a small table but apart from that just a few pieces of clothing hanging from an open clothes rail. It looked like the sleeping quarters of a particularly austere monk. The kitchen was at the back and was obviously where Bruno spent most of his time. The dumb waiter was open but the shelf wasn't there, so it was currently on another floor. There were some papers scattered about on the table.

'Look,' Richard said, and unearthed a supermarket loyalty card. 'So that's where he does his foraging, is it? Lidl in Pornic! I knew the man was a fraud when I tasted those crab cakes.'

He opened cupboards randomly and came across tins and tins of tuna, crab and sardines, cooking sauces, soups, potatoes and pre-packed vol-au-vent cases. The fridge was full of pre-made sauces too and packs of mussels.

'This isn't a professional French chef's kitchen, Richard!' Valérie was clearly affronted by the discovery.

'No. It's more like a nuclear bunker,' he replied and then he heard a noise. He put his fingers to his lips, gesturing that Valérie stay quiet. He heard the noise again, a low guttural sound, a mixture of fear and anger. In the darkest corner of the kitchen a blanket covered what looked like a box and Richard nervously made his way towards it. He looked at Valérie for support as he went to remove the blanket. She nodded and he could see the excitement in her eyes.

He whipped the blanket off and there, in cramped almost battery discomfort, were three scrawny-looking hens. Richard, not a man given to violent extremes of obvious emotion, almost exploded with rage.

Chapter Thirty-One

Richard Ainsworth was fully prepared to admit to almost anyone who showed an interest that he was at heart a simple man. His pleasures, such as they were, hardly constituted vices. His emotions stayed within a narrow scope, rarely straying to either ecstasy or depression. He led what would have seemed to many, at least before Valérie had turned up, a dull sedentary life. He had his films, he had his B&B and then he had his hens. To Richard, his hens were his one constant in an ever-changing, ever tantrum-throwing world. They were his solace, his confidantes and his friends. Olivia de Havilland, Lana Turner and Joan Crawford weren't just hens, they were far, far more than that, they were a part of Richard himself. The sight then of these three pathetic, neglected under-nourished creatures with their searching eyes and beaks spoke to the very heart of Richard's being, his very soul, and he could have wept at their plight.

'I can only put up with so much,' he said eventually with some emotion and through gritted teeth. 'And I will not put up with this.'

Valérie put a gentle hand on his arm. On the one hand she simply did not understand Richard's fondness for the creatures, but on the other she knew him well enough by now that if this was his reaction, it was for him an earth-shattering and enraging discovery.

'We will come back for them, Richard,' she spoke softly, 'but we must urgently find Connor.'

'I'll be back,' Richard said soothingly to the hens, though his voice carried a level of determination that Valérie had rarely seen, and he put the blanket back in place taking a deep breath as he did so.

The Durands' apartment was far more homely than Bruno's, cluttered even, though not in a messy way, more the accumulation of decades of living in the one place. A collection of life built up by two people living – despite appearances, Richard felt – in a close, loving relationship. It reminded him of his grandparents' house, even the ashtrays. There were chipped mugs, antimacassars on worn armchairs, old books. The bedroom was homely and welcoming, the kitchen clean and tidy. There was only really one thing missing, he thought.

'Richard.' Valérie stood in the middle of the lounge, her arms crossed and looking from wall to wall, sideboard to table. 'There are no pictures, no photographs.' He agreed.

'There might be an album somewhere that's not on show,' he suggested, opening a drawer on the sideboard but finding instead various medications for heart and blood pressure, again a reminder of his grandparents' place. Then he found it.

'Here's something,' he said and moved a large, gaudy vase of dried flowers out of the way. He picked up a picture frame from behind the vase and in it was a yellowing sun-bleached photograph. There were three people in the photo standing on rocks, maybe even on the island. The two at each end were obviously Pascal and Lilibet, taken maybe thirty years earlier though they were wearing much the same outfits. In the middle was a young girl with a boyish haircut grinning toothlessly at the camera; she wore a T-shirt with ANGÈLE written on it.

'Do you think she is their daughter?' Valérie asked.

'I think we need to ask them that,' Richard replied quietly, thinking of the face imprinted on the windows upstairs. 'And ask where she is now.'

Valérie nodded in response and then checked her watch. Richard sat next to her on a sagging old sofa and waited for her to show him what Passepartout was up to. He realised that his mood was probably coloured by the poor trapped hens next door, but he felt that the Durands' place had an air of melancholy. There was a sadness to it. Obviously the cave-built living quarters were much older than most of what was on show in the resort/hotel side of the building, and he thought he could see why the Durands wanted it to return to how it was: where they could stand on the rocks, where the birds roamed freely and where Angèle, if that was her name, grinned for whoever took the picture.

'He is such a clever dog,' Valérie cooed, watching from Passepartout's collar camera. He did seem a remarkably skilled operator. Right now he was sitting on a chair on the library side of the mezzanine and so had all of the bedroom doors within view. Bruno was about to go into Richard's room, which for no one reason at all made Richard feel guilty, as though Bruno might find something incriminating. Of course, he wouldn't; it wasn't like Richard was cruelly harbouring living creatures in inadequate housing. He tried to concentrate. Lea emerged from Bernie's room with an empty wine bottle, which she tipped upside down as she showed it to Elise, who shook her head in disappointment as she closed the door to Lea's own bedroom. They then swapped rooms and closed the doors behind them again.

Richard was impressed. 'It looks like they're being very thorough,' he observed, unable to hide his surprise.

'But still no Ian Connor,' was Valérie's sharp reply.

Elise's quarters were smaller than the others. There was a kitchenette rather than a full-size kitchen, but the place was, unsurprisingly, spotless and whereas the other two cave-built apartments had a slightly damp smell, Elise's place did not. There were various dehumidifiers dotted around the place which helped, all dressed with various types of cactus and rockery displays. The theme was definitely yellow too, which somehow added to a sense of freshness. The one armchair in the lounge was directed out to the sea and beyond it the mainland. Richard could imagine her sitting there in her rare quiet moments, but what was she thinking? Of her mother presumably, in a home and fighting the dying of the light. Certainly the brochure on the armrest suggested that. La Maison Repose it read, and had pictures of people in comfortable, well-lit surroundings being helped by staff in white coats.

The staff quarters were beginning to get him down. He had had enough of the island fort and its enormous contrast between what was provided for those who could afford it and what was on offer for those who kept the place going. There were real lives down here, not the games that Connor indulged in or the fantasy life that few people could actually afford. He found Valérie in Elise's bedroom; yellow bed linen lay tidily on a large bed, yellow towels on the rail in the bathroom. On one wall was an enormous wardrobe and Richard couldn't even begin to imagine how it had got there, unless it was built on the spot. He opened it and was hit with more smells, the dehumidifier smell first and then a mixture of lavender wardrobe freshener and moth balls. The lavender notes reminded him again of home. He and Madame Tablier had had a slight falling out at one point when Richard had insisted that all wardrobes and drawers should have lavender sachets in them. Madame Tablier insisted that clothes were better when they smelled of wardrobe and didn't pretend to be anything else; lavender reminded her of girls when she was little, girls 'who tried to be women too soon'. He smiled at the memory and closed the door on Elise's collection of flowery outfits.

'There is nothing here.' Valérie was disappointed with the search. Richard had understood her logic for how and where the teams had been divided and that she sensed Connor was most likely to be hiding where he didn't usually go, or that someone might even have dumped his corpse where he didn't usually go. 'Do you really think there is a secret passage, Richard?' She looked at each of Elise's face creams and shower gels in the bathroom.

'Like I said,' he replied, 'I'd be surprised if there isn't.'

'Are you still there?' Bernie Webb called from the open doorway of Elise's apartment. 'Hello?'

'I told you to stay on the stairs, Monsieur Webb,' Valérie scolded.

'Yes, yes I know, but it's really quite draughty there. I was getting a chill.'

Richard and Valérie both had the same idea at the same time and smiled at each other for their luck and Bernie's dislike of the cold.

'Did you say a draught, monsieur?' Valérie's tone had completely changed and she approached Bernie with some warmth, Richard just behind her.

'Yes, really quite chilly and you know… well, no pianist needs cold fingers; you end up playing "Baby, It's Cold Outside" on a loop.' Valérie, her hand on his shoulder, had successfully guided Bernie back out into the corridor and the stairs. She knelt down, almost like she was sniffing for fresh air and then went to the side of the steps themselves. She ushered Richard over, who gently patted the rocks holding the stairs up. They gave off a dull, empty sound not like rock at all, more like wood. In the gloom it was difficult to see where the fake rock started and the real rock ended, but by knocking on the surface it was obvious that the fake wood formed a door shape. Richard leant against it and it gave slightly.

'Stand back, Richard,' Valérie ordered, and moved back herself as though she were about to take a run-up.

'I don't think we need to smash it down,' he complained, but moved out of the way nonetheless, while Bernie did the same.

'I'm not going to smash it down,' Valérie mocked. 'I am trying to get a complete image so that I can find a handle.'

'Ah, fair enough,' Richard said and leant back on the wall. He'd seen it often enough in films and indeed it had even happened to him, where an innocent person will lean on a wall, step on a tile or even bang their head and purely by accident stumble upon the mechanism that controls the entrance to a secret passage. And he kept trying, moving nonchalantly along the corridor, back to the wall, manhandling any protruding rocks, stamping his feet, but all to no avail.

'Stop fidgeting, Richard,' Valérie barked at him. 'I am trying to think.'

This last admonishment seemed to wake a bored Bernie out of his listlessness and he began to tap his feet on the steps while singing *You better think! Think! Think about what…*'

'Sit down!' Valérie roared, putting an immediate end to Bernie's impromptu cabaret. He sat down heavily a few steps up and glared at her sulkily before kicking the wall beside him in childish frustration.

The squeak as the door hinges worked on the wooden door sounded like an attack of a thousand mice running into the corridor all at once, but once they stopped a dull light appeared where the door had opened.

'Well done, Monsieur Webb,' Valérie beamed. 'You have found the door for us. I knew your irritating habits would come in useful at some point.'

Pleased, yet crushed at the same time, Bernie followed her into the passage with Richard close behind. 'Is she always like this?' Bernie asked, still slightly hurt.

'Oh, yes,' Richard replied. 'If she's in a good mood.'

The passage was another set of stairs going up and the light came from two or three arrow slits in the walls of the old fort. They climbed slowly as the steps were damp and wet, and passed what was an obvious door on their left. Valérie peered through a slight gap in the frame. 'This is the mezzanine,' she whispered. 'I can see the bedroom doors.'

The shaft of light also revealed something else on one of the steps further up and Bernie bent down to pick it up.

'It's Connor's necktie thing,' he said nervously and then looked behind him at the stairs going upwards into darkness.

They carried on climbing until the steps came to an abrupt halt with another fake rock wall in front of it. This one had an obvious handle in it, however. Valérie took a deep breath and took the handle in her hand. Unusually she looked at Richard for support. There was no way of telling what was on the other side of the wall. It might be Ian Connor, who may or may not be dead. It might be Ian Connor's murderer expecting them and therefore armed. Slowly Valérie drew her gun and then flung the door open pointing her weapon as the light blinded them. 'Stop or I will shoot!' she shouted, but there was no reply at all from the empty gym.

'That's disappointing,' Richard muttered, having built himself up for a life and death finale.

From the gym they heard a commotion outside, where the other party of Elise, Lea and Bruno had rejoined the Durands and the pastor. As they approached the group though they realised that it wasn't the pastor at all, sitting on the chair where they had left him; it was Ian Connor, a look of horror on his face which matched the look of horror on everybody else's faces. And they could see why. Inside the dumb waiter, curled up on the serving shelf and with a grotesque look on his face, was the dead body of Pastor Gilbert.

Chapter Thirty-Two

Stunned into silence, the entire group sat around a large table on which was laid the small corpse of the pastor. From afar it may have looked like a vigil to a dead king, such was the fear and shock that gripped those present. All except one. Valérie d'Orçay paced up and down, separate from the others, her arms folded with one hand on her chin and muttering to herself. It was difficult for Richard to make out exactly what she was saying, but it was quite some monologue and looked on the face of it to be a mixture of self-recrimination, confusion and downright white fury. The pastor himself looked peaceful, as had Nevaeh when they had found her, which was ironic because a search of the pastor's body had revealed her contract in his inside pocket.

'So,' Valérie began again, 'I want to get this all clear in my head. First, how could this happen if you two were here with him?' She pointed a prosecuting finger at the Durands, who looked surprised to be involved at all, let alone on the brink of being accused of murder.

'Like I said…' Pascal removed his pipe from his mouth to speak.

'We…' His wife did the same.

'Like *we* said, we went to that far wall over there. We wanted to see what was happening on our balcony.'

'That's right and the pastor, God rest his soul, said he wanted to have a look around and he went into the gym there.'

'That was the last we saw of him.' Pascal shrugged in conclusion.

'And nobody else came up on to the roof while you were here?' Richard asked.

They shook their heads in perfect unison.

Valérie removed Connor's necktie from her pocket, the one Bernie had found on the secret passage stairs, and ran it delicately through her fingers. The natural assumption, given that the pastor had red marks around his neck, was that, like Nevaeh, he had been strangled and the evidence pointed to Connor. 'And where were you all this time, Monsieur Connor?' she asked. 'And why did you scream in the first place?'

The look of complacency had completely gone from Ian Connor's features. Richard had the impression that despite two deaths previously he really still had considered the whole thing a game and that he was controlling it. He now looked exactly like someone who had a bedroom stuck designedly in his childhood, he looked like a little boy lost. He didn't answer Valérie, he didn't even look like he had heard her and he just continued staring at the lifeless Pastor Gilbert.

'I asked you a question.' Valérie adopted a tone that snapped Connor out of his solemn reverie. 'Where were you? Why did you scream?' she repeated.

'I screamed because…' A look of confusion came over his face. 'Because that's what I always do. My mother always said that if I ever felt out of control, I should go to the highest point of the island and just scream my head off until I felt better.' He half-smiled at the memory.

'And where is the highest point?' Richard asked gently, hoping that would be more helpful than Valérie's strict interrogation.

Connor pointed upwards and to the top of the light-house on the fake palm tree. From where they all sat it looked inaccessible, but Connor now stood and opened a small, child-size door on the thick trunk. Nobody had thought to look there and everybody groaned at their own negligence.

'So you were watching us, then?' Valérie's mood hadn't improved with the solving of Connor's disappearance and hiding place.

'No, not really,' he replied quietly. 'I didn't care.'

Lea Boudon stood up. 'We only have his word for this anyway!' she spouted angrily. 'In my experience he's not at all trustworthy!'

'How could you have been up there…?' Pascal Durand spoke as if every word was a struggle and he was trying to work out a tricky mathematical formula. 'When we heard you calling up through the waiter shaft thing?'

'That's right!' his wife confirmed. 'We heard you! That's why we pulled it up!'

Connor shrugged. Whatever they had heard, whatever Lea Boudon said, whatever Valérie was accusing him of, it didn't seem to matter to him at all. He was totally unaffected by anything around him. Richard felt he had seen this kind of thing before and sat in front of Connor who didn't focus on him at all. His pupils were slightly dilated and the eyes bloodshot around the edges. He nodded to Valérie before squeezing through the tree door and climbing the ladder to the small lantern room. It was, unsurprisingly, roasting hot inside. It really was the highest point of the island fort and made entirely of glass, but there was more than that, there was the smell. Richard had been to a few parties at university and had briefly, as his own mother had put it, 'fallen in with the wrong crowd'. The fact that this wrong crowd later became incredibly successful business types, community leaders and self-righteous politicians was neither here nor there; in the late eighties they had all sat in darkened rooms, smoked a lot of dope and practised talking the rubbish that would prove so influential in later life. Richard didn't really get on with the group partly because he lacked ambition and partly because the dope made him cough like a retired miner and thus apparently 'harshed the vibe'. Those memories came flooding back now as the smell inside the lantern hit him hard. Connor had been at it like a hippy at a free love festival, he concluded.

He hadn't smoked it though, Richard now knew that. It came from the heated pot pourri that was covering the whole of the lantern shelf.

He climbed back down, slightly unsteadily, and whispered his findings in Valérie's ear. Her own eyes opened wide at the news and she came to a decision. 'Bruno!' She clapped her hands. 'You and Monsieur Durand take the body of Pastor Gilbert to his room, please. Everyone else, I suggest you either stay all of you together or lock yourselves in your rooms. We will meet again at dinner.' People started to trudge off nervously, debating what they should do. 'Monsieur Connor, you will come with us?'

'What should we prepare for dinner?' Elise asked, her priority always to organise.

Richard shrugged. 'Anything but chicken,' he said unwilling to hide his indignation.

When they reached Richard's room, Ian Connor slumped heavily into the desk chair and rolled his fingers into his temples.

'Have you got any aspirin?' he asked, his eyes half closed in headache pain.

'You can have some aspirin when we have finished.' Valérie had that look on her face that told Richard she was not going to go easy on Connor, whether he was her employer or not.

'But…'

'Why did you kill Nevaeh?'

'I didn't kill…' Connor seemed only belatedly to realise the situation he was in.

'Why did you kill Pastor Gilbert?' she asked, even more venomously if anything. 'What was your meeting about?'

'Our meeting?' Connor looked like he was searching for a memory.

'Yes.' Richard decided to join in before Valérie started shining a light in the man's eyes and demanding to know names. 'You had a meeting with Pastor Gilbert before lunch. It seemed to upset you.'

For a second Connor stared blankly at Richard and then he appeared to recall the episode. 'Oh, that! Yes, well he wouldn't play, would he?' The man looked genuinely upset. 'He said he would give me a generous price for the place if I just gave him a contract now and stopped these silly games. I mean, silly games? Games aren't silly, they're fun.'

Richard looked at Valérie and mouthed the word 'cuckoo', which she didn't understand.

'You like games, don't you, Ian?' she asked, switching to a gentler style of questioning.

'Why do you want to know?' he shouted back suddenly. 'Don't take my games away from me! Please!'

Richard and Valérie sat stunned for a moment. It was clear that Connor was coming down from a severe overdose of whatever kind of dope the pot pourri contained. The dope that was also in a bowl on Richard's desk and which explained, partly, his own fluctuating moods each evening when the sun fell on the desk.

'We're trying to help,' Richard said soothingly. 'We're trying to help you, Ian.' And then he made a decision to throw in his last psychiatry quote to buy them some time. 'Remember what I said before about know thyself? Most of us know nothing about ourselves. Nothing. I want you to say hello to your inner-self, Ian. Ian Connor meet Ian Connor.' This seemed to placate Connor, who sat back and closed his eyes.

Richard beckoned for Valérie to follow him to the window.

'That was brilliant, Richard!' she said admiringly.

'Something Alan Mowbray probably said as Doctor Vengard, *That Uncertain Feeling*, 1941.' He reeled off the details automatically. 'Anyway, look, the man's as high as a satellite and I think we need to get through to him now before he completely comes around. Whatever this drug is, and he may have had it developed in his own labs, it makes people relaxed and talkative.'

She nodded vigorously. 'I agree. And what we need to know is, who stopped his games and why, yes?'

'Exactly. But let's go easy too, he might be quite volatile.'

She nodded in agreement and they both returned to sitting on the bed in front of Ian Connor, whose eyes were still closed.

'Ian?' Richard's voice was gentle, like a parent waking a sleeping child on a long journey. 'Ian?' he said again, his words almost floating on the air and this time Connor opened his eyes and gave a half-smile.

'Who stopped your games, Connor?' Valérie demanded standing up suddenly, her voice like talking barbed wire. 'And why?'

Richard slapped a hand to his forehead while Connor reacted to the verbal assault by looking like a scolded child to the extent that Richard thought he might start sucking his thumb. 'My mother stopped me playing,' he said quietly. 'She didn't like me playing games.'

'Did she not like you playing with Angèle?' Valérie followed up softy, making Richard redundant in the process as she was now playing both bad cop and good cop.

A tear formed in Connor's eye. 'Poor Angèle,' he said drowsily and shook his head.

'What happened to Angèle?' Richard intervened.

'She died,' was his simple answer. 'She died because of the games. People always die in games.'

Richard and Valérie turned to each other and tried to work out what he meant by that. On the one hand it seemed like a damning confession, on the other the confused meanderings of an innocent. Richard was about to ask what game had killed Angèle when they heard Connor's gentle snoring and saw his head sink into his chest.

They left him to sleep off whatever had drugged him, disabling the door lock as they left with Passepartout in tow, heading for Valérie's room. There was no one downstairs in the lounge area and the whole place was eerily silent. Valérie closed her door behind them and walked towards her window incident board, deep in thought.

'Well, at least we've learnt something,' Richard said with a sigh. 'Angèle, who I assume was Pascal and Lilibet's daughter, used to play with Ian Connor when they were children.'

'And that she died in a game,' Valérie finished the thought for him.

'It's all very tragic,' Richard lamented.

'It is, Richard, but it is no excuse to play games again and to kill people.'

'You think he is responsible, then?'

'Yes, I do think that. But why, Richard? Why these people?' She turned back to her board and began pointing randomly. 'Why Lea? Why Albrecht? Why this Nevaeh? What does that have to do with Lane Bridge Holdings?'

Richard followed her hand as it shot out at the names written on the window and suddenly he had it. Standing up and rushing to the window, he stood beside her. 'Say that again!' His voice was full of barely controlled excitement. 'Exactly the same way.'

Chapter Thirty-Three

Richard leant over the side of the wall and looked down at the balcony of the Durands' apartment. They were both sitting outside in the sun, puffing on their clay pipes, every now and then bickering but more often just sitting in a silence that can only come from years together. If what he and Valérie thought was true, they had suffered terribly and lost the only thing that sane couples agree to love undyingly: their child. Richard felt an ache for his own daughter, Alicia, somewhere in the UK and in the late stages of pregnancy. He was going to become a grandparent, something that had been cruelly denied to Pascal and Lilibet. *Oh my God*, he thought again, *I'm going to become a grandparent!* He broke out into a cold sweat and began to feel dizzy before Valérie grabbed his arm.

'Why are you staring at us like that?' Pascal said without looking up.

'It's rude, that's what it is,' his wife joined in.

'Can we come and see you?' Richard asked. It had been his idea to try this way first, rather than go storming down the secret stairs and bang on their door.

'Nothing you can say down here, that you can't say up there.' Pascal let out a cloud of smoke like a Victorian steam train.

'That's right,' Lilibet agreed.

'It's about Angèle,' Valérie shouted over the wall, not bothering to hide her impatience.

The Durands looked at each other before Pascal stood up and stretched. 'Time for an *apéritif* anyway, Mrs,' he said casually to Lilibet. 'You know the way,' he shouted up, before disappearing inside.

Richard and Valérie were each given a seat at the small dining table while Lilibet Durand handed out wine glasses and Pascal opened a chilled bottle of the local Muscadet. He filled each glass and then raised his, but offered no toast to the occasion.

'What do you think you know?' he asked sitting down.

'And what do you think you want to know?' his wife added.

The questions were asked coldly and now, presenting a united front, they made a formidable team.

Richard took a sip of Dutch courage, and sighed. 'I have a daughter too, called Alicia, she'll be twenty-eight next birthday and I don't see her often enough.'

'That's your mistake,' Lilibet answered, taking the lead for once. 'Hug them close.' She downed her glass in one gulp and Pascal refilled it.

Richard nodded in agreement, having come to the same conclusion.

'Monsieur Connor told us that she died playing in a game.' Valérie left the sentence incomplete, hoping it would kick-start a conversation.

'Poor lad.' Lilibet's jaw muscles were tensing with emotion. 'They were very close, our Angèle and Ian, very close. Well, they were the only kids that lived here. We were the only staff then, too. They'd spend their holidays running about the place, climbing rocks, swimming in the sea, hiding in the passages.'

'And bird-watching,' Pascal added.

'And bird-watching. This was before it was all rebuilt, of course. Our Angèle would go to school during the week, staying over there and poor Ian was lonely all the time. He had tutors or his mother taught him.'

'And his father?' Richard asked.

'Seen him maybe twice. He weren't interested in his boy or his wife. They were kept like prisoners here, they were, even though it was her maiden name they named the company after. Anyway, it wasn't right. That Herr Schmid was here more than the dad was.'

'Did they not try to leave?' Richard could sense Valérie's anger rising in her cheeks.

'No! You see, she liked it. She liked it here. All she'd do was sit and read, or do her word puzzles. Oh, she played with her son, but he had no life to speak of and she was terrified he'd leave her if he ever saw the outside world.'

'So he never the left the island at all?' Richard was incredulous; this was like something straight out of the pages of Alexandre Dumas or – and there was that nagging feeling again – Agatha Christie.

'He did once, when he were eighteen.' Pascal was nodding to himself at the memory and a playful smile, the first Richard had seen on him, emerged. A twinkle came into his wife's eye too.

'What happened?' Valérie asked.

'Well.' Lilibet put her glass down and went to fetch the photograph from behind the vase. 'Our Angèle was twenty by now, working at a hotel in Paris and had come back for the holidays. Mrs Connor was sick in bed and had to be quarantined. I forget what she had…'

'Rubella,' Pascal confirmed.

'Rubella, that's right. So, Angèle said to Ian, "Let's go to the mainland for the weekend, have some fun, get away from this stuffy island for once." And they did too.' It was her turn to smile at the memory.

'Madame Connor was furious when she found out,' Pascal said. 'Furious!'

'She banned her Ian from seeing our Angèle; well, she wasn't here much by then anyway. Then one weekend she came back to surprise us, but we weren't here, gone on one of our trips.' Lilibet went silent and stared at the table.

Pascal stood and put his weather-beaten hands on her shoulders. 'Apparently they played one last time, but there was an accident and she fell. Swept away. Never found again.'

'Oh, Madame Connor had called the authorities. Well, Schmid did anyway. That was another time he was here, we had phones here back then. There was a big search but…' Lilibet Durand started to weep quietly and said no more.

'And how did Monsieur Connor react?' Valérie was building up quite a case and it didn't look good for Ian Connor.

'Difficult to say.' Pascal wiped a tear from his wife's cheek. 'He was sent away to stay with his dad somewhere, learn the business.'

'And after that, Madame Connor just sort of faded away in the way that her son faded from her life.' Madame Durand sighed sadly. 'Whatever game they played, we both lost our children. He only came back here when she died and then started changing the place around.'

'Now he's giving it away.' Pascal huffed.

'He always were generous,' his wife said sadly. 'Always giving things to Angèle, he was, always. He gave her a ring once, do you remember?' Pascal nodded. 'Anyways, turns out it was his great-grandmother's wedding ring. Oh, there was such a kerfuffle over that!' She smiled again and Richard was relieved to see it. 'Is there any more of that wine left, Skipper?' she asked, before the tears returned. 'Hug them close,' she repeated, this time as a toast.

'I know what you're thinking,' Richard whispered as they made their way up the secret passage stairs to the mezzanine. 'Connor is taking revenge on this place and his mother. Her name was Lanebridge, the holding company is called Lane Bridge.'

'And everybody here has a first name that spells out Lane Bridge.' She shook her head angrily. 'So dangerous, so cold.'

'Not everyone,' Richard corrected her. 'We have two letter Bs, whereas we need two Es.'

He pushed the door open and allowed Valérie to go through first. Suddenly she sprinted off to the right and shouted a warning as she did so. Richard followed more slowly but saw the emergency straight away. Bernie Webb looked like he was struggling with someone in the shadow of the mezzanine library and there was a hand around his neck. It was difficult to tell exactly what was going on as Valérie was on to it right away and blocked his view, but on her warning the assailant let go of Bernie's throat and must have disappeared once again into the shadows.

'What was that all about?' the singer spluttered, rolling on the ground.

'There must be another passageway here somewhere!' Valérie was all action, but she couldn't find a door or a way of opening the wall. 'Are you OK?' she asked, without looking round.

'I think so, Val,' he tried to sound chirpy. 'It all happened so quickly.' He sat up and started doing Do-Re-Mi voice exercises and pulling at his Adam's apple.

'The show must go on, eh?' Richard asked in quiet admiration of the man.

'Always! Even here. I mean, I have played to dead audiences before, but this is ridiculous.'

Valérie helped him to his feet, her anger and excitement having completely, on the face of it, dissipated. 'I think you will be fine,' she said and started patting him down and brushing dust off his tuxedo jacket.

'Please, madam,' the little man said in mock effrontery. 'You haven't even bought me dinner yet!'

'Will you be alright?' Richard could see he would be, but it seemed right to ask anyway.

'Oh yeah! Me? I once did an encore during an earthquake in Vegas.' He straightened his tie and did a few more la-la-las. 'I'm going upstairs to warm up the larynx,' he declared, before adding, 'it probably needs some strongish lubrication after all that, too.'

Valérie and Richard watched him climb the stairs as they made their way back to Valérie's room. 'Here,' she said quietly and handed him something. 'It's his wallet.'

Chapter Thirty-Four

Richard closed the door behind them and looked down at Bernie Webb's wallet in the palm of his hand. 'So he wasn't being attacked, then? Apart from by you that is!'

'Actually, you know he was.' She sat down on the bed and cuddled a grateful Passepartout, and Richard had the feeling that she wasn't telling the whole truth.

'But doesn't that ruin the theory that Ian Connor is behind all of this? He's locked in his room, probably playing Mousetrap.'

'Mousetrap?'

'Never mind.'

'Anyway, I think Ian Connor most likely has another secret passage in his room.' She shrugged as if it didn't matter, but it did. 'I had a hunch and I thought that this was more important. Open the wallet, please. I want to see some identification.'

Richard grumbled as he unzipped the thin leather wallet. It was more like a card holder than a purse and it didn't contain much. There was an old picture of a woman and a boy that could even be Bernie and his mum such was its age, and there was a driving licence for the state of Nevada.

Richard smiled and then nodded. 'Bravo.' He smirked. 'Bernie Webb's real name is Ernie Robinson.' She beamed a big smile at him, though he also thought there was a hint of relief in her eyes. 'We have our second E,' he declared and turned to the incident chart on the window. 'Lea, Albrecht, Nevaeh, Ernie or Elise, Bruno, Richard, Ian, Durands, they come as a pair, then Gilbert and Ernie or Elise again.'

'Lane Bridge,' Valérie confirmed.

'And that's why these people have been chosen. All of that nonsense on the first night about bad reviews or plugs near the beds, it was just that, nonsense. He wanted guests that would complete the word Lane Bridge.'

'Brilliant, Richard,' she said, 'and you saw it. We make a good team, I think.'

'But you said that we had made a big mistake.' He didn't turn round as he spoke, but he could see her reflection in the window now that the skies were dark.

'Yes, but I was talking about this.' He saw her point to the board. 'I knew we must be missing something.'

'And the rest?' he asked quietly.

'Well,' she stood up and moved next to him. 'The rest, it speaks for itself. I think Ian Connor knows that he is in trouble. I think Lea Boudon is behind the patent court case and I think that Connor has been drugging his high-level entrepreneurs and stealing their ideas for his own. So, knowing that the end is in sight he decides to take everybody down with him: his enemies, staff, even old friends. They must die. The word puzzle – remember, he grew up with them – of their names will kill the company and even the memory of his overbearing mother. It is actually all very Freudian.' She sounded a little bored now that she had solved the puzzle.

'And what if he had killed me, seeing as you placed me as the R in his murder word game?' he challenged.

'Oh, that would not have happened, Richard.' She was almost laughing at the thought. 'I was watching out for you all the time.'

'You used me!' Richard Ainsworth wasn't one to lose his temper. Frustration and indignation were usually about as far as it went; maybe on the odd occasion, extreme vexation, but anger didn't come naturally to him. This though was his second volcanic explosion in as many hours. 'Watching out for me all the time? Is that what you call it? Who do you think you are – James bloody Bond? You can't treat people like that, it just isn't right. I'm not a piece of meat, a toy to be tossed aside like that, job done, move on, wham bam thank you, ma'am!'

She squinted her eyes and frowned. 'Richard, I really think that when this is all over, you should probably take a holiday, you know? You are certainly overtired.'

He stared at her in disbelief. 'I'm supposed to be on bloody holiday now! Instead, I've been kidnapped, set up as a murder victim decoy, seduced – partially against my will – and my crown jewels have become a World Wide Web uproar! Damn right I need a bloody holiday!' She walked towards him, a worried, confused look on her face. 'ARGH!' he added for good measure and stormed out.

He leant against the bedroom door on the mezzanine side and watched for a few seconds as Elise, the Durands and the hen-botherer Bruno went about setting up the dinner table. He had certainly had enough of the place and needed some fresh air. First he had an idea, re-opened the door and, without acknowledging Valérie, he grabbed his laptop from the desk, still mindful that he had a theory he wanted to test out. Then he made his way to the roof terrace hoping the sea breeze would blow away his anger.

He had forgotten that Bernie Webb was going to the roof to test his voice out after the possibly fake attack, but a mixture of fresh, salty air and the delicate notes that Bernie played were immediately soothing. He made his way to the piano and nodded as Bernie sang. *Just make it one for my baby, and one more for the road* – grab one for yourself, Rich.' He nodded towards his glass of wine, before adding his own lyrics. *''Cos it's a bloody long road…'*

'That's a favourite of mine,' Richard admitted as he poured himself a glass.

'It's a favourite of every bloke who's ever been hurt.' Bernie raised his glass in Richard's direction. 'Here's mud in your eye!'

'How's the voice holding out?'

'Pretty good actually, how are you?' Richard was surprised at the question. 'Piano players always know.' Bernie winked. 'This is what Sinatra called a three in the morning drunk song. If you work in enough bars, you can always tell.'

'And you've worked in a lot of bars?'

'Oh, loads! That's how I started out, on the bottom rung of the ladder, before working my way down even further!'

'Why are you here, Ernie, really?'

'Bernie.' He missed a note as he played.

'Ernie. Ernie Robinson.'

'Ah. You know.'

Richard nodded and refilled the man's glass. 'Now why does someone with your talent hide away here? And also, why does someone with the name Ernie Robinson change it to Bernie Webb? It's not all that different in showbiz terms.'

Bernie played a few bars before answering. 'I've seen fire and I've seen rain,' he said, though not singing the song, just playing his piano and occasionally, emotionally, adding the words – words of loss.

'Who was she?' Richard asked softly.

'They.' Bernie replied. 'They. My wife and my son. I'm hiding from them, Rich. I'm a nothing, a no one, not even a has-been. I'm a never-was and they're better off without me.'

'Really?' Richard thought he knew the answer but asked anyway.

'I didn't want to stick around and have them watch a failure disintegrate. Like I say, they're better off without me.'

Richard looked up into the night sky. 'And Connor sheltered you here.'

'He said that families only destroy each other, anyway. That if I stayed here, out of their way, they'd have a better life.'

Richard shook his head at the tragedy of it. He knew a little something about hiding, but at least he'd let people always know where he was. The dinner gong interrupted his thoughts and he wandered over to the mainland-facing wall. For a moment he thought Bernie was singing again and then he realised that it was coming from down below, where he could see the foam of the waves on the rocks. It was a delicate sound, Lilibet, he assumed, singing as she used to do to her Angèle. *Everybody here has lost something*, he realised, *and Connor has been manipulating that.*

'Can you hear that?' he shouted back to Bernie. 'I thought it was the wind at first.'

'It is just the wind,' Bernie called back. 'And you know what?'

'What?' Richard asked, hoping he was about to learn something extra.

'*They call the wind Maria!*' Bernie sang heartily. Richard's sympathy for Bernie Webb evaporated quickly and he even felt that maybe the man had actually done the right thing and abandoned his family for their own sake.

The singing below continued though – was it the wind? The wind certainly carried it, delicately light like musical dandelion seeds. It sounded so fragile, so fleeting, angelic, other-worldly even.

'Do you believe in ghosts?' Richard lowered his voice as the breeze eased off a little.

'Don't you start!' Bernie finished his drink and made for the door to go down to dinner.

'Connor's been on at me all the time about that! "Do you believe in ghosts, Bernie?" All the time. No, I said to him. Though I did play a summer season in Cromer once.'

Richard ignored the joke. 'And does Connor believe in ghosts?'

'Oh yeah, terrified of them. Are you coming down?' he asked, standing in the doorway.

'Not yet,' Richard answered wistfully. He turned back to the singing, but it had stopped. He waited a few moments, before coming to a decision and making his way to the gym.

Chapter Thirty-Five

Richard could hear the voices of everyone as they gathered for dinner, with Valérie loudly directing where she wanted people to sit. She was gearing up for her explanation of why and how Connor was intending to destroy them all, along with his multi-billion dollar company and the memory of his family. From his position in the kitchen, just on the other side of the double doors, he heard her pacing and at one point ask exasperatedly, 'Where is Richard?'

Richard was mere yards away, but he had some theories of his own he wanted to investigate first. He walked silently into the small office and took the calendar off the wall. He rifled back over a year and built up a very good picture of who was here and when. Secretly he thanked Connor for being oddly technophobic when it came to management as he'd have had no chance if it had all been locked on a hard drive somewhere. Business hippy twaddle clearly needed old-fashioned paperwork and he was grateful for that. Having found what he wanted, he went back out to the kitchen and checked the big empty chiller again. It was still empty but – and he kicked himself for not noticing this earlier – there was an open padlock on the handle. Why would someone need to lock a fridge? He could understand Bruno's downstairs secrecy, the man really was a gastronomic charlatan, but here too? Of course, he'd never worked in a kitchen, maybe it was a legal requirement.

He closed the door silently before going back to the double doors and putting his ear against them.

'I have to admit,' he heard Valérie say, 'that I was taken in at first by Monsieur Connor...'

She'd be fine for now, he concluded, but he also knew he didn't have much time and that he had to urgently find another piece of concluding evidence if he was to help her out. He paused. *Does she even deserve to be helped out?* he asked himself. She had admitted to using him and in a pretty raw way too, which on a point of principle hurt him but the memory of which he wouldn't swap for anything. He smiled and caught his reflection in a shiny oven hood. 'You're not doing this for her.' His voice was affectedly deep and melodious, and he arched the eyebrow for added effect. 'This is for you and England!' he added, getting carried away with himself.

Fifteen minutes later he re-emerged into the kitchen from downstairs, the missing piece of the puzzle happily in tow. He grabbed his laptop and tried out his last theory. Clicking on to the hitherto redundant Wi-Fi he typed in what he thought the password was. Ten letters, all in capitals and hopefully no numbers or special characters. The wheel on the screen seemed to turn for an eternity before finally his own homepage downloaded and he saw his bed and breakfast in all its glory, his hens at his feet in the welcoming photo. He felt a pang of homesickness at the sight of them and then anger at the other poor hens he'd discovered in Bruno Mangetout's kitchen. He looked at them in the corner now, having rescued them and brought them upstairs.

He was just about to close the laptop when an urgent notification appeared. It was an invitation to a Zoom call organised by Martin and Gennie Thompson. Should he answer it? He really should have joined Valérie by now, if only in his capacity as her sergeant. On the other hand, although between them they had the answer to most of the questions he had asked of the Thompsons, there were still a couple of things outstanding that would wrap it all up.

He pressed ACCEPT and then jumped back in fright as three different screens opened up in front of him. Martin and Gennie were on the bottom screen and dressed for some reason as what he guessed were Mark Antony and Cleopatra; Madame Tablier was scowling at him through the top right-hand screen and Monsieur Noel Mabit, who had in Richard's absence apparently assumed the mantel of mayor, was looking as regal as possible while wearing the sash of office.

'You've got clothes on, then?' Madame Tablier's perfunctory attempt at an introduction was overtaken by Noel's.

'Monsieur le ex-Mayor,' he intoned seriously. 'After a vote of no confidence from the council committee…'

He was interrupted by Gennie Thompson. 'We haven't got long I'm afraid, Richard, Samson and Delilah are waiting downstairs. We have some of those answers for you…'

'That's great, thank you,' Richard replied urgently. 'Look, I need just a couple more things looking up if that's OK?'

'Monsieur le ex-Mayor!' Noel's indignation caused his sash to ripple wildly and it was Madame Tablier who told him to be quiet.

'Put a croissant in it!' she demanded. 'There's more important things to talk about here. I can't cope!' she added, her voice rising at least three octaves with the stress of it all.

'I will be back soon, Madame Tablier, I promise, it's just…'

'What are these questions, old man?' Martin was quite impatient and Richard thought he heard an equally impatient voice behind the couple. 'OK, Samson,' Martin snapped. 'Keep your hair on!'

Gennie giggled and that set Martin off as well.

'Richard!' The voice was a strong, demanding one and Richard felt his knees buckle, even more so when Clare, his soon to be ex-wife and still equal partner in his bed and breakfast, appeared on the screen beside Madame Tablier.

'Argh!' he whimpered, almost falling backwards.

'What on earth is going on?' she demanded. 'Where are you? What are you up to? And why are you all over the internet and the world's media doing naked fertility dances?'

'Is that what they were?' Gennie asked. 'Fertility dances?'

'No!' Richard replied defensively. 'I was trying to distract a bird!'

There was a moment's silence, before Clare spoke up again. 'A bird?' she asked, her voice soaked in disbelief.

'Are we talking the flying egg-laying kind or the Michael Caine *Alfie* dolly variety?'

Richard's shoulders slumped. 'Look, I can explain everything, I promise. I just don't have time right now.'

'But you must make time, monsieur!' Noel Mabit looked on the verge of tears. 'This is no longer just a civic matter, it is a criminal one.' Mabit shifted awkwardly to one side as Commissaire Henri LaPierre, Richard's nemesis and one of Valérie's ex-husbands, sat smugly down next to him. The man chuckled and wiped an intimidatory finger across his crumb-laden moustache.

'Of course,' LaPierre began. 'I have suspected something like this all along. Monsieur Richard Ainsworth, I am arresting you for fraud, embezzlement of public funds and,' he leant into the camera menacingly, 'anything else that I may dig up.'

'What's he saying?' Clare, whose French wasn't on a par with Richard's, was infuriated with frustration.

'He's arresting, Richard,' Gennie translated cheerily, always happy to help. Behind her Martin could be heard remonstrating with their guests.

'Look, you've waited three thousand years, I don't see what difference a few more minutes will make?'

'Who's Martin talking to?' Clare asked, frowning.

'Delilah.' Gennie's face was fixed in cheerfulness.

'Delilah? Is it a Tom Jones thing? This camera is very fuzzy. Richard, I have repeatedly asked you to update the equipment around here.'

'I wish to know exactly where you are right now, monsieur!' LaPierre talked over her.

'Tell that buffoon to put a sock in it!' Clare retaliated.

Madame Tablier, whose English was improving, said something about *chaussettes* which caused the policeman to turn bright red and Noel Mabit to bury his head in his hands. A door slammed somewhere and Martin returned to the screen.

'Well, that's Samson and Delilah gone.' His disappointed voice garnered a kiss on the forehead from his Cleopatra.

'Maybe we can give Napoleon and Josephine a call later on,' Gennie soothed. 'I know Josephine's Zumba class finishes at nine.'

Richard banged his own forehead on the table in front of him. 'WILL YOU ALL JUST PIPE DOWN, FOR ONE BLOODY MINUTE?' he shouted. 'I haven't defrauded anyone or embezzled anything, I'm not doing naked fertility dances and if you must know, I'm really, really tired. So be quiet for one minute and let me explain.' There was some grumbling down the line. 'I mean it!' he carried on. 'I will shut this thing down if I hear another word.' Finally, there was something approaching silence. 'Now, firstly, Commissaire. I want you to get on to the police in Nantes and have them send over a launch to Le Fort Esprit de l'Air, it's just off the coast.'

'Why should I do such a thing?' LaPierre was behaving quite prissily.

'Because I assume you want to catch a multiple murderer?' Richard was losing his patience again. What was it Lilibet had said? 'Sometimes you do need to get away.' She was right too.

'OK, I will do this, but you must stay on the line please, Monsieur Ainsworth.'

Richard thought about this. 'OK, if I must, but you lot must be quiet if I do so?'

Again there was some grumbling and Clare spoke.

'But Richard…' she began.

'Ah, ah, ah,' he uttered, holding up a finger. He knew this was a very quick way to annoy her, but although her face went red she went quiet.

He saw Gennie put her hand up to ask a question.

'Yes, Gennie, what is it?'

'You said you had a couple more things for us to find out for you?'

'Right, yes! I nearly forgot. And maybe the Commissaire could help with these too.'

He gave them their instructions and told them that he needed the answers urgently, before adding that they were now going into the main room and that their silence was required.

He opened the double doors and all eyes turned to him.

'Sorry I'm late,' he said as calmly as he could muster, putting his laptop on the sideboard. 'Have I missed much?' he added, giving it the full Mae West.

Chapter Thirty-Six

Ian Connor pretended to yawn loudly before struggling against the ropes that had him tied to his throne-like dining chair. 'Your superior here,' he spoke through a grimace, 'is putting the case for the prosecution and the defendant, as you can see, has already been declared guilty!'

The others sat silently around the table, still quietly in awe of Connor – at least the staff were. Lea Boudon was trying to hide her own nerves by picking at her salad. Bernie inevitably was at his piano, but rapt just as the others were.

Valérie sidled up to Richard. 'Where have you been?' she hissed. 'I had to ask Bruno to tie up Monsieur Connor, that is a bad show, you know?'

'What did he use? Some of his underdone spaghetti?' Whatever other crimes it might turn out that Bruno Mangetout Leroux may have committed, it was nothing in Richard's eyes to his treatment of his hens and he wasn't going to forget it.

'Hello, Valérie!' Gennie simply couldn't help herself and Valérie took a step back to take in the full display on Richard's laptop. She closed her eyes in a strong sign that remaining calm was going to be something of a struggle.

'Have you been selling tickets, Richard?' she asked menacingly.

She had a point. It did look rather like a temporary stand had been erected for a paying audience. Awkward introductions were made between the laptop guests and the dinner table guests.

'Valérie.' Clare nodded coldly as she spoke her greeting. 'Are you responsible for Richard's fertility dance, then?'

'I told you it wasn't a fertility dance!'

'It looked like a fertility dance,' Martin interjected.

'And to think he was our mayor,' Mabit wailed.

'I hope they throw away the key!' Commissaire LaPierre salivated.

Richard turned to Valérie and uttered what was fast becoming his own catchphrase just like 'Dogged Dan, always gets his man', and 'I sing what I see!'

'I'll explain later,' he mumbled and then turned to the seated group in the room. 'I'll explain later,' he enunciated clearly.

'Yes, could we get on, please?' Ian Connor struggled against his ropes again.

'Yes.' Valérie decided he was probably right. 'Now where was I?'

'You just said how his mother had trapped him here as a boy...' Pascal Durand said helpfully.

'...and that he was now wreaking revenge on everything as a result!' Lilibet finished for him and this time without an admonishment from her husband.

Connor rolled his eyes. 'Oh, per-lease,' he moaned.

'Lane Bridge stood for everything that Ian Connor came to despise.' Valérie started to pace, with the room and the Zoom call watching her. 'It was his mother's maiden name, a reminder of the woman who ruined his life; it was a reminder too of his parents' marriage and a father he rarely saw growing up. It is the name of his company which is failing. This place itself is in debt and there are court cases regarding intellectual theft and industrial espionage.'

'Richard, concentrate,' Clare heckled, noticing that Richard's eyes had glazed over while Valérie spoke.

'He knows that he and his company are doomed. Madame Boudon, your company is in court at the moment against Lane Bridge Holdings, am I right?'

'Your company?' Connor spat in disbelief.

Lea paused to let her cloud of vape dissipate before speaking and then her face emerged from the smoke as though she was walking onstage through dry ice. 'Yes,' she said proudly. 'My company, Dubloon Engineering.'

'Dubloon!' Connor rolled his eyes again. 'Of course! L. Boudon, Dubloon. Why didn't I see that? I'm really losing my edge.' He shook his head. 'When I drugged you, I thought you were just a secretary or something and that you'd overheard stuff!'

'When you did what, monsieur?' It was Commissaire LaPierre who asked the question from his corner of the laptop screen.

'Oh. Nothing.' Connor was now a picture of innocence.

'I thought it must be something like that!' Lea exclaimed. 'That was the only reason I came back here – I wanted to know your methods.' She looked at Valérie for a further explanation.

'The pot pourri in the rooms,' Valérie explained. 'It is all grown and dried in the lighthouse tree on the roof. Then it is put in the rooms, most likely by Connor himself. It heats up at sunset via magnified windows and, shall we say, relaxes the guests. They become talkative over dinner and Ian Connor harnesses that knowledge to give him an advantage.'

'Drugs and industrial espionage!' LaPierre cried through the laptop speakers. 'Monsieur, I am arresting you for…'

'Who *is* he?' Connor's frustration was beginning to show too.

'He is my other sergeant,' Valérie answered coolly.

'What?' LaPierre spluttered.

'But what about the deaths?' Bernie sang. 'My own compilation,' he added. 'I couldn't think of anything appropriate.'

'Deaths?' LaPierre was struggling to keep up.

'Yes, three murders.' Valérie swung back into action. 'Herr Albrecht Schmid, Nevaeh Ormorod and Pastor Gilbert Rondeau, formerly known as Dan Gilbert.' There was silence as everyone either remembered the deaths or took in the news for the first time.

'And how do you spell Nevaeh?' LaPierre asked.

'It's Heaven backwards,' everyone replied at once.

'But how?' Elise looked on the verge of tears and her voice was cracking as she spoke.

Valérie sighed again, affecting an air of sorrow, though Richard knew she was absolutely loving the whole thing. 'Herr Schmid I think was drugged. When we first arrived Monsieur Connor walked around the room and stood briefly behind the man's wheelchair. Something was administered at that point, possibly by syringe. A post-mortem will tell us exactly.'

'And Nevaeh and the pastor?' Lea asked, shaking her head and giving Connor a filthy look at the same time.

Richard felt like intervening at this point and asking Valérie why someone had moved Schmid's body and then replaced it, but it was a sure-fire bet the answer would be Connor and his games.

'Nevaeh was strangled because she went to Connor's room and told him that she was his daughter.'

Connor laughed maniacally, a really unsettling sound that was going to do nothing for his later defence. 'And I suppose I killed Pastor Gilbert because he was my long-lost son, is that it?'

'No.' Valérie was keeping her cool. 'You killed Pastor Gilbert simply because he wouldn't play your games. It is as simple as that. You despise anyone who doesn't play your games, your games of death.' She stopped speaking and the silence that engulfed the room almost felt like it weighed a tonne. 'And that is why you killed poor Angèle Durand!'

She walked silently around the dining table and returned to her seat at the opposite end, Connor watching her all the way. Gone were the pantomime denials, the affected boredom and the schoolboy smirks, he looked crushed by Valérie's accusation, defeated into submission and he shook his head from side to side but said nothing.

Lilibet Durand stood up from her own chair and threw what was in her glass into Connor's face, but it didn't seem to register on him at all. He just blinked at Valérie in fear. Not frightened like a cornered animal, more as though a

Proustian rush of memories, good and bad, were thrashing at him, as if he were running through a forest and the branches were scratching his face. Lilibet screamed and burst into tears, falling into the arms of her husband, Pascal, at the same time. He managed to calm her down briefly and sit her back down before picking up a knife from the table and walking menacingly in his employer's direction.

'At least,' Richard moved to block Pascal's path, and guide him back to his seat, 'that is what we were all led to believe,' he said loudly.

It wasn't necessarily his intention to break the tension, far from it. Richard for once had been looking forward to his own moment in the spotlight, but his words inevitably caused a stir. Chattering started up from all corners, especially on the internet side of things, where he could see Martin was deep in conversation with Clare above him and the exasperated Commissaire was crossing out the list on his charge sheet.

'Can I add wasting police time?' LaPierre shouted above the din.

Richard felt a presence at his side. 'What are you doing, Richard? What is this?' Valérie's face was a picture of confusion that mirrored the room perfectly. Only Connor sat in silence, staring at the table in front of him as though, in a sense, he had already left the room.

Richard smiled nervously down at Valérie and then coughed loudly to recapture everyone's attention.

'Like I say,' he began, 'that is what we were meant to believe and I thank my colleague, er Valérie here, for setting out that case so, er beautifully, succinctly.'

'Oh, Richard,' came Clare's not necessarily unsupportive voice from the laptop. 'I do hope you know what you're doing.'

Valerie retook her seat.

'As Valérie said, Ian Connor wanted to see this place destroyed. It is a reminder of a painful, largely lonely childhood and he is definitely guilty of stealing the innovations of other businesses by a process of drug inducement. But he did not kill Albrecht Schmid, nor Nevaeh Ormorod, nor Pastor Gilbert and nor did he kill your dear Angèle.' He glanced down at the Durands, who shook their heads at his words.

'How do you know this?' Elise asked, looking more than most as though she had been through an emotional tumble dryer.

'Harry Fielder,' Richard said simply.

The hubbub started immediately as again people asked their immediate neighbour who this Harry Fielder might be? Where had he been hiding? And was it one of them in disguise?

Richard lifted his arms, calling for silence, and was about to continue when he heard a groan from the Zoom meeting. 'Oh, Richard.' Clare was shaking her head.

'Harry Fielder,' Richard began to pace nervously as he spoke and tried not to catch anyone's eye as he moved about, 'was a background artist in British cinema, an extra they're called. He was rarely on the film credits but in the course of a deliberately undistinguished forty-year career from the mid-sixties onwards he worked with some of the best in the business.'

'Richard!' Valérie was tugging at his sleeve as he passed, but he ignored her.

'Steven Spielberg, Michael Caine, Stanley Kubrick, Julie Andrews, Peter Ustinov, Meryl Streep, Sean Connery, Mel Brooks, Peter Sellers...'

'Richard!' This time it was Clare who gave him a verbal nudge.

'He was in Indiana Jones, Star Wars, the Carry Ons, James Bond, Hercule Poirot, Pink Panther, *Doctor Who*, *Mission: Impossible* and *The Bill*,' he continued.

'Everyone's been in *The Bill*, Richard,' Gennie added.

'Well, quite.' He was determined not to be derailed and was now approaching full steam. 'He was in the 1981 version of *Great Expectations*. Joan Hickson played Miss Havisham. Joan Hickson was the definitive Miss Marple on television but she was also, interestingly, in the first Margaret Rutherford Miss Marple film, *Murder, She Said*. Anyway, that is an aside.'

'You do surprise me!' Clare snorted. Valérie, Richard noticed, was oddly quiet.

'At first...' Richard was managing to drown out any heckles now, he could see the finish line and wouldn't be diverted. 'At first,' he repeated, 'I became distracted by the James Bond and Agatha Christie parallels, particularly *And Then There Were None*. A remote island, reluctant but suspicious invitees, Mr U. N. Owen and Ian Connor, *inconnu*. I got lost in my own book about film family trees; for instance, do you know that of the four film versions of *And Then There Were None*, three star actors had been, or at least went on to be, Bond villains? No? Never mind.' Though he was slightly disappointed.

'Richard. Who is Harry Fielder?' Valérie asked the question quietly, which made it all the more intimidating and it was clear that she was speaking for the rest of the room.

'Harry Fielder was in *Force 10 from Navarone*,' he replied urgently. '*Force 10 from Navarone* was directed by Guy Hamilton. Guy Hamilton directed *Evil Under the Sun*, another Agatha Christie strangers on an island story, but he also directed, along with various James Bond films, the 1980 Miss Marple film, *The Mirror Crack'd*.'

'Starring Angela Lansbury,' Clare said aloud.

'Starring Angela Lansbury,' Richard continued, pretending not to have heard her. 'It is a film about vengeance, about a woman's misguided revenge, a child thought lost re-emerging and about love too.'

'For the love of God!' Connor had woken from his doldrums. 'Am I guilty or not?'

'No.' Richard shook his head and pointed across the table. 'She is the murderer.'

Chapter Thirty-Seven

'Me? No, I couldn't be!' Elise, flaming red hair standing out against the subtle lighting, looked from face to face hoping to find support from those around her, but everyone was so stunned by the revelation that they said and did nothing.

'It was you, Elise,' Richard said softly. 'Firstly, you didn't retire. You took a few months off because you had exactly the same kind of burnout that the guests here had. You were doing so much and had so much responsibility that in the end you couldn't cope. You told your friend Albrecht Schmid, who booked you into a clinic on the mainland, La Maison Repose…'

'No, I retired. I didn't mean to come back!' Elise protested.

Richard shook his head. 'No,' he said simply. 'Ever the organiser you blocked out your dates away, but actually wrote on the calendar "Return to Work". It was in the same handwriting as your vote written before lunch today.'

'If Albrecht Schmid was her friend, why did she kill him?' Lea asked.

Richard took a deep breath and knew now he was taking a gamble. 'Martin, Gennie, did you find out who owns La Maison Repose for me?'

It seemed to take an age for them to answer. 'It's a subsidiary of Lane Bridge Holdings,' Martin read. 'Owned in the name of Albrecht Schmid…'

Inside, Richard gave a huge sigh of relief.

'Herr Schmid was here the night Angèle Durand disappeared into the sea, suspected drowned,' Richard continued and nodded sadly at the Durands. 'Yes, Madame Connor organised a search for her, but she knew that Angèle would never be found because she had never gone into the sea.'

'We were playing.' Connor's voice was almost inaudible. 'Pretending we were children again; at least, Angèle was pretending. My mother was furious and demanded to know why Angèle was here. She sent me to my room. I never saw my Angèle again.'

'Your wife, you mean?' Richard lowered his voice to match Connor's. Connor nodded.

'Martin, Gennie, did you find the record of the marriage for me?'

This time Gennie answered. 'The marriage of Ian Connor and Angèle Durand took place on Thursday, 23 September, 2004. Does that help?'

'I think Angèle told your mother of the marriage that night. She also told your mother that she was pregnant.'

Connor looked up at Richard with tears streaming down his face.

'What has this got to do with Elise?' Lea asked.

'It was Schmid who put Angèle in that clinic on Madame Connor's orders, hid her there, imprisoned. He was in love with your Connor's mother, you see, and couldn't understand why your father was absent all the time. He would have done anything for her, even this. Somehow, when Elise was there, probably having sneaked into an office trying to organise things, she came across certain records and especially one of a young girl kept in the grounds. She saw it as a way to bring down Ian Connor who she suspected wrongly of being behind the whole thing.'

Elise stood up angrily. 'This is absolute rubbish!' she shouted, as usual playing with a piece of material, this time a napkin. 'Why would I want to bring down Ian Connor? He's my employer, this is where I live.'

'Because you knew Angèle,' Richard said. 'She was your friend at the Lane Bridge Hotel in Paris, where you both worked. You never knew what happened to her until you stayed at La Maison Repose.'

Elise sat back down, but it was noticeable that her napkin was now tied as a deadly tourniquet.

'I think you tried to blackmail Albrecht Schmid into helping you destroy Ian Connor, especially as he was already thinking of pulling out anyway. But he refused, even threatening to tell Connor the full story and beg forgiveness. So you killed him.'

This time Elise didn't protest, but poured herself some water instead.

'But, Richard, why then move the body?' Valérie asked.

'Who moved what body?' Lea asked with excitement.

'This is great stuff!' Gennie remarked. 'Well done, Richard!'

'I'm not saying it's as good as Samson and Delilah,' Martin added, 'but it's up there.'

Richard decided not to dwell on whether he thought that was a compliment or not. 'The Herr Schmid who came over on the boat with us was not Herr Schmid,' he said simply. 'It was someone else in one of those joke padded fat suits you can buy online. Add a wig and absurdly large sunglasses and you have, as long as there's no real scrutiny, a ready-made Herr Albrecht Schmid.'

'That is why the wasp did not upset him on the quay!' Valérie was looking at him in something approaching wonder and it was most disconcerting.

'I couldn't find a pulse either; the suit – and it was horribly realistic – was too thick. Elise and I left a supposedly dead Herr Schmid in his room, while the real dead Herr Schmid was stored in a locked chiller in the kitchen.'

Everyone took a moment to consider this while Elise picked at a bunch of grapes on the table.

Eventually it was Bruno who spoke. 'So who was in the suit?' he asked.

'I hope it's a kitchen cleanliness inspector from the Department of Hygiene!' Richard responded caustically. 'What a fraud you are! Foraging nonsense.'

Bruno had the good grace to look embarrassed while Richard heard the Commissaire click his fingers, indicating that he wanted him to get on with the important stuff.

'I'll come to who was in the fat suit later.'

'And why did I kill that Nevaeh girl and the pastor?' Elise asked, pretending to be enjoying the nonsense of it all.

'For the same reasons that Valérie said that Connor killed them. Nevaeh said she was his daughter and the pastor didn't want to play the game. They were perfect fodder for your plan to paint Connor as the murderer because you thought he'd been responsible for Angèle's incarceration and, sadly, her subsequent death from a broken heart.'

Lilibet began to sob again and Pascal hugged her close. 'My poor girl,' she said.

'You haunted Connor hoping he would break. The pictures on the window, IAN written on the window, the black-nailed finger in his pasta, even the singing. It was all meant to drive Ian Connor over the edge and make it easier for him to be blamed. It was also why you attacked Bernie in the mezzanine corridor.'

'I thought that was Val, actually.' Bernie spoke up, slurring his words.

'And I thought it was Ian Connor.' Valérie frowned.

'No. It was Elise. You see the game was genuine, Connor's game that is. He really did, does, want to get rid of the island. The guests were chosen carefully spelling out the words Lane Bridge, but think of the order in which they were then murdered. Albrecht, Nevaeh, Gilbert… Elise was working her way through an anagram of Lane Bridge, and it was the Wi-Fi code as well. It was Angel Bride. My bride, Angèle. He even gave her his great-grandmother's ring.'

There was a stunned silence in the room.

'Brilliant, Richard!' Valérie stood up and hugged him.

'But that doesn't fit.' Elise snorted derisively. 'A, N, G, B?'

'Bernie's real name is Ernie,' Richard replied, slightly embarrassed that Valérie was still holding on to him and noticing some jealous glares from his laptop screen. 'Which you knew.'

'Brilliant, Richard!' This time it was Elise speaking, mimicking Valérie's voice perfectly.

Richard shrugged a little smugly. 'And that is how you lured the pastor. I noticed how good a mimic you are, madame. You did a wonderful Bing Crosby on the first night, you mimicked Connor's Irish accent perfectly on a few occasions and there, that *Richard...*' He suddenly stopped speaking as if in realisation of something else, something more haunting and he gulped, looking in Elise's direction. She returned his stare with a very suggestive wink.

'Yes, Richard...' she oozed, her eyes awash with seduction.

The double doors to the kitchen opened slowly and a young girl in her mid-teens emerged in the light that came from behind her.

'Can I come out now?' she asked. 'Are we still playing the game?'

Ian Connor tried to stand up while Lilibet and Pascal both screamed at the same time.

'Angèle! My Angèle!' Lilibet bustled her way towards the girl and picked her up in a hug.

'Not Angèle.' Richard sounded oddly distracted. 'This is Celeste, your granddaughter and Ian Connor's daughter.'

* * *

Richard, despite the sharp sea spray generated by the speed of the police launch boat, was still in a state of bewilderment as he and Valérie sat on the back staring at the quickly retreating island fort. He had barely said a word since introducing Celeste to a family she didn't know. It had been heart-warming to see Lilibet and Pascal fuss around her. They had accepted the loss of Angèle years before and they had never expected in their wildest dreams that they could ever be this happy or fulfilled again. Even Ian Connor seemed to mature at the news, apologising profusely to Lea and promising to withdraw from the court case and also offering hefty backing to her engineering company. Lea had refused the offer and looked delighted to be able to do so, especially as she had other things in mind judging by the way she was still holding on to Bruno. Richard, letting the mêlée continue around him, had taken a small sip of wine while quietly closing his laptop and avoided any more contact, eye or otherwise, with Elise. He was utterly drained by his performance.

'But how did you know it was one of these fat suit things?' Valérie asked, still in awe at Richard's work.

'Eh? Oh, the glasses were sticky, which meant they'd been taped on for one thing, but it was the finger. That wasn't a fake joke finger in Connor's salad, that was Schmid's fake finger. Well, the pretend Schmid anyway.'

'And Elise persuaded Celeste to dress like that?'

'Yes.' He shrugged. 'Just another game. She had no idea obviously, but Elise was just going to use her to haunt Connor because the likeness to her mother was so strong. The little one was happy to play and she had a nice bedroom through the back of Elise's wardrobe.'

Valérie shook her head. 'I am very proud of you, Richard,' she said, though he didn't reply, which made her feel uncomfortable. 'So what will you call them?' she asked, nodding at three nervous-looking hens sitting in a box cage between them, who in turn were looking at Passepartout on Valérie's lap.

For the first time Richard smiled. 'Well,' he said, 'I'd like to call them Harry Fielder, Guy Hamilton and James Bond…'

'But they are ladies!'

'Actually,' he replied, 'they're dames. Dame Angela Lansbury, Dame Elizabeth Taylor, they were both in *The Mirror Crack'd…*'

'Directed by Guy Hamilton.'

He was astonished. 'Yes!'

'And the third one?'

'Dame Margaret Rutherford,' he said proudly.

'There is nothin' like a dame, nothin' in the world!'

'Are you going home, Monsieur Robinson?' Valérie asked quickly before Bernie could embark on a further chorus.

'Yes,' he said with a touch of defiance. 'If they'll have me, that is. I wouldn't blame them if they didn't, though.'

He wandered off around the small deck.

'I am sorry, Richard,' Valérie said quietly.

'Sorry?' he replied, not used to such a word coming from Valérie's mouth.

'Yes. You said that I used you…'

'Oh, that!' he replied, embarrassed by his own mistake. 'Don't think anything of it. Really.'

'I think that sometimes you do not like me and my methods.' Her voice was suddenly small, smaller than he had ever heard it. He had a decision to make, he had one more classic film psychiatry quote in him, but dare he?

'Now, it isn't that I don't like you, Susan, sorry… Valérie,' he corrected himself quickly, 'because after all, in moments of quiet, I'm strangely drawn towards you, but well – there haven't been any quiet moments.'

Valérie smiled warmly at him and Richard turned back to look at the island fort one last time as a ticker tape went across his mind's eye. *Cary Grant*, it read, *Bringing Up Baby*, 1938.

Also available

Death and Croissants
(A Follet Valley Mystery 1)

Richard is a middle-aged Englishman who runs a B&B in the fictional Val de Follet in the Loire Valley. Nothing ever happens to Richard, and really that's the way he likes it.

One day, however, one of his older guests disappears, leaving behind a bloody handprint on the wallpaper. Another guest, the exotic Valérie, persuades a reluctant Richard to join her in investigating the disappearance.

Richard remains a dazed passenger in the case until things become really serious and someone murders Ava Gardner, one of his beloved hens... and you don't mess with a fellow's hens!

OUT NOW

Also available

Death and Fromage
(A Follet Valley Mystery 2)

Richard is a middle-aged Englishman who runs a B&B in the Val de Follet. Nothing ever happens to Richard, and really that's the way he likes it.

Until scandal erupts in the nearby town of Saint-Sauver when its famous restaurant is downgraded from three 'Michelin' stars to two. The restaurant is shamed, the town is in shock and the leading goat's cheese supplier drowns himself in one of his own pasteurisation tanks. Or does he?

Valérie d'Orçay, who is staying at the B&B while house-hunting in the area, isn't convinced that it's a suicide. Despite his misgivings, Richard is drawn into Valérie's investigation, and finds himself becoming a major player.

OUT NOW

Also available

Death in le Jardin
(A Follet Valley Mystery 4)

On the surface, Richard Ainsworth has life where he wants it. Middle-aged navel gazing and Olympic levels of procrastination are exactly what rural life in France should be about.

Then crisis hits his posh B&B when redoubtable housekeeper, Madame Tablier, is accused of murder. Even more surprisingly, it's the murder of a former fiancé, turned brother-in-law. None of which the stubborn old woman denies.

Valérie d'Orçay is having none of it and their investigation leads them to a strange tourist garden village, where backbiting, recriminations and even former colleagues provide a deadly scenario more tangled than knotweed.

OUT NOW

Also available

Death and Boules
(A Follet Valley Mystery 5)

Saint-Sauver, home to Richard Ainsworth and Valérie d'Orçay's detective agency, is celebrating the 25th anniversary of its town twinning with Anglethorp Spa in Lincolnshire.

Events are planned, a huge *brocante*, street parties and the centrepiece, an exhibition boules tournament between the two towns and a team of international boules all-stars. Everything is going well, the sun shines, the wine flows and the *entente* is very *cordiale*.

Until the mayor turns up dead in an antique dresser having apparently been killed twice. Inevitably Richard and Valérie have very different views on the subject and engage in their own battle: who will solve the crime first?

OUT NOW

About the Author

Ian Moore is a leading stand-up comedian, known for his sharp, entertaining storytelling and observations. He has performed all over the world, in luxury, in war zones, to royalty, to the Russian mafia and on one occasion, to nobody at all. A TV/radio regular, he won four out of five days on *Richard Osman's House of Games* but having failed to win the prized dartboard is still shunned by his three children.

Ian lives in rural France with his wife, children and a menagerie of animals that do as they please.

He is also the author of the critically acclaimed Loire Valley Mystery series, which began with *The Man Who Didn't Burn*, and two memoirs on life in France contrasting with life on the road as a comic, *Vive la Chaos* and *C'est la Vie*.

Acknowledgements

I've always loved the film versions of Agatha Christie novels, even the really bad ones. There's something about her name that gives a whodunnit film at least a bedrock, however deeply hidden, of real quality. I feel that Richard would agree and I wanted this book to be a doffed cap in the direction of the great Dame. With that in mind, enormous gratitude goes to Agatha Christie herself and to all the filmmakers and creatives who keep having a go. I will always devour what's produced, so keep them coming, though having said that I've never made it past the first thirty minutes of Kenneth Branagh's version of *Death on the Nile*.

My editor Abbie Headon has stuck with me since I was first published in 2012, and she is an absolute diamond. I'll admit to getting a little cranky during the edits of this one, mainly because I got carried away with things. Abbie, with her endless patience, reigned me back in and the book is much better for her calm judgement.

A huge thanks as always go to Farrago Books, to Pete Duncan, Matt Casbourne and Josephine Cassaglia, and Jayne Lewis a simply superb team who punch way above their weight in publishing terms. Bill Goodall, another calming voice in my diva-like ear, is my agent *extraordinaire*.

Lastly, my thanks go to you, dear readers. I get quite a lot of messages from readers telling me how much they love these stories and Richard and Valérie. All of those messages mean so much, thank you.

Note from the Publisher

To receive background material and updates on further humorous titles by Ian Moore, sign up at farragobooks.com/ian-moore-signup

Everyone is wanting *Moore!* – praise for the *Follet Valley series* and Ian Moore

'**A joyous read!**' Alan Carr

'A writer of **immense wit and charm**' Paul Sinha

'A very funny page-turner. **Fantastique!**' Adam Kay

'Ian is **one of my favourite writers**; this is hilarious and a great mystery too' Janey Godley

'**Good food and a laugh-out-loud mystery**. What more could anyone want in these dark times' Mark Billingham

'**Like going on a joyous romp** through the Loire Valley with Agatha Christie, P. G. Wodehouse and M. C. Beaton. A delight' C. K. McDonnell

'Ian Moore is a **brilliant, funny writer who perfectly captures the foibles of rural France** but judging by this book I will never be visiting his bed and breakfast' Josh Widdicombe

'**Beautifully done. Very funny indeed**. I can't imagine how one plots something like that. Tremendous work' Miles Jupp

'I'm so **punchdrunk from the sheer entertainment of it** I've got a sore jaw. Encore!' Matt Forde

'This is like **two great books in one**, a tricksy whodunnit, and a really, really funny story' Jason Manford

'Such a brilliant read, smart, funny and **his sharp writing captures the nuances of "Anglo-French" relations beautifully**' Zoe Lyons

'This book is **a fun and funny read** and I'm very much looking forward to the next one' Ian Stone

'**Funny, pacey and very entertaining**' Robin Ince